SO-BAF-087

❧ *A Walnut Sapling on Masih's Grave*
and Other Stories by Iranian Women

FRANKLIN PIERCE
COLLEGE LIBRARY
RINDGE, N.H. 03461

A Walnut Sapling on Masih's Grave

❧ and Other Stories

by Iranian Women

EDITED BY

JOHN GREEN
ANN ARBOR, MICHIGAN

FARZIN YAZDANFAR
CHICAGO, ILLINOIS

WITH A FOREWORD
BY EVELYNE ACCAD

HEINEMANN
PORTSMOUTH, NH

Heinemann
A division of Reed Publishing (USA) Inc.
361 Hanover Street
Portsmouth, NH 03801-3912

Offices and agents throughout the world

Copyright © 1993 by Heinemann

All rights reserved. No part of this book may be reproduced in any form or
by any electronic or mechanical means, including information storage and
retrieval systems, without permission in writing from the publisher, except by
a reviewer, who may quote brief passages in a review.

Editor: Lisa A. Barnett
Production: Renée Le Verrier
Text and cover design: Gwen Frankfeldt

We would like to thank the authors and translators who have given their
pemission to include material in this book. Every effort has been made to
contact the copyright holders for permission to reprint borrowed material
where necessary. We regret any oversights that may have occurred and
would be happy to rectify them in future printings of this work.

Library of Congress Cataloging-in-Publication Data
A walnut sapling on Masih's grave and other stories by Iranian women
/ edited by John Green, Farzin Yazdanfar; with a foreword by
Evelyne Accad.
    p. cm.
    Consists of stories written between 1945 and 1989.
    Includes bibliographical references.
    ISBN 0-435-08626-X
    1. Short stories, Persian—Women authors—Translations into English. 2.
Persian fiction—20th century—Translations into English. 3.
Women—Iran—Fiction. I. Green, John. II. Yazdanfar, Farzin.
PK6449.E7W35 1993
891'.55301089287—dc20   93-19755
                                                                      CIP

Printed in the United States of America on acid-free paper
98 97 96 95 94 93 EB 1 2 3 4 5 6 7 8 9

PK
6449
.E7
W35
1993

❧ Contents

Contents

🌿 *Introduction*

Before you is a collection of short stories translated from Persian to English, all written by women between the years 1945 and 1989. It presents a sample of the work of Iranian women writers in the modern historical period, writing in several short story styles.

The selections were made in fits and starts, with a few reversals and serendipitous decisions. We have even selected several pieces by relatively obscure writers, works whose settings and tone we feel evoke something of the relationship between these writers and the sexually segregated culture to which they belong.

The reader will also find here stories by some prominent writers, and by prominent women with no literary pretensions. We have made no effort to present anything that could be called a literary canon, or part of one. What we have tried to compile is simply a readable and interesting group of stories in a variety of styles and perspectives within the parameters of gender and language of origin.

The prominent writers represented are Mahshīd Amīr-shāhī, widely acclaimed for her 1987 novel *Dar Hazar* (At Home), the respected novelist and short story writer Mīhan Bahrāmī, Sīmīn Dānishvar, well known for her best-selling

1969 novel *Savushūn* (Mourning), Shahrnūsh Pārsīpūr; and Gulī Taraqqī.

Amīrshāhī and Dānishvar have both been translated and anthologized elsewhere, which left us with a limited range of their works to choose from. Amīrshāhī's thoughtful *After the Last Day,* one of her own favorites, is the only story here that explores a relationship between sisters. Her *Peyton Place,* one of a series of humorous pieces she wrote about the teenage girl Sūrī, was chosen by translator Michael Beard. Amīrshāhī's great skill as entertainer and satirist shines through in this charming episode.

Dānishvar's *The Story of a Street* is autobiographical, drawn from her experience in north Tehran during her life with her late husband and fellow writer, Jalāl Āl Aḥmad. Mīhan Bahrāmī's *Ḥāj Barekallāh* is a fictional look at philandering and infidelity as seen through the eyes of a group of Iranian women, against the cultural backdrop of the Shi'ite passion play.

Pārsīpūr's *Sara* is one of her early stories that casts revealing light upon her later major novels. It illustrates the marginal role of a woman and her symbolic pregnancy in the male-dominated society of Iran. Pārsīpūr's, like Amīrshāhī, has never accepted the traditional female role prescribed by Iranian society. In her short stories and novels she chooses to raise issues of sexuality and to assert a female identity inconsistent with the traditional Iranian standards.

The less prominent writers include three whose writing has been published in literary journals, and two writers whose work has appeared in the popular press, but who have not been taken seriously by the literati. The former group is represented by Fāṭimah Abṭaḥī, Mahdukht Kashkūlī, and Gītī Nīkzād; the latter by Shukūh Mīrzādah'gī and Zhīlā Sāzgār.

Abṭaḥī's 1980 story is an oblique commentary on the fledgling Revolution. Editor John Green has translated the poetic epilogue and presented it with the story as originally published in the journal *Kitāb-i Jum'ah.*

Kashkūlī's story was chosen by editor Farzin Yazdanfar and translated by his Chicago colleague Frank Lewis. One of four stories set in the years of the Revolution, it features a male protagonist caught in an ambivalent and tragic relationship with heroism, sacrifice, and loss.

Nīkzād's story is another favorite of Yazdanfar's, and also of contributor Mahshīd Amīrshāhī's. Mīrzādah'gī's contribution is the other story in our group with a male protagonist, and is useful as well for its informative depiction of rural ritual and sexual roles. Sāzgār was a contributor to the women's magazine *Iṭṭil'āt-i Bānuvān.* Although the selection here, *There is No Truth,* is not typical of the maudlin tales of family crisis and romance favored by such journals, it is an interesting contemporary variant of the animal fable, whose popularity is much older in the Middle East than the short story itself.

Finally, we have two prominent women who are not known as literary artists, the late educational activist Zahrā Khānlarī and historian Humā Nāṭiq. Each has produced only one short story. Khānlarī's 1945 tale of the village girl Gawhar is the first short story by a woman to be published in Persian. Despite its technical shortcomings, it is a very important artifact, rich with carefully researched details from Iranian rural society.

Nāṭiq's 1980 story is a fictional account in journalistic style of an educated woman's attempt to come to terms with scarcity and environmental destruction in northern Iran during the first year of the Revolution. Sadly, the environmental destruction depicted in this story has continued unabated on a devastating scale in that area.

The question of sexual identity in relation to literature is a popular academic topic. Some critics, such as Cynthia Ozick (in *Women Writers at Work: The Paris Review Interviews,* ed.

by George Plimpton; New York: Penguin, 1989, p. 304) have written about the writer as being "genderless." Yet in a sexually divided society such as the one in Iran, there are two distinct realms of experience delineated by gender, and much of what goes on in the world of the women is concealed from the men. While the writing itself may be similar, Iranian men and women see and do different things in life, and it is the women writers who have done the most to portray their side of the Iranian gender gap. Bahrami's *Haj Barekallah* and Abṭaḥī's *The Walnut Sapling on Masih's Grave* are two examples of stories told in terms of the thoughts and habits of secluded women.

This women's fiction from Iran is not always feminine, however, as is illustrated by Nāṭiq's 1980 story. Both male and female Iranian writers frequently conceal themselves behind characters with whom they have little in common. Gulī Taraqqī and Sīmīn Dānishvar are two good examples. In her story "The Great Lady of My Soul," Taraqqī tells a personal story through a narrator-protagonist who is a middle-aged man in circumstances quite unlike her own. This story has been discussed by Michael C. Hillmann in an essay entitled "An Autobiographical Voice: Forugh Farrokhzad" (in *Women's Autobiographies in Contemporary Iran,* ed. by Afsaneh Najmabadi, Harvard Middle Eastern Monographs; Cambridge: Harvard University Press, 1990, p. 38.)

Taraqqī's *One Day* shows a different shade of her artistic voice, portraying the emptiness felt by a divorced woman in a reunion with her estranged children, during which she encounters a conflict between her love for them and her personal commitments and interests.

We regret lacking the space to include more of the post-revolutionary Iranian women writers whose achievements we admire, for the contributions by women to Persian fiction are growing rapidly. This anthology is but a small sample of a much larger existing and forthcoming body of work.

On Transliteration

There are two transliteration systems, one that emphasizes pronunciation (used in the text) and one that is the Library of Congress standard (used in the bibliography). The latter system emphasizes orthography, and we employ it because of the need to present information to readers about books in the same form it is found in most American libraries.

Persian terms in the text are transliterated using the system proposed by Naser Sharify in his *Cataloging of Persian Works* (Chicago: American Library Association, 1959). The bibliography uses the system presented in the American Library Association and Library of Congress Romanization Tables in Cataloging Services Bulletin Number 119 (Fall 1976). The spellings for the names of authors are the ones established by the Library of Congress, and may or may not conform to a particular transliteration system.

We also include a glossary of Persian terms. Terms throughout the text that appear in the glossary are printed in italic.

John Green and Farzin Yazdanfar

❧ *Foreword*

EVELYNE ACCAD

We
in the stubborn genesis
that shapes our freedom
shall keep
the eye of the pilgrim
the mission of the stars.

Andrée Chedid

A *stubborn genesis,*—a careful, sensitive, soft, yet strong pen to shape freedom and to draw new vision for Iranian women, for other women in that part of the world, and for women and men all over the world—this is what is at the core of these short stories by Iranian women. By well-known and unknown Iranian women writers, women experienced in creative writing and women at their first trial in the field, they all give voice to their particular experience, reflection of a society in turmoil. They mirror their inner and outside world, managing to go beyond the often cruel and restrictive walls of their existence.

Among the many themes developed, the tension between individual freedom, happiness, and collective adaptation to traditions and conventions comes out sharply. Most of the stories are realistic with vivid descriptions of the various communities the authors belong to, and some use symbolic as well as surrealist language to better express their search for a way out of their imprisonment.

A Walnut Sapling on Mashi's Grave is a very sad story about
a mother giving birth to a child who is taken away from her.
The mood of the city, the expectations concerning a forthcoming revolution come out strongly. Symbolism success-
fully blends the condition of women with the Iranian revolution. *After the Last Day* and *Peyton Place: Tehran, 1972,* by the
prominent writer Mahshid Amirshahi, take us into the lives
of women with humor and great narrative skill. *Haj Barekallah* is well written with suspense, sensuality, revelation about
women's roles, and the importance of love. *The Story of a
Street,* on the evils of polygamy, the roles of children, mother,
wife, is narrated with sharpness and sensitivity. *Congratulations and Condolences* is quite telling about today's problems,
especially as they are reflected in violence and the problems
of Iran, both past and present. *Gowhar,* on the tragedy of
polygamy—a woman driven to madness because of it—is a
very powerful story; I will probably use it in one of the
courses I teach on women and literature. *The Starling Spring*
is informative on Iranian rural sexual rituals and unusual in
its use of a male narrative point of view. *A Visit with the
Children in the Upper Village* renders the aftermath of the
Iranian revolution and is striking for its ecological awareness.
The Tale of the Rabbit and the Tomatoes is short but sharp and
well narrated. *Sara* is a strange, information story on the
Iranian revolution, giving us insights on the desire to give
birth to martyrs and what it requires. *There Is No Truth* is a
surrealist story, its roots lie in the long Middle Eastern tradition of the animal fable. *The Great Lady of My Soul* also talks
through a male character, giving us strong indirect insights on
some of the problems of revolutionary Iran, bringing out the
distress and anguish of post-revolutionary Iranian society.
Someday describes a mother looking forward to her grown-
up children's visit, followed by her disappointment in their
lack of communication, questions about her life, the anguish
and memories this visit brings her.

The short story is a genre particularly adapted to present a wide variety of authors in a relatively short space. It is a form which has witnessed an interesting and dynamic development in the Middle East in the last few decades. Often used for publication in the literary pages of daily newspapers, later collected into volumes, many young authors started their careers this way. This concentrated creative form draws its imagination from socio-cultural contexts undergoing rapid changes. Its roots go back to Middle Eastern tradition, found in the animal fable, the oral storytelling, the folk tale, and *A Thousand and One Nights*, as well as in Western models of the mid-nineteenth century and beyond.

Collections by women from that part of the world are relatively few and I am so glad to see this one out in print with so many fascinating accounts of women's lives in pre-revolutionary and revolutionary Iran. The book is informative, educating, as well as entertaining. What Charlotte Bruner says in the preface to her second anthology of women writers from Africa is also true for these Iranian women: "They are no longer isolated voices crying from a wilderness, they are reaching an audience at home and abroad, they are aware of each other . . . they provide role models for others, new and as yet unheard." (*African Women Writing*, Charlotte Bruner, ed, Heinemann, 1993, p. vii.) A link between women from various continents with similar yet different experiences is being created. The editors of this volume and the publishers ought to be thanked for helping strengthen that bond. Ultimately, the women in this collection are to be praised for their courage and their openness in the midst of the difficulties they face, their struggle for freedom, and their search for identity in a culture that provides them with so few alternatives.

❧ *A Walnut Sapling on Masih's Grave*

FĀṬIMAH ABṬAḤĪ

Masih has been born. I must pray. I must make offerings to the saints to secure his well-being. I must say prayers. I light long candles for Masih. I light them in all the mosques and churches. How like all the other women I've become! I'm so anxious! I put my hand on his forehead several times a day. I'm afraid his little body will be overcome by the filthy heat outside and he'll get a fever. I look at his skin. I count his veins and contemplate his breath. Was his birth a miracle? How does a morose person like me become so light-hearted and kind? I gave birth to Masih. No one makes statues of me. I was afraid I'd give birth to a stone. Did I give birth to this bundle of life? He smells so good! Oh Holy Virgin and child! The statue has come to life. He must survive. I must pray for him. I pray for all the children, even those who will be wicked people.

How depressed I was that day in the darkness of the Isfahan bazaar, behind my dark glasses. I just wandered around alone. I wasn't looking for anything. I was heavy, dragging the weight of my being this way and that way. The quilt shop. They had piled up a mountain of cotton on one side. An old man was sitting among the colorful satin quilts

This story was first published in *Kitāb-i Jum'ah* 9 (Sept. 27, 1979), pp. 21–30.

and the cotton. I thought of God. I sat on a pink satin quilt. The old man sewed very rapidly with a needle. I removed my glasses. The lamplight shimmered on the satin, depressing me more. I knew the sun was shining on the blues of the mosques outside the bazaar.

"How long does it take to make a quilt? Has the price of cotton gone up? Has the satin mill shut down?"

He gave me tea. I buy a blue quilt for Masih. I always keep it clean. I lay it out in the sun once a week. I wash the windows. The house must be sparkling clean. I show Masih the sun and the snow-covered mountains through the clean windows. The pigeons, doves, and sparrows that conquer the city year after year in the fall.

"Where are the little birds?" They've gone. The birds have flown. "Where do all the sparrows come from?" Perhaps I won't be so depressed this fall. That day in the Isfahan bazaar I wanted to cover my head with a pink quilt, have a bitter cry, and then go into the midst of the sunlight and the blues of the mosques and scream.

Crying for nothing. Like that swarm of sparrows. They say the fall is a season of creation. I always cry more in the fall, with the women's morbid black chadors, and the sallow-faced, skinny children who must live under their mother's chadors, go to the *rowzeh*s and weddings, and whine all the time. The smoke-blackened street altars, the bent and leaning white candles. "How many candles do they light in a day?" I lit a candle too. For what? I fled from the midst of the women. I reached the plaza and lost myself among the blues.

If Nanny Masumah hadn't left, I would have made a pilgrimage with her to the shrine of *Emāmzādeh* Abdollah. She always made her offerings there, for her daughter Puran, for me, for her grandchild, and for a canary named Nanny Masumah, which I was unable to care for properly. She'd put on her splendid velvet coat that was worn smooth in places, and she'd put on her white lace shawl over her head. Her shoes sparkled like the ruby in her ring. My disposition improved a little because of her. You couldn't tell whether she was crying or not through her thick glasses. She had made me a doll with those same feeble eyes, one that had turquoise earrings and velvet clothing. She had shortened her own coat to make clothes for my doll. If Nanny Masumah hadn't left I'd have made a doll too and given it to that girl who used to sit by herself and cry in the middle of the road to the shrine of *Emāmzādeh* Abdollah . . . We would have set out together and made the trip. I would have bought a large candle for Masih. I would have carried the candle on my shoulder. When she used to water her walnut sapling in the garden, or sit and look at it, the sun was so pretty coming through her lace scarf! Now the sapling is getting big. This time I know it has nothing to do with Puran. She's gone and she won't be back. She won't even miss the walnut sapling.

She was always dancing and laughing. She was always dancing and crying. She was always making dolls for all the children. She was always watering the flowers and idly caressing their leaves. She would be intoxicated by the smells she loved. She went mad with joy every time a flower unexpectedly came up. She was always reciting prayers, making offerings to the saints, and doing prostrations. Even when there was no Puran she was already her mother. She was always drinking tea, and she ate very little. She always patiently went to the baker's and the butcher's and she cleaned the vegetables with that same patience. She always looked out the window at the garden while she was sweeping. Her clothes were always neat, giving a holy smell. Sometimes she would wear her sapphire ring. Occasionally she said "My father, may he rest in peace, made me a blue and red wooden horse."

She laughed and cried, and I could never tell for the life of

3

me whether she was crying or not, even when she was dancing. Sometimes she said "I pledged an offering of 100 tomans in return for my grandson's protection. I'd do anything for him. He's going to school. He's become a little gentleman, praise God! I want to buy him a toy electric car. Did you see how pretty the table vegetables turned out? It's delightful!"

She made a little satin blanket for my canary, Nanny Masumah. Every day at sunset she'd put her cage in front of the television and sat there alongside it herself so the bird wouldn't get depressed. "Sing, Puran *Khānom*! Chirp, Fati *Khānom*! Watch, I won't let the cat come and eat you. Don't be afraid!"

Sometimes, when she had heard nothing from Puran, she was quiet and somber. She would water the flowers sadly. The sadness and heaviness of several *emāmzādeh*s was visible in her face. "Nanny Masumah! I've shown your doll to everyone!" Silence. She didn't see me. She didn't see anyone. She was looking somewhere far away, perhaps at the height of the walnut tree in the years after her death. Her smile resembled the cramped expression of homeless nursing infants. Her blouse and lace scarf were like the great waves of the ocean, and she like a small piece of coral beneath the water. She no longer heard my voice. Puran's letter finally came. Nanny Masumah danced, laughed, and cried again.

On hot summer days she made fans. She served *sharbat* and drank tea. "I used to make date-nut candies and fried noodles dipped in sugar at weddings. I could do everything. I used to make delicious cookies. I made colorful stockings for Puran and the relatives' children. Now I'm old and can't do anything. 'Now that you're old, Hafez, get out of the tavern.'"*

I hadn't seen her wearing her velvet coat for some time.

---

*Quoting Ḥāfiẓ.

Ammeh *Khānom* said she had given it to a beggar who had no coat. They gave her one of Khosrow's coats. One day she showed me her ring and said, "If you look carefully you can see the image of that red and blue wooden horse in it."

I know she won't be back again.

This fall I hold Masih in my arms and watch the sparrows through the filthy window panes at sunset. I don't take him out. The crowds outside have become annoying. The ugly and pointless shouting makes me moodier. Nanny Masumah, with her beautiful silence, has gone and she won't be back.

Nanny Masumah didn't have time to make dolls last fall and winter: she spent the hours standing in the oil and bread lines. I never saw her talk so much. She repeated all the rumors she heard to us: "They say *Āqā** is coming back. They say this is the end of the line for the oppressor shah. I heard shooting when I was at the bakery today. I was afraid to death. Soldiers stopped a young man right before my eyes. Such a young man! Like a redwood tree. He started to run away and they shot him and martyred him. All martyrs go to heaven. May God give that soldier who shot him an early death, and may the grief of that remain with his mother!"

"Fati *Khānom*, let me tell you about a dream I had: I dreamed I was going to visit the *Āqā*. I didn't know the way, and you were with me. The *Āqā* wasn't there. His wife was there. She had us sit down, showed us all kinds of honor and respect, and brought tea for us. I told her the soldiers were bothering me in the bread and oil lines. I woke up just as *Āqā* was arriving. I wasn't happy. What business does the likes of me have seeing the *Āqā*'s blessed face! He wouldn't visit the dream of a black-face like me. The *Āqā* has work to do. He has to take care of everyone."

---

*Referring to Ayatollah Khomeini.

She had purchased a glass kerosene lamp that was painted red. She put her ruby-colored lantern in the kitchen window and kept it lit all the time. She'd say "I'll keep this lamp lit until *Āqā* returns and everything is put in order." She was careful not to leave the window open, to keep the wind out, and to prevent street urchins from throwing rocks at the window that might hit the lamp. She was more concerned about the lamp than her trees.

"Everything will be alright when the *Āqā* comes. There will be abundance and we'll have plenty of everything. People will no longer die of colds. The *Āqā* will come. Roses will grow beneath his feet. He'll be surrounded by the smell of rosewater. Light will radiate from his glorious presence."

Everything shone when Nanny Masumah spoke of the *Āqā:* her eyes, the lens of her glasses, all the windows, and my heart.

One day Nanny Masumah, Ammeh *Khānom*, and I went to the Behesht-e Zahra Cemetery. The mothers were not crying for the deaths of their children. They were singing anthems by the gravesides. We sang anthems too, and shared our little tin of halvah with everyone. The graves were one with the sky. We sat quietly beside a flower-covered grave with no headstone and watched the sparrows pecking rapidly, eating the grains of wheat and millet scattered over the graves. If I had died Nanny Masumah would have planted a walnut sapling over my grave. She would have scattered wheat and read the opening verse of the Koran over me every Friday. Mothers were sitting quietly by the graves. I looked at a statue of the virgin and her child. Death was so beautiful. I wanted to die too. This time I would die without crying, because of the earth. I would remain in the earth and always smell the sky from among the rocks and the earth. I'd smell the bitter walnut tree that stretched up to the sky. They brought in a corpse. They were holding up a blood-soaked shirt alongside it, singing anthems. We sang anthems too, walking behind the corpse and the blood-soaked shirt.

Nanny Masumah wanted to plant the entire garden with Damascus roses. She had put the *Āqā*'s picture up on every wall. The lamp was lit. I was having fantasies in anticipation of Masih. When Masih came I told him a story:

"Once upon a time long ago, when there was still much time to pass before you would be born, there was a wicked demon living in a distant land who tormented everyone. He wouldn't let the children play and he wouldn't let the adults rest. Not a single heart was happy and not a single pair of lips ever smiled."

I made a stern face, and Masih grimaced. But I wasn't about to let his little heart be sad; I went on at once with the rest of the story.

"Until one day, a holy man came with a demon-killing sword. He went up to the demon, unsheathed his sword, invoked the name of God, and hit the little demon on the neck so hard it made thunder and lightning. The little demon turned into a column of smoke and rose up into the sky. A black cloud appeared. The cloud turned to rain and there was a great deluge! It washed all the blood from the earth and made it green again. Everything dried out, faces smiled again, and the world was filled with praise and joy."

Masih smiled, with his lips, his eyes, and his little heart.

The day *Āqā* was to come, Nanny Masumah, even cleaner and neater than usual, wearing henna and face paints, took several stalks of roses, gave her lamp to Ammeh *Khānom* for safe-keeping, and went to meet him. She had wiped away the tears from around her eyes with cotton and tea. She had put on a new velvet coat.

When my canary died Nanny Masumah's voice was broken with sorrow. She thought the canary had died because of her own neglect. She wouldn't look in my face. She folded the little satin blanket up in plastic and put it in the cage. She

7

filled the cage with artificial flowers and put it in the closet. She buried the canary in a flowerpot with a geranium and sang a song from her own province in a broken voice.

I was depressed again. I had distressing dreams. I dreamed Masih was kissing my face and trying to make me stop worrying. Masih was born at the first light of dawn. Several stern men in black were carrying his little coffin on their shoulders in the last light of sunset. I was afraid. Nanny Masumah's face was filled with foreboding. Her new velvet coat was covered with greasy stains. The lamp, whose red paint was flaking and dropping off, was still lit. She had put her sapphire ring back in its box. Her voice was broken, just like the time Nanny Masumah died. She no longer spoke of the *Āqā*. In the early mornings of winter before the first light of dawn she cleaned the snow off the walnut sapling. The snow and Masih weighed me down. I sewed and knitted clothing for him, and I was afraid. I woke up in terror every night. Every night they broke down the door and came and took my Masih. Men with covered faces who never spoke, wearing long black capes. They broke down the door with the stocks of their rifles.

One day Ammeh *Khānom* said to Khosrow, "Nanny Masumah is sick again. She won't eat a thing."

No one watered the flowers. It was spring and the garden stayed dry. The only thing left was a crooked pine tree. Nanny Masumah, without her glasses, lay beneath a filthy quilt, her red and swollen eyelids fixed on the ceiling. I knew a letter had recently come from Puran, so it had nothing to do with her. She had changed completely. The henna and makeup were gone from her hands. I took her gaunt, cold hand into mine and she withdrew it. She neither saw nor heard me. Nor did she hear Puran's voice. Her white and brown hair dangled messily from beneath a dirty scarf.

"Nanny Masumah! Say something to take the burden from your heart. Let me go get you some tea."

I went to pour tea and found the lamp extinguished. A dirty, greasy lamp with a smoky chimney. It was surrounded by dirty cups and plates. I cleaned and relit the lamp. I could see the kids in the street through the window, hiding under their mothers' chadors. They all seemed to be afraid. Nanny Masumah did not drink the tea. She stared at "noplace" with her swollen eyelids and dried lips. She had turned away from me. I sat beside her so quietly and rubbed her cold hands, so that she saw me and felt the warmth of my hands. She suddenly started crying, a quiet, controlled crying, not like my hysterical crying. She wiped away the tears with a corner of her shawl. Her crying dried up the whole garden. It dried up all the gardens where Masih and I walked in the evenings. The desert. The hot, salty desert of her lips that drank no tea.

She put her glasses on again. She straightened her hair with trembling hands and tucked it under her scarf. She sat on the bed, looked at me, and said, "Excuse me, I've inconvenienced you." I brought her tea, she drank.

She got out of bed the next day. She put on clean clothes and went out and sat by the dry garden. Then she went into the kitchen and extinguished the lamp. I knew she was crying and trembling. She was so depressed! I was so depressed! She tied up her bundle and said goodbye to us. She bought an electric car at the end of the street and set out for her own province. I wanted so much for her to be with me when Masih was born. I don't know whether she can still make children's dolls or not.

I'm so tired! The women have taken their sallow, skinny children into their arms and set out for the *emāmzādeh*s and monasteries to make their offerings. I remain in this room. The milling crowds in the street bother me. Fall is approaching. No one sculpts our image when I'm showing Masih the sparrows. Oh holy virgin and child, I'm so depressed!

Masih is growing up in this very room. Perhaps one day

when the city calms down I'll go into the street and buy him a wooden horse. Masih is growing up and I'm getting old. I pray so much it's aging me. One day they knock on the door, and men with covered faces come in and take him. I remain alone in this room behind dirty window panes. I pray, do prostrations, water the geraniums on the porch in the evening, and scatter seeds for the fall sparrows.

Esfand 1358 [Feb. 20–Mar. 20, 1979]
Translated by John Green

A Walnut Sapling on Masih's Grave

The old owl with the turquoise eyes
Looks down again from the heights
Of the snow-covered peaks
He laughs
At the tired rain
Falling on the sad earth
And the night-flying lovers
Whose flights of fancy have rent their breasts
And remained barren

"I remain
Forever on this rocky height
With a sheathed heart
I sing"

Alas, my anthem
Has dissipated in the murmur of the rain

I know he has averted his eyes
From the center of the earth
He knows not that his wings are of wax
He sits on the snow-covered peak
And watches the distant sun with a smile

FĀṬIMAH ABṬAHĪ

*Born in Tehran in 1948, Abṭahī lives in Tehran and is a gradu-
ate of Tehran University. She is a painter and a musician, and has
written and produced children's television programs for Iranian television.*

This is from *Stories by Iranian Women Since the Revolution,* translated by Soraya Sullivan.
Austin, TX: Center for Middle Eastern Studies, 1991: 71.

🌺 *After the Last Day*

MAHSHĪD AMIR-SHAHY

To my sister Mahvash

You had put on jasper-green clothing and gathered your silky black hair above your head. I knew you were worried. I could see it in your eyes. You always speak with your eyes—always, since you were a mere toddler. When you were happy—and how seldom you were happy—your pupils would expand and the whites of your eyes would turn blue. When you were sad your eyes would settle back into the sockets. You don't know this yourself.

You sat beside me. "Worried?" I asked.

"Yes."

I laughed and put on my sunglasses so you wouldn't notice if any tears came.

"I promise not to do anything foolish," I said. "I've become much wiser you know."

"Not so much," you said, "but you did promise. . . ."

"I'll go to bed early," I said. "I won't get angry, and I won't take a husband, OK?"

"I'm serious," you said.

This story is from the collection *Ba'd as Rūz-i Ākhar* [*After the Last Day*] (Tehran: Amīr Kabīr, 1348 [1969]), pp. 7–21.

"Do you want me to go to bed late, then?" I said. "Do you want me to take a husband?"

"Don't make me mad," you said. "Can't you see how worried I am about you?"

Of course I saw, and I felt like crying. In all my life no one has ever been as beautifully worried about me as you, not since I was a very small child. When I would go to get my school report, when I had a match to play, when you didn't like my friends, you were simply worried.

"Will you write?" I asked.

"You know I'm bad at letter writing," you said.

For a moment a hint of shame replaced the look of anxiety in your eyes.

"You are quite good at it," I said. "You're lazy, lazy. If you don't write . . ."

But it makes no difference at all if you don't write. Your heart will be close to me and my heart will be close to you. We're often separated from one another. The first time you were twelve and I was fifteen. I was so giddy I couldn't even cry. The round glass in my window was filled with your face. Then the airplane turned around and I no longer saw you. I burst into tears.

How many letters did I write you during that year I was away? I don't remember. A great many. You wrote some too, and you wrote so beautifully. But you are lazy about writing. When I was going to school and you were at home, you wanted to come with me.

"I'll become a porter," you'd say.

"Eh? Why?" They'd ask.

"'Cause I don't go to school," you'd say, and I don't know where you had gotten that idea.

Then you went to school too. I used to solve your problems. Mother used to do your homework. Even then you were wiser and more intelligent than I, and later a much better human being as well.

"You must write," I said.

"I'll try," you said. "Forget that for now. You promised to take care of yourself. You promised not to tire yourself out. You promised not to smoke cigarettes."

"Cigarettes?" I said. "When did I promise not to smoke cigarettes?"

"Come on, you smoke too much," you said. "So cut down a little." And you were annoyed.

"Well, you smoke a lot too," I said, "so you . . ."

"Are we competing then?" you asked. There was neither anxiety nor shame in your eyes. There was feigned annoyance. You had wanted to trick me into giving my word, but your eyes, like your entire being, are incapable of lying, and I wasn't fooled, because I know I'm not competing with you, and I know that you know I'm not. How can I compete with you? You're so much better than I am that you actually think of me as your better. Always and everywhere you stand in my shadow so only I am visible. Is it possible to compete with you?

I only competed with you during those early days. Those days when I didn't know you, when my nursemaid was assigned to you and Mamma was always in bed with you beside her, and I was only in the room when you nursed. I would press myself against Mamma's side and watch you sucking. Always hungry, you drank the milk ravenously and then slept under Mamma's breasts.

"Thank God this child has a good appetite," Mamma would say with satisfaction.

Then they brought in Nanny Shekar to nurse you, the nursemaid was mine again, and mother got out of bed. And the competition ended.

"No, no competition," I said. "Forget that. I'll cut down if I can, but I won't promise."

"Let's see," you said. "Now what else did you promise to do?"

"Hey, drop it," I said. "We only have a few more hours."

Time was more of an issue in my relationship with you than with any other person or thing. Every moment we were together and every instant we were apart time was present and felt. From the day you came into existence, time existed. Before I knew there were twenty-four hours in a day, sixty minutes in an hour and sixty seconds in a minute, I felt time because of you.

Several hours before you were born Father took me to his office so I wouldn't be a nuisance. He tried to tell me you were on the way, but I didn't understand. I only understood that a little baby was in Mamma's belly—and I couldn't understand why it was there—and it was going to be coming out—and again I didn't understand why. If I had been in Mamma's belly I would have stayed there.

I remember Father's office, the sound of the clock on the wall, and the clerk who would bring in one piece of paper and take out another. I remember that the clerk was completely outside my world and the expectation of your arrival, and, although I didn't know precisely why, that the sound of the clock was directly related to the fact that you were on the way.

Then the nursemaid came. I was delighted to see her and jumped into her arms. Uncharacteristically, however, she didn't pay much attention to me. She talked to Dad.

"Is it over?" Father had asked. He put out his cigarette and lit another one.

"Yes," said the nursemaid, hanging her head.

"Is this one a girl too?" Father asked.

The nursemaid said nothing.

"What's wrong with a girl?" Father said laughing.

I didn't know what they were talking about. I watched stunned.

"So why are you quiet?" you said.

"I want to apologize for upsetting you the other day," I

said, "but I don't know how to do it. I'm depressed, but I don't know exactly how to apologize. Well, I apologize anyway."

"Why are you apologizing?" you said. "You didn't do anything."

"Every time I argue with you I'm as sorry as a dog afterwards."

My arguments with you are never really arguments. They are always crude, tasteless jokes that get carried too far. Do you remember the day I poured salt in your mouth? That was a joke too, and maybe in my six-year-old mind I thought if I poured salt in your mouth it would be a joke worth its salt. You were three years old.

"Close your eyes and open your mouth," I said. You closed your eyes tightly, so tightly that they resembled my drawings of the sun: only one spot surrounded by the rays of your eyelashes. You opened your mouth eagerly and I emptied a handful of salt into it. You coughed—and I thought you were choking. When you stopped coughing I went off and cried to myself. For several days whenever they gave me anything good to eat or when I was able to get something from Mamma's cupboard, I put it in your path. I couldn't come to you and say "this is for you." I was afraid you'd think I was giving you salt again.

"That's it—sorry as a dog," I said.

"Hey," you said, "for God's sake don't talk this way. Cowering doesn't become you. Anyway, what happened that day was my fault."

And you smiled at me from the bottom of your velvet eyes, just like the first day you laughed for me. You don't know the time I'm referring to. You don't remember. I'm talking about the beginning of my own world. I'm talking about the day you came into the world. Your arrival in the world was the beginning of my world, because your birth is my earliest memory. Is a person's world anything other than his memories?

They put me on the edge of Mamma's bed. I threw myself on top of her and squeezed her tightly.

"Can I kick you in the tummy now?" I said to her.

"Oh! My poor darling. You waited nine months for that!" said Mamma.

Mamma told me these things later. I didn't remember myself. But I remember Mamma saying "Don't you want to see the baby?"

I hugged her tighter. I don't think I really wanted to see you.

"If you only knew how pretty she is," Mamma said. "She has a little hand this size, a little foot this size."

My curiosity was aroused. I wanted to see your little feet and hands, and they showed you to me. You were asleep in your little bed. Your feet were nowhere to be seen, you had made fists of your little hands, and you were frowning. I didn't like you.

"Do you want to hold her?" Mamma said.

I frowned and stuck my chin into my collar.

"See how pretty she is," Mamma said.

"She's not pretty at all," I said. "Why is she so red?"

"Because she's just been born," said Mama.

"So what," I said, "Why is she so red?"

"That will clear up in a few days," said Mamma. "She'll be white. You were just like that when you came into the world."

I choked. "I was not!" I said.

How often I wanted to look like you later when we grew up. I always wanted to look like you.

Mamma laughed. Becoming angrier, I said "I was not! I was not!"

"Don't yell. She'll wake up," Mamma said.

You waved your little hand in the air a few times and sucked your lower lip. Mamma pulled the blanket away from you and inched the mattress under you. I saw your soft red feet and held them in my hand.

"I'll make her some slippers out of almond shells," said Mamma. "What do you think?"

I squeezed your foot.

"I'll make her a hat out of a walnut shell too."

I looked at your head. "She's bald," I said.

"No, she's not bald," Mamma said. "She's got a lot of hair. Other babies have no hair at all."

"So what else will we do with her?" I said.

"We won't do anything with her," said Mamma. "We'll cuddle her and kiss her."

"I mean how will we dress her?" I said impatiently.

"Ah, how will we dress her. Let's see. What can we do. We'll make her a skirt of tulip petals."

Later when you got older you had a red velvet dress with puffed-out organdy sleeves and a white bib. You looked like a red flower in it, but every time you put it on I remembered the tulip that was to have been your garment.

"And what else?" I asked.

"We'll make her a chador out of onion skin."

"What about her hat?"

"Her hat? Ah, her hat! No problem. One day she'll wear a hat, another day she'll wear a chador."

"What else! What else!"

"That's all. Then she'll come to the door of your room with her almond shell slippers. 'Tik tik tik.' She'll knock on the door. 'Tak tak tak'."

I was delighted. "Tak tak tak. Tik tik tik. Tak tak tak." And I woke you up. You opened your eyes. So much softer than my doll's eyes. And you were so pretty. You laughed. I'm sure you laughed, with your large black velvet eyes and your long black lashes canopied over them. I wanted to hug you but I was embarrassed to say so and Mamma pushed the matter no further. I stood next to you waiting for another laugh. You didn't laugh.

I hugged you. I put your head on my shoulder and kept it there until the tears welled up in my eyes disappeared.

"Oh, I'm such an ass," I said. "I've messed up your hair."

"To hell with my hair," you said. "Talk to me."

I have so much to tell you. Whenever I have a lot to tell you, important things, all I do is talk nonsense. I don't say anything important. I talk about my diet, about the tea at the office, which smells like cowslips and tastes like plaster, or about the candies in Monavar's cupboard that stretch like gum. It was the same way then as well. Did I ever speak of Grandfather's death? Of Mamma's going away? I didn't, because you knew everything, without my saying a word.

You were seven when Grandfather died. I was ten. For several days I didn't even look into your eyes, because that would have been speaking too. The first time I realized that you talk with your eyes was two years before Grandfather died: when Mamma went away. After that, every time something bad happened I didn't have the courage to look into your eyes, because all the pain of the event would settle there. And with each look layer after layer would pile up on one's shoulders and crush one with their weight. I didn't talk to you, either of Grandfather's death or of Mamma's leaving. Instead, I spoke of inconsequential things. "The teacher plays favorites," I'd say, or "I'm not on speaking terms with one of my friends," or "Ask father's permission for us to go to the cinema," or "If my foot hadn't slipped I'd have scored."

I won't talk about that other event now either. It's still too soon. They still haven't taken out the stitches and I'm still weak and in pain. Perhaps I would not talk about it later either. What is there to talk about anyway? Should I say I tried unsuccessfully to kill myself? What a joke. Suicide is a beautiful and heroic act, provided one succeeds. If a person doesn't die, it's a joke.

The moment I opened my eyes you appeared before me, in the jasper-green dress you were wearing when you left.

"Talk to me," you had said.

"Did you pack everything?" I said. "Don't forget anything."

You glanced casually through your bag. "No," you said, "I've got everything. What shall I send you from there?"

"Letters."

I tore up the letter I had written you. Your letter, Mamma's letter, and Father's letter. I had written only those three. The ritual was fully performed. It all seems so funny now. I had written to Mamma telling her to try to comfort you. Who could have comforted Mama?

How lucky I am. Not because I didn't die, but because when I was about to die I was sure you and Mamma would be grief stricken. Perhaps this idea kept me from dying. I want to live now, for Mamma, for you, for myself. If only the pain would stop soon, if only the stitches would heal, so I won't have to explain when you come back, and I'll be able to wave my hands when I go to meet you, as I did the day you left.

When you come your face will be in every round window, even when the airplane turns around. I'll wave my hand comfortably and painlessly.

"Talk to me," you'll say.

I'll say, "The tea at the office is as bad as ever," and "I've lost five pounds. The yellow shoes you sent matched my purse perfectly."

Translated by John Green

MAHSHĪD AMIR-SHAHY

The author spells her name Amir-Shahy in the Latin alphabet, whereas it is spelled Amīrshahī in the Library of Congress. Born in Kermanshah, she was sent to a boarding school in England and then trained as a physicist at London University, but abandoned physics later to pursue a career in writing. She currently lives in Paris, where she continues to write fiction. Her published works include a long list of translations from English to Persian, such as P. L. Travers' Mary Poppins, *E. B. White's* Charlotte's Web, *James Thurber's* Fables for Our Time, *Giuseppe Fiori's* Antonio Gramsci: Life of a Revolutionary, *Lawrence Durrell's* Justine, *and from the French into Persian, Shapour Bakhtiar's* Ma Fidelité. *While living in Iran prior to the 1979 revolution, she contributed short stories, articles, and translations to such journals as* Alifbā, Nigīn, Farhang va Zindagī, Rudakī, *and* Āyandigān.* *Of her writing, she says ". . . I have no mission, and I am not a committed and responsible writer. I have shown no talent for creating stupendous works, and so must confess with embarrassment that readers will probably understand my stories."** Following the publication of her novel* Dar Ḥazar *in 1987, there has been renewed interest in Amīrshāhī's work. Since then she has made two trips to the United States to give lectures and readings, and has been very active in Paris and elsewhere encouraging Iranian writers to take a public stand in defense of the rights of novelist Salman Rushdie.*

---

*Mahshīd Amīrshāhī, personal communication.
**Mahshīd Amīrshāhī, introduction to *Muntakhab-i Dāstān'hā* (Tehran: Intishārāt-i Tūs, 1351 [1972]).

❧ *Peyton Place: Tehran, 1972*

MAHSHID AMIR-SHAHY

Saturday night Mama and the whole mess of them were supposed to go visit that new son-in-law of poor old Uncle Erfagh. I thought I'd stay home and work on my algebra. Then I was going to watch "Peyton Place." The fact is, before that night I'd never seen "Peyton Place." Not once. Promise not to tell Mehri.

Not that it's important. But I tell you: they're all talking about Betty and Allison as if Betty and Allison had grown up with them. On Sunday when we got together to work on trigonometry problems, I was just starting to read out the first one when Mehri asked Homa, "Hasn't Allison been getting a little thin?"

Homa said, "No she just looks thinner because she cut her hair."

Rokhsar said, "I think it was a big mistake. It looks awful on her."

Homa said, "If you ask me it looks rather smart. A lot prettier than Betty, anyway." And if I hadn't started grumbling, "Hey, we've got these trig problems here," they would

This story is a translation of *Piytun Pilays* from the collection *Bih Sīghah-'i Avval Shakhs-i Mufrad [In the First Person Singular]* (Tehran: Intishārāt-i Buf, 1350 [1972]), pp. 35–52.

never have stopped arguing—which one was prettier, Betty or Allison.

Okay, okay, when they talk about it that way you're not going to say who are these people, I've never heard of them. And lately it's not just Mehri and the girls either. Even in our house, Simin and that whole crew; they're all talking about "Peyton Place," and just as bad. Simin's husband Amir even. The nights he plays poker are the only times he misses it. Simin's the worst though. Let her miss a program. She sulks around the house like a dog on a leash until she can phone enough people to piece the story together. She's never satisfied. She always thinks she's missing a piece. Or take Maliheh. Let someone mention anything they saw on television and listen to her make fun of it. She says she never watches television. But then a few days ago Simin was complaining that she had missed another program and what should I hear but Maliheh giving her a blow-by-blow account. I got there just as she was saying "That was when Rodney was kissing Betty."

Simin gasped. "No! Kissing her? And after they've been divorced too."

"Well, there you are," said Maliheh, meaning, "Simin, you're so old-fashioned."

Simin is always scared Maliheh will think she's old-fashioned. She knew what Maliheh was thinking and said "I mean you can't help but feel sorry for Steve. How beastly for him."

"Who's Steve?" I couldn't help but ask.

Maliheh started to explain, but it was still awfully boring, and I asked, "Maliheh, aren't you the one who never watches television?"

Simin said, "Suri. You're getting in the way. Don't pay any attention to her, Maliheh. Go on. And then? Then what did Betty do?" Maliheh went on. She filled in the rest as if I hadn't said a word, or as if she'd said there was nothing she liked better than watching a little television now and then.

But as I was saying Mama and the whole mess of them were going to Uncle Erfagh's house. The whole dynasty was invited. Back on the actual day of the engagement ceremony Uncle Erfagh hadn't invited anyone because the forty days of mourning for Grandma weren't up yet and it had to be a quiet occasion. That's why no one had yet seen our relatives-to-be. We hadn't really sized them up yet, and that is what everyone was dying to do. We may not have seen them yet, but everyone who had any inside information had put it on the table.

Like that night at Maliheh's parents' place. I must have told you about this. That's all they talked about. It started with grumbling about Uncle Erfagh's hurry and why hadn't he waited until the forty days were up.

Maliheh's mother said, "I beg your pardon, but young people these days just don't have any respect. If they'd waited a few days more what would have been the harm?"

Apparently she forgot what a hurry she was in to get her Maliheh married off to Brother. She didn't even wait for Uncle Hosein to get back from his trip: "These young people," or so she was saying back then, "I beg your pardon but young people these days—the world belongs to them anyway. We old folks will just have to go along with them."

Then Aunt Fakhri said, "It's the fault of us grown-ups for letting it happen. Showkat ought to know about this. Showkat, aren't you ashamed of yourself? You don't really think your little Parvaneh is going to be left stuck on our hands, do you? She's such a pretty little thing. Well off too. So what if this match doesn't work out. There are lots of men. Scratch a dog's head and you'll find a suitor."

Listen carefully now. This is the same Aunt Fakhri who got so excited when some diseased moron turned up asking for me. Don't tell anybody. And she was saying, "God knows he's a good boy. These days you don't find husbands just anywhere. You might have a regular full moon for a daughter, an heiress, perhaps, sitting at home just dying for a husband . . ."

That was when Mama got a little angry and said, "Really, Fakhri, it's not as if I had a little misshapen homunculus or a beggar for a daughter. And she's not dying for a husband yet, thank God. It's not time yet for that kind of talk."

It was a good thing Mama cut her off because if she hadn't I would have become the topic of one of our endless family conferences. And that poor dope and I might have ended stuck with each other. But never mind that, I was talking about Parvaneh and her fiancé. Uncle Hosein asked Brother, "How's Erfagh doing financially?"

"I really don't know," Brother answered, "but Parvaneh's a nice girl. Good looking too." He seemed to be blushing a little.

And you would hardly believe the look Maliheh gave him. Brother was interested in her before he married Maliheh, but I always suspected that when they confiscated Uncle Erfagh's property the family changed his mind for him.

Mama's brother Ardeshir said, "Well, if you ask my humble opinion, Uncle Erfagh is fumbling at the bottom of the sack. The end. Kaput. And there is the reason why he is consenting to give his daughter away to this individual."

Uncle Hasan asked, "And the groom's family? They're doing all right?"

"Unlimited resources, my dear sirs," replied Uncle Ardeshir, "Unlimited resources. This groom's father had, before the Second World War, perhaps one suit of clothes. During the war he sold used tires and now he is wealthy. You couldn't count it."

Uncle Hosein said "Yes I know him all right. But devil take that kind of wealth. When his wife was dying everyone said to take her overseas for treatment but he wouldn't do it. He was afraid for every little shahi he spent. All he'd say was, 'Our doctors here are just fine, thank you.'"

I broke in with a question. "Do you mean his wife is dead, Uncle Hosein?"

Uncle said, "No, she's alive all right. Fat as a bear too."

I wanted to say but then he wasn't so far wrong, but Uncle Hosein's wife, Fati, who went overseas for what she called, in English, her "check-up" once a month, said, "The point is how stingy this man is."

I said, "I was thinking the point must be that his wife got better," but nobody paid any attention and Uncle Hasan said, "If they'd just give me that money . . ."

"To dump it into the toilet, I suppose," said Aunt Fakhri.

Uncle Hasan didn't seem to hear. You don't know in our family what an extraordinary talent they have for not hearing things. But he added, "I saw this villa in Nice . . ."

Simin's husband said, "Before you get to Nice you'd lose the money for the down-payment on that villa at Monte Carlo. Why don't you be a nice fellow and hand that money over to me for safe-keeping?"

"Fine," added Simin, "so you can go chase women."

"Womanizing?" he replied, "Me? I wish."

Aunt Fakhri said, "Listen. You kids don't know the value of money. When I was a youngster like you . . ."

But Simin's husband said, "Now now, Auntie, you're still young. And you're still a regular full moon too."

Aunt Fakhri gave one of those piercing laughs that reminded me of the shrieks that came out of her when Grandma died, and said, "You little rascal. Aren't you the clever one."

I said to Simin's husband, Amir, "Shall I tell her what you were saying about Aunt Fakhri's youth and good looks? Shall I?"

Aunt Fakhri said, "Yes, go ahead. He is sweet. Well, what did he say?"

Simin looked ready to spring at me and Mama was biting her lip. Simin's husband just said, "Now, Auntie, you were talking about money." And in my direction he made a threatening gesture.

Aunt Fakhri said, "That's right. I was saying, if I had that much money . . ."

Uncle Hasan whispered into Maliheh's father's ear, "She'd bury it all in the garden." Maliheh's father started to laugh but his eye fell on his wife. His voice died out and Uncle Hasan's laugh became a solo performance.

Maliheh's mother glared at her husband and said to Uncle Hasan, "You were addressing me, Sir? Anyway, I only say I neither want that sort of money, nor, I beg your pardon, would I want for a father-in-law a man who used to sell used tires. Now if Erfagh ed-Dowleh gave his daughter to some aristocrat down at the heels, what harm would that do?"

Simin's husband said, "It wouldn't do any harm, but there wouldn't be that much difference either. Only we would have had that down-at-the-heels aristocrat to gossip about instead. I can hear it now: 'The clumsy fool—he's let the family fortune just melt away.'"

What Amir said was right. It was funny too, but Uncle Ardeshir didn't give anyone a chance to agree with him. He cut him off before the burst of assenting laughter and said, "Really, Sir, I must protest. Of course there is no dignity in being beggars. All I want to say is that one should not seek one's wealth by every means available. Money is a good thing provided one gains it in a respectable and honorable way. As a porter for instance, or a garbage collector . . ."

Honestly sometimes Uncle talks such nonsense that it could break your heart. Do you know of any porters or garbage collectors, no matter how respectable or honorable they might have been, who have amassed considerable fortunes in their porterage or their street cleaning? Well, do you?

That was when Mother's mother Khanom Jan spoke up. "Well, let us hope the little bride is happy. The rest doesn't really matter."

There was a general nod in agreement, but Uncle Ardeshir intervened again. "Nonsense, Khanom Jan. They've married the girl off to money, and money doesn't buy happiness."

The uplifted heads about to nod in agreement with Khanom Jan started to redeploy themselves to agree with Uncle Ardeshir. But Khanom Jan said, "Thank God you've never had to understand what it really is to be without money. If you really understood that, my dears, you'd know what sort of things money does buy. Health, education, comfort. Maybe happiness too. Yes, even happiness."

Even when Khanom Jan says something you really wish weren't true, you think about it for a little and you see it's true all right. With Uncle Ardeshir it's the other way around: even when he says something right it sounds a little off. I mean he always sounds like a school composition. No matter how true it might be it's so insipid you just can't bear it. What he said just now, for instance: "Money doesn't buy happiness." How often do you think I've been assigned that one to write an essay on? And every time I've tortured myself for quite a while trying to demonstrate that money doesn't buy happiness. If they give that assignment this year I'll include what Khanom Jan said. If they lower the grade, let them.

I thought Uncle Ardeshir would back off after what Khanom Jan said, but did he? His voice seemed to have gone up one notch. "I wouldn't expect that of you, Khanom Jan. A young girl should marry someone she's really in love with. How is money going to change that?"

So I said, "But how do you know that Parvaneh doesn't love him?"

Maliheh's mother lifted one eyebrow even higher than usual and gave Father's sister Aunt Fakhri a look which said,

"I beg your pardon, my dear, but you see how shameless this generation has become."

Uncle Ardeshir said, "Pardon?"

This is another of Uncle Aredshir's strategies. When he really can't think of an argument sufficient to break his opponent's teeth, either it's "Here is my humble proposal" or "I just wouldn't expect that of you," or if that doesn't do the job, he lets on that he hasn't quite heard. But he does it with such lofty scorn that he seems to say, "I didn't hear you, but then nonsense like that is hardly worth repeating." But since I really had him this time I didn't back down, and enunciated carefully, "I only asked where you had heard that Parvaneh didn't . . ."

At that point Brother broke in, "And how would you know that she is in love with him, you little sneak?"

Brother's replies are always like that, repeating the tone of your voice just to reverse the flow of your argument. Usually I don't answer, but this time I couldn't help myself. "I know, because Parvaneh told me. She said they're both in love with each other."

Actually I hadn't seen Parvaneh since the New Year holidays, and anyway we don't talk much when I do see her, and honestly I didn't know whether they were in love or not. But the way the family was going on about it, it seemed that if the groom's father ever did sell used tires in the street she wouldn't be allowed to fall in love with the son if she wanted to. And they hadn't said a single word about the son or what kind of person he might be anyway.

They just went on and on about the father. These aristocrats with their pedigrees don't do a damn thing to keep up their names, or fortunes for that matter—and what's more they don't really like each other, but if a poor soul comes along without any ancestors to boast about and manages to get rich, they all act as if it were their heritage he'd used to do it. At any rate, Uncle Erfagh's new son-in-law didn't sell used tires. It was his father. And what's wrong with selling used tires anyway? Do you know? I really don't understand it, but I can assure you that in my family whenever they want to make someone an outcast they just say his father sold used tires after the war. What do they do themselves? You'd think all we did in our family was scientific research and plans for the betterment of mankind. Really.

But you can't say all these things to them. And I didn't. The little I said had the specific effect of closing Uncle Ardeshir's mouth a few degrees, and then to get Brother angry. Now the reason Brother got so mad was that he had expected Parvaneh to pine away over him the rest of her life. Here the boy gets married and goes about his own business; the girl however should sit on the shelf like a bottle of pickles, gradually ripening into an old maid. Now let Maliheh say whatever she wants about how equally men and women are treated.

But I was telling you about Parvaneh and her husband. In fact I was pretty worried. What if the husband turned out to be a good-for-nothing and Parvaneh wasn't in love with him after all?

Simin asked, "Tell me the truth, Suri. She told you herself?" It was clear that Simin really wanted it to be true so she could use this love story as an example to her husband for the next few days. You don't know how romantic Simin is, and how frustrated she gets because he isn't. At all. When Richard Burton married Elizabeth Taylor, Simin wouldn't talk to Amir for a week.

Maliheh had her eyes glued to Brother to see what he had to say.

Brother aimed a smile in Maliheh's direction. Barely. Which made her even more uncomfortable. "Don't be silly," he told Simin, "You still don't know her? Do you really think that she understands what love is? And lovers?"

Simin's husband said, "Be fair. This at least she understands. Better than us anyway. And you keep on talking
about engagements and marriages in front of her. She looks
like a monkey on a hot roof."

"Madame, why aren't you thinking about getting Suri
married off?"

Mama's eyes narrowed. Amir continued. "As the man in
the story says, let's talk about selling the livestock for a
while." Ho ho ho. More laughter.

Simin's husband said, "Really. I'm serious."

Uncle Hasan said, "You? Serious?" Now it was my turn to
laugh.

Simin's husband said, "What did I tell you—talk about
selling the livestock and look at her cheer up. Madame, Parvaneh's future husband has a younger brother. It wouldn't be
a bad idea if you could tie Suri to his beard."

Mama said, "Oh really?" She had been quiet all this time.
Amir said, "Yes indeed."

Mother's brother Ardeshir gave a few mighty puffs on his
pipe and said, "That's a surprise. I didn't know. What's this
boy like?"

"A perfect gentleman," Amir replied. "He's studied
abroad. He's quite educated." Then he pointed me out to
Uncle Hosein and winked. I caught myself listening very
carefully. I could have kicked myself. Simin's husband said,
"She'll be dreaming from now till Saturday when she will
finally set eyes upon him."

But Simin said, "Oh no. The party's on Saturday? What
about 'Peyton Place'?"

I said to Amir, "If you're going to talk, just keep on talking. But I'm not going anywhere Saturday."

Simin's husband said, "Oh yes. You can't say you're not
going to eat and then complain that the portion you've been
served is too small. Don't worry. They'll take you along."

Simin said to Mama, "Can't we change the day?"

I said to Simin's husband, "Take me? The hell they will. I'm not going."

Brother said, "Hey, watch your tongue."

I said, "You'd better watch yours."

Uncle Ardeshir said, "You are invited, young lady."

I said, "Mama, didn't Uncle say that it wasn't necessary for me to go and you agreed, didn't you?"

Mama said, "Give me a minute to see just what Amir is saying. Amir, how old is he? What does he do for a living?"

I said, "I'm not going anywhere Saturday."

Brother said, "Oh hell. As if anybody cared. The spoiled brat."

Simin continued to ask anyone and everyone, "But can't we meet some other day?" But no one answered her. It was clear that the spectacle of Uncle Erfagh's son-in-law would be more interesting than "Peyton Place." But just between you and me, if the film of our family beats "Peyton Place," then "Peyton Place" must be pretty bad.

But no matter how entertaining it was going to be I wanted to stay home Saturday and after homework watch "Peyton Place." Do you think they let me? I had just settled down to my algebra when Mama and Uncle Ardeshir came into the room to prod me into getting ready. Nothing I said made any difference.

I said, "I can't. I have piles of homework."

Uncle said, "Don't be stubborn now, Dear. The radio said school's going to be closed on account of this snow. Get up and get ready." And he didn't wait for an answer. He went down to tell Ali Agha the driver to put the chains on the tires and park Uncle's car in the courtyard. The gate is eight meters wide, but Uncle Ardeshir still can't quite manage to thread the car through it.

I was so busy being mad that I forgot I should be happy about school being closed. Mama didn't waste a second though. She threw the closet door open and handed out my dark blue velvet outfit with the rabbit-fur coat. I said, "I'm not wearing that."

Mama said. "My closet is open too. Go ahead. Take whatever you want Darling and put it on. But do be quick. We'll have to pick up Khanom Jan on our way."

If I had wanted to go to a party of my own Mama wouldn't have let me near her closet. But now when they wanted to take me it was, "Go ahead. Take whatever you like."

So I took a whole hour. I threw everything out of Mama's closet and spread out every earring and necklace there was. Finally I put on my own grey pullover and black trousers, and then I tied a black scarf around my neck.

You should have seen the look on Mama and Uncle Ardeshir's face when they saw me. It was as if the ceiling had fallen in.

Mama said, "Surely you're not going to go in braids?"

I said, "When I don't braid it it gets messy. And that might be hazardous to Uncle's reputation."

Uncle said uncomfortably. "We'd better go, Madame. It's useless. Totally useless."

I was about to say, "What a fuss just to visit someone who used to sell used tires. What if we were going to a party at an honest street-cleaner's house?" But at that moment I slipped on the snow and fell. I didn't even get to start my speech. My pants got soaking wet. And I never got to see "Peyton Place."

Translated by Michael Beard

❧ *Haj Barekallah*

MĪHAN BAHRĀMĪ

The sound of the trumpet was cold and cutting, like the strike of a sword cutting through space, the distance, and the wall, and brought with it anxiety, like a cold breath. The sound of the trumpeter was despondent, as if calling a dead man who is sleeping in a far-off place, waiting in vain.

They always came to the square early in the morning because the summer days were long and hot. But the trumpeter played his horn an hour before the chanters to assemble the crowd. The lament singers chanted. They were young. They wore headdresses on their heads and abas on their shoulders. Their black headbands were old and worn. They conversed together in the middle of their singing, with prying eyes that searched the crowd around the square. When singing, they pointed in this direction and that with their hands. And the verses they sang were old and depressing. My mother would say, "They learn the verses from each other and pass them on from one generation to the next."

Among them, sometimes there was a child whose childish voice sounded high and out of harmony. They would dress him in an old green gown and a little black turban and

---

This is translated from the story "Ḥāj Bārikallāh," published in the journal *Nāmah-ʾi Kānūn-i Nivīsandigān-i Irān* 2 (Tehran: Intishārāt-i Āgāh, 1358 [1979]), pp. 85–106.

hang a stained canvas on his chest that made the women weep before the passion play.

My mother would say, "The *ta'ziyeh* operators have several wives. They train the children when they are still in diapers."

But Uncle's wife would say, "They bring some of them from other places." And she would look up at the ceiling, ask God for forgiveness, spit in the space between her thumb and index finger and say, "Their sins will be on their own heads. They kidnap them. . . ! May God have mercy. And they take the girls to be given away as temporary wives. They are capable of any sinister thing, so it brings them bad luck and misery."

And she was right. Their poverty was obvious from their old clothes and the ill omen of their portraying martyrdom. Sometimes when the show was not going well, it was carried out like a puppet show. In one corner, the blood-colored ink stains, the red- and green-colored feathers on helmets, and shiny lead armor were mingled, children would wail over straw-stuffed headless bodies, women would throw straw on their heads, and in another corner, the *ta'ziyeh* operators would be making rounds, but before the brass collection bowl could be held before the people, they had reached home.

Near the time for the call for noon prayers, the trumpet would sound off for the last time, the patched tents would be gathered up from the square, and martyrdom would disappear like dust into the air. My mother would shake her head and say, "It all has to do with belief. People have lost their faith." She would sigh, and our eyes would meet. Her glance had turned somber with regret. Then, despondently, both of us would leave the house to go to the *ta'ziyeh* performances at Bagh Tuti and Baghcheh Alijan. We were both young then.

The *ta'ziyeh* performance would last from dawn to two

hours before dusk, and it was so crowded, as if people had sprung from the ground, the trees, and the roofs.

The performance itself was elaborate and costly. When it was performed for the notables, they would bring jewels and costumes from the shrine's endowments and also Arabian horses with bejeweled saddles and paraphernalia from His Holiness's private property. The king would sit on the portico of the shrine, the khans were honored to stand at his service, and the ladies would sit behind the net curtains, eat candy and Sepahsalari bread, and curse the favorite maidens of the king.

For the Mokhtar episode, the male cook would prepare food. And once when Haj Barekallah was going to be there, they had brought in Zellossoltan's ivory throne. But that day, the *ta'ziyeh* was disrupted and the ivory throne was almost destroyed in the commotion. The commotion arose because of Haj Barekallah and the Alamdar clan, who were in charge of the shrine's endowment.

As my mother explained, "Haj Barekallah is tall and broad-shouldered and has a good voice. He wears a black velvet costume with a steel helmet, black feather, and a silver-studded belt. He rides a brass-colored horse, takes the black banner, and comes to 'Mokhtar's court' to avenge the 'Sire of the Martyrs.'"

"Horr-e Shahid-e Riyahi wears a white shroud over a red gown, holds a Koran in one hand and a sword in the other, kisses the stirrup of the King of the Martyrs, and attacks the army of the infidels single-handedly."

"Dressed in green, Abbas carries a sheepskin of water on his shoulder and with his hands chopped off, he sets out towards the Euphrates. The women start such a commotion, as if an earthquake has struck. They send him Western boots, agate arm bands and other gifts. Many women who had it good lost their luck and became homeless over Haj Barekallah."

My uncle's wife said, "His voice drives you out of your mind. When he holds a note and sings 'Life's table is not worth setting,' men and women alike really get stirred up, and those who are in love with him faint."

They spoke about him and their faces, like flowers that have been given water, opened up. Coriander flower chadors, braided hair with tassels and yellow two-rial coins and especially shiny, starched scarves blossomed in Russian-made mirrors; womanhood, like a plant, set roots in youth; and bodies with a bittersweet heartbeat helped awaken drowsy emotions.

We sat in twos and fours, wove shawls, nightcaps, and scarves and embroidered them with our sorrows.

In those days, a man passed through the dark corners, through the hardness of the high walls and the unspoken thoughts of the houses, invoking a sweet belief in his uniqueness. He shone in the women's conversation, with his colorful sparks of silk and steel. Wherever women gathered, they spoke of him, in the "Uprising of Mokhtar" and "Abbas the Water Carrier."

But the men treated this story differently. They did not like the scent of the women's joyful daydreaming. At that time, Uncle, Haj Amu, had apparently suspected or heard from someone that the women in the inner courtyard took pleasure in the *ta'ziyeh* and tried to keep on top of it before anything could happen.

Haj Lotfollah Dulabi, who was my mother's uncle, was sitting that day in the most prominent place in the room on a little mattress with a cushion for his back, and there was not a sound except for the monotonous high-pitched chirping of a canary whose cage Uncle liked to hang near the window. Khatun proved her good fortune with this same canary. When she joined the household, Uncle gave the canary away to someone. Uncle's wife said, "Khatun couldn't stand looking at the canary. She somehow got rid of it."

Pushing the charcoal chips with the tongs around the brazier closer to the hot charcoal in the middle and chewing on his blonde mustache, Uncle suddenly interrupted Mash Karam with a groan and uttered a "God save us" loud enough to take Mash Karam aback. The women were eavesdropping in a corner behind the door. Uncle's voice was harsh and threatening, "Karam, put a stop to the women's activities. I don't want to hear them talk about such things as *ta'ziyeh* any more."

Karam shifted his weight on his heels, brought his head forward, and said, "Khan, forgive me, but it is not my fault; it was you who started it all."

Uncle roared, "Whatever I did was for the reward in the next world. And there it will become completely clear, if our deeds are indeed looked into." And he added more quietly, "Watch out that something doesn't happen to make me end up wearing a cuckold's hat in the middle of all this mess."

Mash Karam shook his white beard, crouched, and said, "Khan, I swear by everything that is dear to you, such a thing will not happen in this house. I will be all eyes, watching everything, as long as I have breath in me. Besides, everybody knows, they have already bought up all the two-*abbasi* seats, and the one-*shahi* seats, the rooftops, and the narrow window ledges!"

Uncle roared, "Bastards! You see what I mean when I say they are doing business with the Imam's name? I spit on their sense of honor!"

A small glob of spit fell into the brazier. Uncle picked up the opium pipe, straightened out the needle, and stuck it into the hole of the opium bowl. His fingers were accustomed to this and were nimble. His eyes looked for the box. He stuck his hand under the little mattress. He used to say that his friends introduced him to the opium pipe when he was eighteen.

Karam moaned, "Khan, what could a miserable wretch

like me do? They have sent someone to the building who gave a message to Zeynal saying that they always have respect for the Khan because of the tent. And the ladies will not give up . . ."

Uncle stormed and Mash Karam retreated.

"Bastards! How they put ants into people's pants! I had pledged the tent for religious mourning, not to dishonor myself on account of the women. This is no religious mourning. It is debauchery. God save me! Come, don't let me foul my mouth. Tell them the *ta'ziyeh* is finished."

He blew into the opium bowl hole, shook it over the tray, and picked up the saucer containing the opium rolls. The rolls were picked moist. They were cylindrical and the color of light mustard. Uncle smelled the saucer and breathed out with delight. All those who watched this scene seemed to be relieved.

The voice of Uncle's wife was heard, along with the laughter of Behjat Moluk, who had suspected something and could not stand the sight of Khatun from the very beginning. The moment that Khatun had set foot in the Khan's bed, Behjat's luck had changed.

But there was a depth to Uncle's wife, and she was patient. She had seen the passage of the years and the women who occasionally shook up the house, and Uncle's wife would not show her displeasure with their variety and looks. With the arrival of every new temporary or permanent wife, she would go on a pilgrimage, have her hair cut and dyed with henna, proudly and steadfastly prepare the old bed, and patiently await the Khan's desires.

Behjat Moluk was younger. Uncle had married her to have children. Later on, when she began to blossom into a full-fledged woman, he had extended the temporary marriage vows to ninety-nine years and Behjat had become Uncle's favorite. She could talk well and was full-figured, had a healthy color and, as the women in the inner courtyard would say, she could hold a china bowl on her rump. She knew how to have a good time and whenever there was a drum or a tamborine around, she could dance pretty well, too. But when she realized that her happy days were over with the coming of a seventeen- or eighteen-year-old girl from Varamin who combed her curly hair down to her waist and whose pomegranate breasts could hardly be contained within her blouse, she became a close companion of Uncle's wife. She would resort to witchcraft and beat her chest, but nothing could calm the burning in her heart. Uncle's wife was not fond of witchcraft and curses. She had an ache in her heart. But it seemed both of them shared the same pain.

In those days, the women would sit in the inner courtyard, knit shawls and nightcaps, and talk incessantly. Uncle had forbidden the women to come to the outer courtyard.

Master Farajollah would sew the tent ordered for the *tekkeh,* and the house would be all prepared for entertaining the master and his apprentices, who had set up their work in the outer courtyard.

When the women were tired of gossiping and knitting, they would go behind the lattice woodwork of the door to the outer courtyard to watch Master Farajollah, who had six fingers and wore an embroidered cap over his pockmarked face. The women knew that Master Farajollah had been circumcised just before he turned sixteen years of age. They said that they had pickled it in a vat and they laughed heartily.

Master Farajollah measured the canvas, drew a line on it, crouched up, bent over, and straightened up. His heels were cracked. He wore black percline pants with a wide crotch and a long pant string that swung in front of him. The women laughed at his swinging pant string, and at what was swaying in his crotch, saying it weighed one stone!

When he was finished cutting, they put the layers together and the apprentices sat around the parlor. Master Farajollah performed ablutions. They sprinkled some rose water on themselves, chanted salutations, and the master used a packing needle and silk thread to stitch the tent. The apprentices chanted salutations again.

The master stitched for days, chanting in praise of the imam, and the apprentices chanted salutations and sewed the seams, and the women giggled behind the tile lattice work.

Master Farajollah had very skillful hands. When he stitched, it looked as if a lever were going up and down. He himself sewed the lion figures, which were made of reddish leather from the chest of calves, in the four corners of the tent over the air holes, which were shaped in a hexagon. The lions had a dull smile and crossed eyes, with a crooked sword held forward in one paw. Their faces had a stupid human gesture. I don't know why, but the design was taken for Uncle from the British Embassy.

While the commotion was going on about the *tekkeh* tent, Khatun was a new bride. She looked like a little fairy in a story book, with her white satin chador, velvet embroidered vest over a taffeta petticoat and an agate pendant trembling between her two breasts.

Behjat Moluk, making fun of Khatun, said that on her wedding night, she put on anklets with golden bells so that when she walked she would not step on baby jinns. Behjat pounded her heels on the ground and with an angry laugh shouted, "Shameless slut, she wears nothing, absolutely nothing under that vest. And on her necklace she wears a snake charm. That is why the Khan is so crazy about her." She then pounded on her knees, saying, "May I be struck blind if I am lying, the slut even puts perfume on the backs of her knees!"

She talked in frustration and the other people in the house

looked around to see if Khatun was passing by, with her unknown perfume, which they said was European, rising from her satin chador.

When the tent was finished, they gave a banquet and the garden parlor was packed with city guests and the headsmen of the surrounding villages. They came to the Khan's house, group by group, from early evening, kissing the tent and pledging religious vows.

In the morning, they took the tent to the *Tekiyeh-ye Dowlat* and handed it over to the religious endowment people. Asheykh Fazlollah had said, "Just this one deed will earn the Khan's next world."

The call for the Twenty-eighth-of-Zul-Hejjeh noon prayers was being sung, and Uncle's wife was praying that at that time the following year she would be a pilgrim. Her prayers seemed to have substance. Rings of green and blue light would pour on the ground from behind the stove and flow on the wet stones.

Suran, the old black woman with her red loincloth, came to the bath alcove with a copper bowl of henna in one hand and a pitcher of soaked gum tragacanth for the hair in the other. Uncle's wife sat in the alcove on a scalloped tray with a lace loincloth rolled up under her belly. Three layers of white skin were rolled up from under her breasts all the way down to under her navel, and when she moved, her wide, round buttocks spilled and shook over the edge of the tray. Uncle's wife had clear skin, not yet wrinkled with age. She washed her small, ring-filled hands in henna solution and put fresh henna on her nails, leaned her head that had been dyed with indigo and henna against the wall of the hot-water pool, and closed her eyes. Next to her sat Behjat Moluk, who was still undoing her tightly braided hair, putting the gold two-rial coins from the tips of her braids in a copper bowl next to her, and watching the proceedings around her. But part of her mind, and the half-closed eyes of Uncle's wife, were on Khatun, who had just entered the bath and was standing on the step to the hot-water pool.

Khatun was of medium height, with skin the color of ivory. Her breasts were round and firm, with rings around the nipples the color of quince blossoms, which looked like fruit. Her wavy hair reached her waist and shone like silk.

That day, she wore a gold chain around her waist attached to a small lock under her navel. Seeing the lock, Uncle's wife and Behjat looked at each other and shifted uneasily. The excruciating tolerance would now end, and if Khatun was pregnant, it was all over.

At this time, Khatun went forward, poured a pitcher of water over the shoulders of Uncle's wife. She then poured another pitcher of water over the head of Behjat Moluk, who had not yet gotten herself wet. They both shifted, saying a poisonous "thank you," and Khatun, embarrassed, pulled up the loin cloth which had slipped down to rest on a tray at the foot of the alcove.

There was silence. The bath had been reserved for the family, yet one could only hear the sound of water pouring into the hot-water pool.

The master bath keeper's wife came in with a tray of *sharbat,* held the glass before Uncle's wife, and said laughing, "God willing, we will have a banquet after your pilgrimage, madam. Have some refreshment." She paused and said, "I am not worthy of it, but I have a request," and said nothing else.

Uncle's wife threw an intimidating glance at her face and took the glass of *sharbat.* Khatun turned around and looked up with curiosity. Drops of sweat danced on her face. She asked what it was and the bath keeper's wife said humbly, "To tell you the truth, I was too shy to ask, but I was hoping you would allow me to be at your service and come to the *tekkeh.* I feel quite depressed."

Behjat Moluk looked at Uncle's wife. The bath keeper's wife lowered her head. Uncle's wife took a sip and said nothing.

The bath keeper's wife continued, "Last night my husband was describing it. I swear to God we were dying to see it. He said it is all in the hands of the Mo'inolbokka'..." And she sighed with yearning, "What will happen, only God knows..."

Uncle's wife put the glass on the tray and said in a sad voice, "If the Mo'inolbokka' agrees! His Reverence has sent a messenger . . . for the sake of His Majesty, who is supposed to be there." And turning to Behjat, as if only speaking to her, she said, "They say they are going to bring the European ambassador to see our Muslim mourning rites . . ."

Behjat Moluk said, "Maybe he will be lucky and convert. Don't you remember the one who went to His Reverence at the Sham Bazaar *ta'ziyeh* and converted?"

The bath keeper's wife put the tray down, brought her head forward and asked in a whisper, "My lady, please tell me, after all that happened. . . ?"

Uncle's wife did not wait for her to finish. She glared and said, "Speaking behind other people's backs is a greater sin than adultery. One should not talk about it. Besides, the gates to a city can be shut, but people's mouths cannot!"

Behjat Moluk said, "The Mo'inolbokka' has had it up to here. The last time he came before the holy shrine in the middle of the square and held his beard in his hand, tears streaming from his face like spring clouds, the poor man looked at the crowd and said, 'I tell you, today, right here, that tomorrow, on the Day of Resurrection, before God, as I have been a mourner of Hoseyn for fifty years, I will grab him by the gown and plead with him that whoever has fabricated this about me must answer to His Holiness.'"

Embarrassed, the bath keeper's wife picked up the tray

and held it in front of Khatun. But Khatun shook her head and the bath keeper's wife looked offended.

My mother said that the Mo'inolbokka' was a dwarfish hunchbacked old man who wore a seersucker turban with a Na'in-made aba and a long camel-hair gown. He had a full beard dyed with henna and a pockmarked face.

Abol was a child when the Mo'inolbokka' adopted him. Abol was now seventeen or eighteen years old, with a sallow complexion, long face, narrow nose, and large black eyes and eyebrows, and he had a new growth above his lip. He wore a white cotton gown and a shirt with a starched collar. He wore spats and carried a pocket watch in his vest. He shaved every morning and had the hair on the back of his neck trimmed every week. He wore a fez on his head sideways, and what hair! Thick and garish. That is why they talked behind his back. The children followed the Mo'inolbokka' and sang:

> "Sheykh Hasan sings a merry song:
> I have Abol and customers a mile long
> Sheykh Hasan says, I have a stash
> I have good merchandise and I want cash."

And Sheykh Hasan held his beard up towards the heavens, raised his eyes to the sky and cursed.

Uncle's wife said, "Nothing holds people's mouths shut. Without knowing anything, they make up things."

The bath keeper's wife said sadly, "Without them, you couldn't have a real *ta'ziyeh.*"

Uncle's wife said self-importantly, "Many have tried to mediate. When His Majesty comes, Sheykh Hasan can't say no. They are supposed to perform the martyrdom of Ali Akbar. Zellesoltan has made a religious vow."

The bath keeper's wife, losing control, asked, "And is Haj Barekallah sure going to be there, too?"

Khatun was scrubbing her heels with a pumice stone and listening to them. She got up and walked towards the hot-water pool.

Uncle's wife said, "It won't do without him anyway."

The bath keeper's wife absentmindedly sat on the step with her pants and petticoat on, hit herself on the knee, and said, "It will be a bloody mess. May God help us all. They say the Alamdar clan is ready for him."

Uncle's wife said, "God only knows, we have also heard things. But, God knows, it is all their own doing."

Behjat Moluk said, "Closed up in the corner of the house, we don't hear about anything."

Uncle's wife leaned her head against the wall and appeared to close her eyes. But Behjat Moluk was not as diplomatic as Uncle's wife and couldn't hold anything in. She confessed, "When I cannot figure something out, I get a rash."

And despite Uncle's wife, she asked the bath keeper's wife, "Haven't you heard anything about Gelin Khanom, their daughter-in-law?"

The bath keeper's wife said, "To tell you the truth, let those who say it be blamed . . ."

From the hot-water pool, Khatun shone on the step like a light. Her pink satin loincloth was stuck to her body and her round navel was reflected in Behjat's staring eyes. Her white shins were like crystal and her small hands, which were dyed with henna, were reflected in the wet stones. The voices became remote and she appeared to me to be the image of the daughter of Fakhimotojjar surrounded by courtiers.

The daughter of Fakhimotojjar is an only child. She is fourteen years old, with fair skin and eyes the color of honey. She parts her hair over her arched eyebrows, with a Flemish diamond-studded emerald hanging in the part. Her wedding gown is of blue satin, and she has a gilded Banares-made scarf with gold sequins over her head. She wears a gold velvet petticoat and Fil d'Ecosse stockings and is watching the door from under the wedding tent.

Khatun sat at the edge of the step embarrassed.

The bath keeper's wife was swearing on everything holy and Uncle's wife was staring at her mouth.

All the women in the wedding room knew about the condition that had been set and anyone who had heard about it was shocked.

The bath keeper's wife swore again, "His first wife was gorgeous, the daughter of Alamdar, from a good family, and had three babies all in a row. At the wedding, everybody talked about that, too, and about men's fidelity."

Behjat shook her head. Khatun was sitting sideways and wanted very much to ask something, but did not have the courage. Uncle's wife was leaning against the wall of the hot-water pool, relaxed, and was dozing off.

But Behjat Moluk was excited with eagerness and envy. A light shone in her eyes from a hidden desire, the fact that the suitors of Fakhimotojjar's daughter were clamoring after her. The fact that in place of a dower the bride had asked that the groom come to the wedding chamber in such a suit. The taste of love awoke in her mind and the light of her heart was aflame. The women moved their heads together and a fragrant steam surrounded them. The conversation became animated and it was as if the wedding had been transported to the bath!

At the house of Fakhimotojjar, the mirror hall has been set aside for the men. Fakhimotojjar, in a cashmere gown and a sheepskin hat, with salt-and-pepper whiskers, is sitting in the parlor, both content and discontent, and around the hall there are men in turbans and bazaar merchants sitting at small tables filled with pastry and candy, decorated with flower pots of geraniums with red flowers in bloom.

The reflections of the guests in the mirrors make the room look crowded, but there is no sound. The man performing the wedding ceremony, his long beard reaching cumberbund around his waist, delivers a sermon. The candle flames trembling in the crystal tulips, the scent of willow and frankincense in every corner, and the joyful delight of women have created a commotion. Women who have married twice and widows are left outside behind the doors, while happily married women, women of good fortune, surround the bride from seven directions, sewing the symbolic seven silk threads. The bride's nanny boils milk and honey and chants prayers of love.

The Koran is open on the bride's lap and she has two good-luck figurines in her fist. It is said that the closer together the two figurines get, the more in love with her the groom will be. The condition set for the wedding is passed from mouth to mouth and travels outside the house, and everyone in the neighborhood and the city learns about it . . .

The Alamdar family has heard it too. They bite their lips, but do not say a word. Women are trembling with curiosity and excitement. As Behjat put it, "They are sure to get a rash now."

An animal-like glow sparkles in Khatun's eyes. Everyone is watching the mouth of the bath keeper's wife: "The daughter of Fakhimotojjar had seen Haj Barekallah in a *ta'ziyeh* performance at the shrine and had fallen head over heels in love with him, in the performance where he held the sheepskin of water in his teeth, with an arrow piercing his eye, going to the Euphrates River to bring water for Sakineh . . . She had said that in place of everything else, she wanted the groom to come to the wedding in a green gown, backless armor, an emerald-studded arm band, a helmet and a shield, and to come to the wedding chamber in the same clothes! God save us, what falling in love can do!"

Uncle's wife said, "May God save them from how they

will end up. A greedy rooster jumps on every hen. When he is finished with one, may God help the next."

But Behjat's eyes were wet and her face had flushed like brushed velvet. It was obvious then that in the sad house of the Khan, she was living in constant pain, a pain that had robbed her of the opportunity to blossom.

The women sat in a circle with their heads together and an innocent, unfulfilled passion drifted through their steamy, languid conversation. Like hand-trained pets, they needed caressing and love more than food. This rare elixir was necessary to give them a shiny gloss. How is one to know that a woman's imagination reaches an obstinate need, a need that I saw that day in the hopeless lethargy of Uncle's wife, the withering of Behjat, the pained perseverance of my mother, and the blossoming flower of Khatun, and realized that together we had shared a unique secret whose simple and childish manifestation was the falling in love of the daughter of Fakhimotojjar?

On the first of Moharram, to shut her up, Uncle's wife took the bath keeper's wife to the *ta'ziyeh* performance at Sar-e Takht-e Barbariha. There they were performing the Moslem *ta'ziyeh*. On the third and the fifth were the *ta'ziyeh* in the bazaar, which they left for in the morning, leaving us at home. The little girls were burning with eagerness for the eve of *'Āshurā*. They had imagined thousands of things and made preparations for that day. It had just become fashionable to have the front of the chador embroidered. Fingertips were sore from needles. My mother had bought me a pair of suede-heeled shoes which had a strap and buckle, and whenever I could, I would take them out of the closet, put them on and walk. In those shoes, I felt tall enough to reach the edge of the roof, but I would not test it, because I was afraid I couldn't. The soles of the shoes had not yet touched the dirt.

The eve of 'Āshurā came and I put on my shoes and silk chador. Until dawn, I looked at the glass panes of the door for signs that the sun had come up. At dawn, I got up and by the time morning prayers were over, I had run out of patience.

My mother said, "Do you want to wear those? You can't stand up in those heels. When the riders come, everyone will stand up. You are not used to high heels yet."

I said, "I can. I'll get used to them."

"If you stand, you won't be able to sit anymore. . . ," she said.

"I won't have to stand," I said. "I'll sit from the beginning."

She replied, "If you want to see His Majesty, you must stand up. You can't see him sitting down."

"I will stand up . . . I will stand up," I said. "If I can't, I will take off my shoes."

"Do as you wish," she said. "But in front of the building in the coach house, if your uncle sees the buckle and high heels, he won't let you go."

And I saw in her kind eyes a desire for me to wear the shoes. I put a few jasmines in my collar and braided my hair in two parts, but did not let my mother see it. As we were leaving, the smell of flowers filled my facial veil and I was afraid they would find out. Khatun came in a different carriage. Zeynal was sitting in the outside seat. When we reached the *tekkeh,* there were two entrances with soldiers on guard around them. They wore red felt uniforms, leather boots, and felt hats with insignias, and their mustaches were frightening.

The men went to the right, to the men's section, and the women sat behind the net curtains.

From early morning there was no room to stand, and no matter how the guards drove away the children with their clubs, they could not establish order. I had to stand in those

high-heeled shoes. There wasn't even room for me to bend
down and take them off.

The sun had just come up when the prime minister, the
dignitaries, and the khans came. An hour later, His Majesty's
carriage arrived; when they played the bugle and the dignitaries stood up in respect.

Women and children were climbing over each other and
craning their necks to see him. His Majesty accompanied by
his retinue went to the pavilion, sat down on the chair, and
glanced around. You could have heard a pin drop in the
tekkeh. Women sang his praises and uttered endearing
phrases about him. His Majesty's face shone like the sun.
Upon a signal from the *tekkeh* keeper, the crowd shouted
salutations three times. Then His Majesty asked for a robe of
honor to be brought, the bugles sounded and the riders came
into the *tekkeh*.

They entered in rows of four on bay horses. They wore
red felt uniforms with gilded, embroidered shoulder epaul-
ettes, cardboard fezes with tassels, tight riding britches, and
Circassian sabers at their sides. Under the light of the chan-
deliers that hung from the ceiling, the insignias, embroidery,
and filigree work on their uniforms sparkled, instilling awe in
one's heart. The horses were thoroughbreds, with blinders
over their eyes, mirrors on their foreheads, a multitude of
colored feathers over their heads, cashmere shawls hanging
in front of their chests, and their saddle paraphernalia laced
with leather and velvet.

With the commotion of the *tekkeh* and the sound of
drums and bugles, the animals had become restless, but the
riders were pulling their reins, and their march around the
square was performed in a most orderly fashion.

When the riders left through the large gates of the *tekkeh*,
the crowd shouted salutations several times for the health of
His Majesty, the continuation of his reign, and the blindness

of his enemies. Then, there was silence and Sheykh Hasan came to the square with his mourning chanters.

The square was actually a round platform in front of the pavilion which was covered with carpets, with the alcoves of the dignitaries and the khans overlooking it. The rest of the alcoves were in a circle at greater distances from the square, and the place for women was farther than the rest, opposite the pavilion, in front of which a net curtain was hung.

Sheykh Hasan, who had a piece of paper in his hand, bowed and recited some poetry addressed to His Majesty in a resounding voice that did not match his small frame and his age. We could not hear him, but they said that the poems were in praise of the king, and His Majesty ordered a robe of honor to be granted to him.

Sheykh Hasan bent over, kissed the robe of honor and the dust before the king's feet and, walking backward, left the square. The mourning chanters stood in the four corners of the square. A heavy, expectant silence followed that was split, as with a sword, by the sound of bugles.

My mother said, "They are singing of the martyrdom of Akbar and Abolfazl going to the Euphrates."

Abol was small and thin. Just as they had described him, his face looked like the figure of Majnun, the famous lover, printed on the hand-stamped cloth. When he entered the square, the women began to whisper. His delicate body moved in a white suit and the armor that was too big for him. He wore an arm band and an amulet. In the farewell scene with his mother, his movements were gentle and feminine, and when he sang, as if flushed with embarrassment, his sallow complexion would disappear and his large, dark eyebrows would stand out.

Behjat Moluk said, "Let those who say it be blamed, but it is God's doing that his color is like that of a hashish addict.

This itself will disgrace him. May those who dragged him into this be layed up on the mortuary slab."

But how Abol made the heart of the assembly tremble with his delicate and euphonious voice, and how his fighting and falling to the ground brought excitement to the assembly. But the excitement did not last long.

When Akbar's corpse was on the ground, the audience was moved. The women, with tearful eyes, began to wriggle and push and shove to get a better view from behind the net curtain. Behjat told my mother, "If you stand up, you can see better. Haj Barekallah has come."

From where I was standing, I stretched my neck and from behind the backs, the heads, and the shoulders of the women, I saw him riding a horse in a green velvet suit, green helmet, backless armor, and an emerald arm band and belt. He carried a green banner in one hand on which something in Arabic was inscribed, and in the other hand a Koran with a sword on it. On the back of his horse hung a goat skin. His bay horse stopped its hooves in front of the pavilion, neighed and, together with its rider, bowed. Then he turned around and rode to the middle of the square. The women let out a frenzied wail upon seeing him. My mother said, "This name was given to him by His Majesty. His real name is something else. When he was singing, His Majesty said, 'Barekallah [bravo],' several times, 'Barekallah Haji!' And this name stayed with him from then on."

Behjat Moluk said, "They carry Haj Barekallah over their heads. They give him anything he asks for. Let them be blamed who say it, but those who fall in love with him circle gold five-rial coins above his head and give them to beggars. Anisolmoluk, Aghdas Duleh, many of the women, have fasted forty days for him. God save them from how they will end up."

Haj Barekallah dismounted in the middle of the square

before the corpse of Akbar. He was tall and muscular. His helmet, with two green ostrich feathers, was placed over his ivory-colored forehead like a crown. His eyes were green and his face clear as marble through which light would pass. His twisted blonde mustache hung from the two corners of his lips down to his chin and gave his mouth a pleasant dignity. He came near the corpse of Akbar, composed and dignified, stood by his head, and remained silent for a moment.

You could not hear anyone breathe. He then lifted his head and began to sing at the top of his lungs. The first words flew in waves to the ceiling. When he warbled his voice, his throat made a sensual shiver.

The *tekkeh* suddenly became silent. No living creature made a sound. Through the air holes in the ceiling, the dim, pale rays of the sun shone on the square, and it seemed to me that the light emitted from him towards the sky. There was something ethereal in his tall, green stature, and I could see this thought in the sad, desirous eyes of other women as well.

When the Prince of the Martyrs* kissed the Koran, tied the sword to his brother's waist and Abbas took the reins of the horse and left for the battle field with a long farewell, an earthquake of wailing and crying shook the *tekkeh*. In the midst of the ruckus of the weeping and wailing of the crowd, choked up and stunned, I was mesmerized by the scene and on edge, waiting for something to happen. Perhaps an angel, a light, or something would come to the gathering. A miracle might happen, a miracle like those I had heard about. Or maybe the end of time would come.

It seemed to me that in this loud excitement, there was a relationship between the earth and the heavens, and angels with small, fat legs and curly hair, holding stars and Mohammadi roses, were flying in the light that flowed from the air

---

*Meaning Imam Hoseyn.

hole into the square, and that the one who was circling the square with the horse behind him, singing battle cries, was the reason for this relationship. There was now an astonishing commotion in the *tekkeh*. Men beat themselves on the forehead and women on their chests. And Abbas, who had to cut through the enemy lines to reach the Euphrates, had to circle half way around the square to reach the river. From around the battlefield, he was showered with arrows and while singing, he would hold up his shield to defend himself. Wherever he passed, he would carry with him the excitement of the mourning ceremony. As he reached the front of the net curtain and the women began to elbow each other to get a glimpse of him, making such a ruckus that the guards came, their warning to keep order only increasing the women's excitement, suddenly Khatun rose up from amidst the women, came forward, climbed up the stakes which supported the tent post and, with her face visible, like a sleepwalker oblivious to all other people, threw a package towards Haj Barekallah. Still continuing on his way, with his face flushed, as if wanting to defend himself, he took the package. For a moment, his eyes circled the crowd and met Khatun's. I saw a change in his face from where we were. He paused for a moment. At one moment, hundreds of moist, intruding eyes witnessed this scene and the wave of excitement and wailing washed it away. I did not see anything more, but that picture has always remained with me. Something unspoken, frightening, and magnificent. Perhaps it was a merciless desire or a passion that I had not known until that moment, and its first encounter, like the flowers one dries between the pages of a book, left a bitter, lasting fragrance in me. As my mother said, that day, in those luminous eyes, the look of Satan shone, and from then on, nothing remained but blind, silent time.

When Uncle went on a trip, he gave the key to the cellar to Mash Karam. It was more than a week after *'Āshurā*, and during this time Uncle's inner courtyard had turned upside down. My mother tried to get the key from Mash Karam, but he kept that key with his other keys on the shawl around his waist and was even on guard at night when he slept. I saw him several times respond to my mother's insistence with, "The Khan will have my head if I give up this key."

In the early days, the shouts of anger and insults and the sound of pounding on the cellar door would reach the outer courtyard rooms. But after four or five days, the shouts turned into despairing cries and the pounding stopped. In the following weeks, even the cries stopped. My mother was burning like a tree trunk on fire, but could not do anything. Mash Karam had sharp, cold eyes, like an executioner.

It was the end of Moharram when Behjat Moluk returned from the city and went into the inner courtyard, straight and quiet. She neither sat by the veranda nor unpacked her bundle. In the withering of her frightened glance, the sleep of death had settled. My mother ran forward. They did not say hello. They just shook their heads. Behjat put her head on my mother's shoulder and wept for a while. My mother waited, consoled her, and was about to leave when she heard the news. She stood and looked at us. Women stood around her silently in black scarves and chadors. She said quietly, "From God do we come and unto Him shall we return." And she said no more. Her face had hardened like stone, and her eyes were shiny and frightened. The news of death always stunned her. She sent me to Mash Karam.

Mash Karam was sitting in front of the cellar on a camel felt mat smoking his clay pipe. His sunken eyes over the protrusion of his cheek bones were sad, like an owl's. When I told him, he put his clay pipe on the ground, lifted his head to the sky, and said, "There is no God but God, Who alone is grand!"

He put his hand into the shawl around his waist and untied the key to give it to me. My mother took the key from behind me and said to Mash Karam, who was afraid, "You see how transient the world is?"

Mash Karam did not answer. He seemed to be crying.

They opened the cellar door. It was so dark you could not see a thing. Except for a dim light which shone from the ceiling on the stairs, there was no light, and the grey light of dusk remained outside. The weakened, mildewed stairs turned towards the floor of the cellar, which was brick. There were traces of kerosene lamp smoke on the walls, but there was no light in the cellar.

Eyes became accustomed to the darkness. Moss, mildew and weeds that looked like snake tails hung from the walls, and there were spider webs between their dark stems.

My mother, chanting the name of God, advanced. Boxes of crushed charcoal, vats of vinegar, and earthenware containers were arranged by the wall and mud-covered carboys were placed on the ledges. Here and there old junk lay decaying. At the end of the cellar, over a ledge in which an area had been hollowed out for cooking, a piece of wood was installed from which a rope hung, and in the hollow of the wall, Khatun's eyes shone like those of a wounded wolf.

My mother said, "God forgive us." She said no more and stopped in place. Khatun moved, and a sigh broke in her chest, but she said nothing. My mother went forward and said, "Can you stand up?"

There was no answer. The light in Khatun's eyes went out and her rapid, frightened panting signalled to us the bad news. My mother shook her head and said, "Yes . . . I knew it. May God help us . . ." But stretching her arm, and in a kinder tone, she said, "Doesn't matter. Give me your hand. Get up . . . get up. You are young. You are young. Everything will be easier . . . " Then she paused and said, "And your hair will grow back . . . Give me your hand. Get up."

The sound of Khatun's breathing could be heard like the growling of an animal. Our eyes could gradually see her in the dark, crumpled up in the corner of the hollowed area. Her white satin vest was blackened by dirt and smoke and her head looked bald in spots. The short hair that had escaped the scissors frizzled up around her forehead. As we went forward, we could see the traces of the wounds from her whipping in the corner of her lips, on her chest, and on her hands, which were covered with dried blood and blackened. Her eyes, with an animal look, gazed at the broken bowl of water and the bread crumbs that a mouse was carrying away. From the ceiling above her head, wet spiders and centipedes were lethargically moving in the webs and mildewed vegetation.

As if speaking to someone else, my mother said, "It is no one's fault, dear. One must not relinquish control to the heart. Even if Zeynal had not told Haji, someone else would have. Everybody is the same. You brought it upon yourself. What woman would have dared to leave her husband's house, with servants and carriages, to go after a ta'ziyeh singer? God save us. I don't want to talk. You brought it upon yourself. You ruined your position as a lady. Don't you know that he has had so many affairs? Hadn't you heard the story of the daughter of Fakhimotojjar?" She paused, looked at Khatun, who sat gazing and dazed, and added in a reprimanding tone, "Besides, didn't you consider the Khan's reputation? You were lucky that he didn't see you on 'Āshurā in the midst of the crowd; otherwise, he would have chopped your head off right there. What did you have to go and throw a package to him for?"

There was silence. The sound of Khatun's panting broke from her choked up throat.

My mother sighed and said, "Get up. Satan be cursed. I'll take you out." She stretched her arm to take Khatun. She pulled herself back. Her panting had become more rapid. My mother said, "Get up. Thank God that the matter has ended here. Well, woman, a married woman and falling in love? And then so daring and careless?"

Khatun seemed to sink into the corner of the hollow in the wall, because you could not see her anymore. My mother crouched up by the hollow in the wall. She knew that she could not take Khatun out, but she could not bring herself to leave her there in that condition. She was helpless, when the light of a lantern appeared. The light made the wounded and blackened face of Khatun visible. Behjat put the lantern on the ledge and sat by the hollow in the wall. She took Khatun's hand. She caressed it several times, then kissed it and wept. My mother also cried with her. But Khatun stared at them in silence. Behjat told my mother, "She doesn't seem to have her wits about her."

My mother nodded and mumbled something. She could not think of anything. Behjat looked at Khatun for a moment. Again, a light shone in her eyes and faded away. She gestured to my mother. They both went forward and took Khatun's hands. But she growled like an animal and pulled herself back. A struggle ensued. Khatun was kicking and putting up a fight. She had become so strong that they could not subdue her. Finally, both stopped, helpless and tired. My mother leaned against the wall and put her hand over her heart. At that moment, she seemed old and broken.

Behjat was staring at Khatun, who was looking at her with shiny, victorious eyes, biting her bloody lip. And her growling filled the ash-polluted air. Behjat looked at her for a moment, then bent down, put her mouth to Khatun's ear and told her what had happened. Even though her voice was very low, it resonated in the space, and the light of the lantern turned red with it. A story like this cannot be told more than once and cannot be heard more than once. But it was repeated forever, repeated forever.

It was next to a stream in Zahirabad or Safa'iyyeh. At

night, they would set up a party. God knows, maybe they would bring prostitutes, too. They had brandy, hashish, opium, and music. Abol would put on a petticoat, tie castinettes on his fingers and dance. The things they did! They did it themselves. It was Thursday night or Friday night in this holy month. They had poisoned him at one of those parties. Apparently, they had put poison in his drink and finished him off. Now, there is the daughter of Fakhimotojjar, with her wedding chamber arranged, with the baby she carries in her belly, and his poor wife with three orphans. And when his mother heard about it, she hit herself on the head with a brick and her eye popped open like a grape . . . She said that after him, she did not want to look at the world. Sheykh Hasan . . . had gone to His Majesty, hoping that his blood would be avenged . . . processions were formed . . .

They said he was lying on the mortuary slab like the champion Sohrab, with his calm face . . . eyes closed, like he had been sleeping for a thousand years . . . When they poured ablution water over him, the chants of "Oh Hoseyn" rose.

Behjat took a long breath and carelessly and sadly said, "Oh well . . . everyone knew he had thousands of enemies . . . The *ta'ziyeh* is all finished . . ."

Khatun was about to leap like a tiger when she bit her lower lip so hard that a narrow stream of blood flowed down her chin. Her panting was rapid and fragmented and her chest went in and out like a bellows. As if she had just seen her, Behjat let go of her hand and stood up. She took two steps backward and took my mother's arm involuntarily. My mother's lips moved, but I did not hear anything. Sound had died around us.

Suddenly, like a sparrow that has opened its wings, Khatun flew out of the hollow in the wall, opened both hands, pounded them together, and shouted out so loud that it shook the walls, the lanterns, the mildew, and the spider webs and tossed those of us around her into different directions, and ran to the stairs.

At the top of the stairs, she threw Karam into a corner with a shout and jumped to the door. Zeynal ran to catch her. She shouted again, and her spittle spattered on his face, crushed him against the wall with her fist, opened the door and, with her head and feet bare, in the same short vest and petticoat, ran into the alley.

Her shouts in the alley resonated behind the high walls of the icehouses. At that time of the night, most people were at home. Doors opened and shadows came out. The men, along with Zeynal, who was carrying the lantern, chased her. But there was no sign of her, except for her cries, which were becoming weaker. They said that her cries could be heard for an hour in the darkness of the rows of summer crop fields and then faded away in the slopes of Bibi Hills.

At dawn, Zeynal returned home with the lantern turned off.

January/February 1978
Translated by M. R. Ghanoonparvar

MĪHAN BAHRĀMĪ

Bahrāmī was born in Tehran, and is a graduate of Tehran University. She studied psychology for a short time at UCLA, but did not earn a degree there. An accomplished painter, Bahrāmī has also worked as a translator. She published her first collection of short stories in 1985.

This is from *Stories by Iranian Women Since the Revolution,* translated by Soraya Sullivan. Austin, TX: Center for Middle Eastern Studies, 1991: 38.

❧ *The Story of a Street*

SĪMĪN DĀNISHVAR

Fall was undressing the trees along the street in broad daylight. A pair of little feet wearing galoshes rustled the leaves in front of me. I looked at the body that owned the feet, wearing a grey girl's school uniform and bent over with the weight of a bucket it was carrying. The faint sound of a rubbish cart going "talak talak" arose in the distance. Then the neighborhood street cleaner rounded the corner pushing his cart. With every lurch, orange peels, turnip peels, and tissue papers fell out of the cart into the leaves. I went up to the girl and took the bucket of water. Her little hands and the tip of her nose were beet-red. The street cleaner came up to us.

"Give it to me. I'll carry it," he said.

He came with us, bringing the bucket of water and a lot of talk. I always got the street's news first-hand from him. We had just moved to Tajrish, and built ourselves a little house in the vast desert at the end of one of the streets. He pointed to a green door and said, "He divorced his wife and now he's living with an Armenian," and then "Hajji Jom'eh had moved up here. You can't imagine what they did in that

This story is from the collection *Shahrī Chūn Bihisht* [A Land Like Paradise] (Tehran, 1962).

garden, dancing and singing all the time. Lady, you wouldn't believe all the chicken legs and salad they've thrown into their trash can. Those heathens ought to collect that food and give it to a couple of poor people. I even found a silver knife in their trash, and when I returned it Soghra was so happy she nearly fainted; but one person sleeps no better than the next when he's six feet under."

"What did you do with the chicken legs?" asked the girl.

We came to the gate at a big garden where the *howz* was always filled to the brim with water and its greenhouse full of flowers. Mashhadi Safar, the street cleaner, grinned broadly. "They're going to resurface the street any day now. That gentleman has personally ordered it." I had known for a short time that Mr. Motlaq, on our street, owned a garden and was also a Majles deputy. When we reached the girl's house, which was a little ways down from our house and had a dirt roof, I asked her, "Don't you have water?"

"No. Our cistern is empty."

"You can come to our house and get water. Have you lived here a long time?"

"We came after you did."

"Who do you live with?"

"With my mother and my brother."

The girl began knocking on the door as I looked at the little town that had taken us in, and which now slept in peaceful oblivion in the semi-darkness of the sunset. A poet who had fled the crowds some time before us had settled to the Northwest of our house. Extending in a line from where the poet's house stood were the earthen homes of the villagers, with their lumpy red gables and walls covered from end to end by an A-shaped rain cover made of ochre-colored tin. Just the width of a street from our house, these houses abutted the desert in tight formation, extending down to the village graveyard at the other end.

Beyond the graveyard there was more dry empty desert

that went out to a hill. Some people, I don't know who, had built a few houses on top of the hill. At night when the lights in those houses flickered like sparks in the distance, it looked like fairies, genies, and demons were having a rendezvous in the middle of the night up on that fearsome height.

I went down this little street just about every day. It connected the highway to the desert, then to the graveyard, then to the desert again. I had gotten used to seeing the neighbor girl on my way. She wore the same grey uniform every day, and her tightly-braided hair was always tied with a white ribbon. She would have a book and a notebook under her arm in the mornings, at noon she would have a basket, and at night she would have a bucket of water, but she was always stooped over, her teeth chattering from the cold. She would be in a rush when she saw me in the evenings. At noon, she would only say hello, but we would talk a lot in the mornings. I knew she was in the second grade, and that her mother was harassed by her brother.

Fearing the ingratitude of God's creatures, the first snow of Winter fell at night. When I got up in the morning and looked out at the village from our front porch, it looked like they had covered everything with a white blanket. The crows were sitting on the lamp posts lest they contaminate all that whiteness. The neighbor's wife was cleaning the snow off her roof with a broom and a dustpan. After emptying a few scoops of snow into the desert, she would straighten up, put her hand in front of her mouth to warm it with huffs of air, catch her breath, and resume working. A boy in shirtsleeves stood beside her with a bow and arrow. Still angry with the sparrows for migrating for the winter, he shot his arrows at our windows.

I got the urge to go outside. Where the street curved Mashhadi Safar gave the good tidings that they had begun laying the asphalt. When he sensed my surprise he motioned to the Majlis deputy's garden, which had gone into hibernation midway along the street under a chandelier of snow-covered branches.

"You may be absolutely certain that the Majles deputy made a phone call and our Mayor fell all over himself to have them start laying asphalt right in the snow."

Then I saw the laborers, who were attacking the trees along the street with heavy axes.

When I went home at noon all the ash trees, the street's arboreal royalty, lay scattered on the ground like fallen heroes. The next day there was no trace of the trees, nor promise of summer shade, nor any sign of the firewood cutters.

At noon the next day I was on my way home, tired and overwhelmed by the struggle with the street's mud and ooze. A roaring truck with a billowing smokestack approached me, rumbling along the road through the fallen leaves, snow, and ice. I waved it down and asked the driver if he had read the sign at the end of the street. He looked at me as if I were a fool.

"If we don't bring in the bricks how will you have a roof over your head?"

"Can't you bring the bricks on the road beside the graveyard?"

"The dead would follow me," he said with a roaring laugh. "Do you know who I'm bringing bricks for?"

I knew, and was silenced by the power of his logic. The truck whistled by so close to my ear that I nearly fell over. Building materials blocked the street in front of the deputy's garden. I tore my socks walking over some bricks and then passed more easily through a narrow passage they had left for pedestrians. The neighbor girl, whose grey uniform now had ink smudges in several places, was walking in front of me. She politely invited me to go in front of her. An automobile was sounding its horn, but it could neither get through nor go back. The little girl's galoshes were buried in snow, mud, slime, branches, and sticks, but she was happy and her face was flushed. Her eyes sparkled.

"My grandmother bought me a red raincoat. My mother's going to town to get it this afternoon. It's just like the one Shahla has. It has a hood too!"

I again urged her to come to our house for water. She opened her mouth as if to speak, but said nothing. At noon my husband and I expressed our dismay at the way the Mayor and the Majlis deputy had decked out this pretty little street like the bazaar of Damascus.

"We'll feel better after they get the asphalt down," I said.

Our housekeeper, who was lighting the stove, said "That's pretty naive. When we lay asphalt it's to keep the people from complaining. I grew up here. They've been promising to resurface this street for six years, and to cut down the trees so the trucks can get by. Every year he pulls something else; this year he wants to fix up his buildings and turn them over to the Americans."

That night as we returned my eyes caught the sight at a distance of a dark figure sitting on the steps in front of our house. I thought it was a dog at first. Stray dogs would often take shelter on our porch and our housekeeper would kick them as if he were driving off dead spirits. The dark figure stood up as we approached. It was the neighbor girl, trembling like a sparrow. She said hello.

"What are you doing here dear?" my husband asked.

"My mother didn't come back from the city. The door to our house is locked."

"Why didn't you knock and go in?" I asked.

"I was afraid of her." She burst into tears.

My husband picked her up and carried her inside.

"She's like a sparrow someone took out of a cat's mouth," he said.

Our housekeeper approached at the sound of our voices. "Sir, her shoes are filthy and I just swept. She's been here several times to get water and I didn't let her in. She's got a truckload of mud on her galoshes. How many gunny sacks must I wear out scrubbing the cement?"

We took her inside. I got a blanket and took off her wet clothing. She was embarrassed and kept hiding herself under the blanket. She was like a skinny chick with about half its feathers gone. Her body had neither the plumpness of a young girl's nor the delicacy and luminosity of a child's. She was past childhood but her body showed no signs of maturity. I wrapped the blanket around her and lit the stove.

"Don't go to any trouble, don't go to any trouble," she kept saying.

"I hope she doesn't get pneumonia," I told my husband.

"My mother went to get an overcoat for me in the city," she said.

I could tell that she was upset, as if she wanted to get over being embarrassed with us, but didn't know how.

"Do you go to school?" my husband asked. "What's your dad's name?"

"Don't pester her," I said. "The poor kid can't take it right now. She's scared."

"No, I'm ok," she said.

My husband buried his face in a newspaper. I stroked the girl's wet hair. She looked at me with her hazel eyes and laughed. Her face showed that even adolescence would not be able to bring out the beauty in her. Her teeth were partly missing and in poor condition. She gradually became one of us.

"A dog got hit by a truck this afternoon. The truck was passing the graveyard. The poor dog was completely squashed. It was close to your house. Blood was coming out of him. Your housekeeper took the dog and dragged him onto the snow. Blood was coming out of him. He dragged him onto the snow, then threw him on a rubbish heap. He's still there. Did you see him?"

An hour later there was a loud knocking at the door. I opened the door to find a woman with her chador fallen down, clutching the wall with her hand.

"Help me," she said when she saw me. "My daughter's lost. I told her to wait for me in the janitor's room at school . . ." Then she collapsed like a spring and sat on the steps.

"Your daughter's here," I said simply.

The mother hurried inside and took the girl and the blanket in her arms, like a mother cat recovering a kitten with unopened eyes.

I wiped my eyes and went to get tea.

The mother was fat, spoke little, and sighed continually, as if short-winded or upset. She finally got up and left. She held the child as if she were holding a china flowerpot and was afraid of dropping and breaking it.

The next evening the neighbor lady came to our house again and asked to use the telephone. She gave me a number written on a dirty piece of paper and I dialed it for her. She then folded the paper carefully and put it in her pocket. She spoke loudly: "It's me, Fatimah."

"Tell your man to come to the telephone. Don't worry, I won't bite him. This is important."

"What other nastiness? It's bad enough I've given up everything for you, out here wandering in the desert with my kid's life slipping away. What did you say?"

"May God reward you. You're pregnant too. And lord have mercy on my child."

A long silence. After several minutes she raised her voice again. Her voice was trembling this time.

"Sir. Sir. Is it you? I hate to bother you, but this has cut me to the bone. I'm no more than a common peasant woman."

She was sobbing now. "Last night when I came to town to see grandmother, Badry had a bad cold. She's burning like a cast iron stove now. I'm out in the wilderness here . . ."

She could no longer continue. She cried out loud. I went to her and her face was wrinkled and contorted.

"Oh God of the God-forsaken," she said, very loudly. She had dropped the receiver on the table. A man's irritated voice was coming out of it.

I picked up the receiver. The voice said "Fatima, I'll be there in an hour. I'll bring a doctor too."

I took Fatima into the other room. I looked at her; there was no sign in her face of the accumulations of a moment earlier. When had she wiped away the tears, then? I consoled her anyway.

"Don't be so upset, *khānom*. A cold is nothing these days with all these new medicines."

Her face suddenly darkened. "She has pneumonia," she said.

"Pneumonia isn't dangerous now either."

"My dear lady, I'm no more than a captive woman. Their dad's having a passionate affair with his young mistress, and I have to stay by the graveyard so the mistress won't be upset. God forbid *khānom*, didn't I get pregnant? I delivered a baby too, but did anyone pay any attention? Now, this new wife is the center of attention and she isn't even pregnant. When I got married my husband was Mirza Hasan. Now he's Dr. Hasan Khan. I helped this very Mirza Hasan build a courtyard with my own hands, and I was even the daughter of Commander Mohammad Khan. Now this sluttish typist can't get along with me in a big house because she thinks it's too tiny for both of us. Oh lady, time has gone back. Better that one with no future had never been born."

"Which Commander Mohammad Khan?" I asked, although I knew no one by that name.

It snowed several days in a row. It was no longer possible to get through on the street, especially since the deputy had decided to destroy the *jū,* and replace it with underground concrete pipes. He didn't want the people to see water in the channel when they and their newly-planted little trees got thirsty. Workers were hollowing out the *jū* and heaping dirt and ice on the street with shovels. Cement pipes and building materials were stacked alongside and on top of one another. It was noon, and I, unable to go anywhere, was weaving ideas. I was thinking of writing a letter to the mayor and searching my mind for a good poem to put at the beginning. Then it occurred to me that we would all be needing boots, canes, hand lanterns, three meters of rope, and first-aid kits to negotiate that obstacle course. What a way to walk the straight and narrow path.

The sound of a group chanting "there is no God but God" diverted my attention. As if that wasn't enough, for some reason I got an uneasy feeling in my stomach. I had seen them carry coffins down this street to the graveyard a number of times. Moreover, they were bringing the coffin from the beginning of the street and our house and our neighbor's house were at the end of the street. Despite all this I found myself thinking "It couldn't be the little girl? She never got to wear her red overcoat." I looked behind me. Then most of the laborers and I stood on the snow-covered concrete pipes, bricks, and rocks to allow the coffin and the mourners to pass.

They had draped a cashmere shawl over the coffin and there was a turban sitting on it. It was evident from the size of the crowd, the turban on the coffin, the flag in front of it, the fact that all the mourners were trying to get a shoulder under the coffin and that even some of the laborers walked a few steps with it, that the friendless girl had not died. The body moved so slowly. I said to myself "If that friendless little girl died, would they put her in such a big coffin? Or would they wrap her in a towel and carry her by hand?" They wrap very small children in a sheet, and such a thin one. That time I did see a dead child they had put him in a fruit sack. You could see his head. Would a friendless little girl have an entourage of mourners? She would have two for sure. No, her father might come too. I would definitely go. They would bear her up in their arms, as if carrying a gift for someone. A gift for the dirt. Anyway, when someone's house is right next to the graveyard it's very easy to bury them. God shouldn't let any little girls die, no matter how skinny, and her teeth . . . People get so sad when little chicks die. Chicks that never get a good look at the springtime. Death is so hard in the winter. Oh God, this world of yours is so full of frightened, lovely little girls and chicks that get smashed underfoot by larger creatures.

I decided to visit Badry and ask how she was doing. Her mother was ill at ease when she met me at the door. I was nervous myself. When I was taking off my galoshes on the sidewalk I heard her voice singing loudly "tick, tock, what does the clock say . . ."

I saw Badry when I pulled back the curtain to the room. She was sitting on a *korsi* holding a book. A notebook and pen and ink were scattered out over the *korsi*. She put down the book and stood up when she saw me. Her whole face broke out in a smile. She hadn't changed. She was wearing the same faded school uniform. I sat by the *korsi*, which was giving off a charcoal smell. Badry was about to sit there too, but her mother told her sharply, "Lie down so you'll get well soon." Badry obeyed and laid on the *korsi*, but uneasily.

On a shelf there was a colorful bird in a cage whose name I didn't know. There was a bow and arrows by the cage. There was a clock on another shelf with persimmons arranged around it. The sound of the clock made me uncomfortable. The mother gathered up the persimmons, laid them before me on a plate and went to make tea.

"Our house is bad," Badry said, getting up. She took out a raggedy doll from somewhere and put it on the *korsi*.

I didn't know what to say. There was nothing to be said about the doll. It was so pitiful. I couldn't tell a story either, because stories are supposed to be told at night.

Badry started talking herself. "We used to have a big house. They had built a rail around the *howz* so we wouldn't fall in. Every afternoon when my brother came home from school I'd hold onto the rail and throw bread to the fish with him. A school of red and silver fish would swarm around the bread. They'd grab everything with their little lips and pull it under." Then she imitated the fish. "When we were at home my brother used to be nice to me. He gave me a lot of things. But now he doesn't have anything to give me. He even hits me. He says when he grows up he'll hit my mother too. He wants something from my mother every day. Now he wants her to buy him a racing bike. Or at least a pair of pigeons. Pigeons cost three tomans apiece. Oh God, let me die. He swears terribly. Yesterday he was about to break the glass in your greenhouse with an arrow. I begged him not to. He's afraid of your housekeeper too. Your housekeeper almost hit him twice. Once he had gotten hold of Mash Taqi's son's bicycle and kept riding back and forth on it. He ended up running into your housekeeper and everything that was in his basket fell on the ground. Your housekeeper chased him, but he couldn't catch him. My brother kept laughing and dancing around. Another time his ball hit your house. It bounced hard off your door. Your housekeeper opened the door and said 'now I've got you.' I was standing nearby about to die of fright.

"'Go ahead and hit me if you mean business,' my brother said, 'so I can tell your mistress and get you fired.'"

"'Do you think I'm afraid of her?' your housekeeper said. 'Who's that bitch?' Then he said something really bad and he never did give the ball back. It's still in your house."

Badry's mother came in with a tray of tea and protested the girl's sitting up. I put my tea on the *korsi*. Right then the front door opened and slammed shut so hard that the cup on the *korsi* shook. Then a twelve- or thirteen-year-old boy came in. He looked like an escapee from the zoo. He came into the room with muddy shoes, picked up his bow, grabbed two persimmons off the *korsi,* and put them in his pocket.

"Say hello," the mother said. But the boy didn't have time.

"I hear your ball is at our house," I said.

"So what? I'll fix him so good you'll even think it's funny yourself. Mom and Dad . . ."

"You should have told me personally. He's not educated and you are. You shouldn't . . ."

"What do you care?" he interrupted. "Why did you come to our house?"

"All the dirt in the world on my head!" said the mother. "Son, you ought to be ashamed."

"Eat rotten eggplant, you runt!" And he left just as he had come.

I wanted to relieve the mother of her embarrassment, but I didn't know how. She was pale, chewing her chador.

"How high is Badry's fever?" I said at last.

"I don't know," she said. "I don't know how to take temperature. Her dad will take her temperature when he comes tonight." Then, as if to apologize, she added, "The child needs a father. A woman can't control a boy."

As I went home I thought, "Are most boys like this, and then they become Dr. Hasan Khans when they are men?"

Our housekeeper had been gone a week. I was flipping through a cookbook looking for a recipe for *khoresht-e fesenjān*. I was sick of having lunch in the cafes in town so much and eating so many fried and boiled eggs at night. I was reading "how to keep the meat balls from falling apart" when someone knocked on the door. It was the neighbor lady, asking "Your husband isn't home?" Her mind at ease, she came in, but in silence. I told her about the latest headache. She cursed our housekeeper in a way that I had never heard in my life. I thought she had come to get her son's ball. But no. She had some fearsome business with me.

"Dear lady, I've come to ask another favor of you. May God give you life. The whole neighborhood says you speak every domestic and foreign tongue. I wanted you to employ your worldly expertise by calling my husband's other wife and telling her a couple of things directly. I got to the real heart of the matter with her last night. I come to you in her best interest as well."

"I don't know your husband's other wife. Anyway, I even have trouble taking care of myself. You can see that I have to use a book to cook *khoresht*."

"My husband's other wife—no offense to you—I don't know how to put this, but she's like you. If there's one thing that paper shuffler can't comprehend it's domestic skills. She wastes seventy tomans a month on an incompetent and stupid maid. She won't touch the whiteness of yogurt or the blackness of coal. She can't, in any case. She's got fingernails the size of shovels, covered with pigeon-blood lacquer. The only thing she knows how to do is expose her chest and go to some dive holding hands with our man. She's digging her own grave consuming so many harmful substances. What a disaster! I wanted you to help, call her and give her some advice. Make her understand, with your powers of persuasion, that it's not good to put me and my children out in the desert. Oh God, by the lock that I kissed, by my fortune, give this woman whatever she wants, as long as she helps me get what I want."

I looked at her. Her face showed no sign of illness. I asked her to come and sit down. It was unthinkable to disappoint her. All her hopes rested with me.

"Dear lady, even if you do know all these foreign and domestic tongues, if you don't help us women, or as my son says, if you don't get our rights for us, then what good is it?"

"I don't have any idea why you left your husband's house," I said. "I don't know. I don't know anything about it."

She interrupted me. "*Khānom,* I'll tell you the whole story from the beginning. Several months ago I had gone one day to the bathhouse, and I wish I'd gone to the undertaker's instead. Nanny Akbar, holding a scrubber, was shaking her head at me. '*Khānom,* I don't blame you for losing weight. What time is it now? Time for the noon prayer.' 'What do you mean you don't blame me?'" I asked. My stomach was churning like it was full of vinegar and garlic. I had known my husband was hiding something for quite a while. He was coming home late at night with absolutely no enthusiasm. He had either already eaten dinner, or if he ate with us he complained bitterly about everything and slapped us around. He didn't pay any attention to the kids either, he just yelled at them. The older woman looked at me with kindness, as if I had gangrene. My stomach was in a fit. I felt terrible, and I knew something was afoot, but I had no idea what had happened to me. I went to see Mortaz Hindi.

"'Don't be afraid,' she said. 'Your fortune is good and your star is in the house of Saturn.'" I felt better. Up until that time the bathhouse masseuse had explained everything from garlic to onions for me, but I won't bore you with that. I didn't realize, dear lady, how much had been taken from me. I hurried out of the bathhouse and took a taxi to the address the masseuse had given me. I knocked on the door of a ramshackle house. A fat little woman opened the door.

"'I want to speak with Ms. Monir,' I said.

"'She's at the office,' she said. 'She'll be here at two in the afternoon.' *Khānom,* I waited right there until two. My stomach was churning with hunger. I watched for her at that house. You can't imagine how I felt when I saw our man drive up in a car with Monir sitting right beside him. I ran into the front hall of another house where the door was open. How can I describe how I felt? I nearly passed out. At least our man didn't stay there with his mistress long. As soon as he left I pushed open the door and walked right in. I opened my mouth and said whatever came into my mind.

"That damned Monir came back, saying 'What's wrong with you, sister? Who are you talking to?'

"'I'm talking to you, you bed-hopping shrew! You steal the peoples' husbands and now you're talking about sisterhood! Drop dead!'

"She's such a little bitch. She came and took my hand, led me into the living room, sat me down, and gave me a cup of water. *Khānom,* even though I was about to die of thirst I didn't touch that water, even as I sat there perspiring. I thought I'd have a heart attack, and God knows my heart is weak. You get the picture now . . .

"What did I say? Yeah. I looked the woman over real well. She was a blonde. Her hair was exactly the color of adobe bricks. And skinny as a skeleton. It looked like her stomach was sticking to her back. But I swear to God she wouldn't look at me. She never said a word. Of course that was because she's such a bitch. Do you know what I told her? I have two children. For fifteen long, hectic years I've toiled in this man's house. It's made my hair turn white. I've put up with all his complaining and we've been getting along alright for two years. We have things under control. Dear lady, I cried like the rain in spring. The woman listened well. Of course *Khānom,* she knew, she had the upper hand. I was the one who was humiliated.

"Finally, she said 'God knows I had no idea the Doctor had two children. At first he didn't even tell me he was married. Then I heard it from the bathhouse masseuse. I reprimanded him and he said it was none of my business. Anyway it was already too late. I had been engaged to him for a month. When I reproached the Doctor he said 'Yeah, there's an old woman who helps my mother and does the housework.'

"*Khānom,* as soon as I heard her say 'old woman' I just about blew up. 'Am I old?' I said. Older than your grand-mother. I'm sure she must have put an amulet under her blouse beforehand to keep my hands still. If not I'd have grabbed her hair and choked her to death with it. And she conducted herself with sinister skill. She played dumb and apologized to me. 'Of course you're not old,' she said, and 'by God, I'm really sorry. I don't know what to do . . .'

"But I'm boring you. I ended up going home with an awful feeling. It was sunset. The children and their grand-mother were sitting by the front gate. They ran up to me happily when they saw me. I told them not to touch my heart because it was broken, and went straight to bed. But for those two stripling kids and the fear of God I'd have taken opium that very night and done away with myself. Why else do people take opium? I couldn't eat a thing for a week.

"If only our man would come to the door and ask about me. If only he would buy an apple and bring it to the kids to give to me. What a miserable turn of events. When we were poor this same Mirza Hasan would buy sacks and sacks of fruit and bring them home. One night when I was feeling terrible he came in with his mother. They sat by my bed. I turned to the wall and started crying. Our man said 'I'm a Muslim man. I can have up to four wives. Don't waste your energy being melodramatic. If it's too much for you, you can leave the house. Have I refused you a divorce?'"

She wiped her eyes and held her nose in a corner of her chador.

"I wore black the night they got married. I went into the gathering dressed in black from head to toe carrying a water-pipe. There weren't that many people. *Khānom,* my hands were shaking so I almost dropped the waterpipe on the car-pet. My legs were so wobbly I said 'I'm going to fall flat on the floor right now.' My rival-wife-to-be, that is, the chaste bride, got up and came and took the waterpipe from me. I was more relaxed near his mother. The impudent woman came over, gave me a handful of sweets, and kissed my neck. She drank the blood of my blood. But I didn't have the nerve to speak out. As of the next day she would be the lady of the house and I would be the cook. At the end she talked so much I had to leave, and now, dear lady, every time I think of her I realize that that house with that other wife is 100 times better than this shack in the desert. God forbid that any man should be deprived of his children.

"I almost lost my precious little girl. She got consumption. She still hasn't gotten over it. You saw my son too. Can I control him? He always says 'You're the bungler who made our father throw us out of our house.' His classmates here are the children of gardeners, waterworks employees, and street cleaners. He learns from them. Even your housekeeper almost took him under his wing. He had taken him for a walk and bought him some ice cream. He had rented a bicy-cle and was riding him on the handlebars. I swear to God it's true. Mashhadi Safar the street cleaner saw him, and he's a devout man. He didn't make a scene, however, he just tricked my son by telling him his father had come home. I was sitting down when I saw my son come running up to the house with Mashhadi Safar close behind.

"'Where's my Dad?'" my son said.

Mashhadi Safar winked at me.

"'He came and left again, I said. You weren't here.

"I've been boring you. That's enough. Now, dear lady, if you could just do this for me, it would be like going on the highest holy pilgrimage for you."

I took the telephone number from her and went to the phone. The person I called—Monir *Khānom*—was a woman with a sleepy voice. She accepted my apologies for interfering in their lives and listened patiently. The neighbor lady had also pressed her ear to the receiver. Her chest heaved up and down, and sometimes she shook her head. Monir *Khānom* acknowledged that "the Doctor" had spoken with her and convinced her that the other wife and her children ought to return to the house. She agreed, saying "Really, why should the Doctor have to support two households? What's done is done now, but on the condition that 'Fatimah *Khānom* must give up sorcery and witchcraft, she must not bury a donkey's head in the basement nor throw a hoof in the brazier, nor put an amulet on the bottom of the front door, nor put concoctions to assure marital harmony in the water, the tea, and the food.'

"*Khānom,* when I came home from the office, Fatimah *Khānom* used to say prayers and spit in my face. I heard 'deaf, dumb, and blind, they are devoid of wisdom'* 100 times in my ear. You must agree that one would soon weary of this sort of life and be afraid of eating for fear of getting sick."

---

*The Holy Qor'an, Surah II, v. 171.

I promised for Fatimah *Khānom*. When I replaced the receiver she was bent over, kissing the threshold in front of the door.

We finally had a sunny day. When I came from the bathhouse in the morning the street had not yet been asphalted but the repairs on the Majles deputy's house had been completed. An American tenant had also arrived and there was smoke rising into the air from all the chimneys. Three jeeps and a Cadillac were parked in front of the big garden in a line. Our housekeeper, who was now working for the people who owned the vehicles, was wiping the Cadillac's windshield. His hair was so shiny it looked like he'd had a six-month permanent, and it was dripping with oil. When I passed the jeep with my boots, my bag, and all my equipment, he sounded the Cadillac's horn. I didn't turn my head, but I heard him laughing. By God, he had even gotten a gold tooth. Poles, planks, and building materials were still strewn in the street. The *jū* was now covered, but mud was oozing out of it into the street. I had sent my letter to the mayor without a poem. When I got home I found Fatimah *Khānom* waiting for me, her face covered with ceruse and bright rouge, smelling of rosewater, and wearing a silk chador with flowers on it. I asked about Badry.

"She's better."

"No more fever?"

"No." She was silent. After a moment she said, "Dear lady, do you have a six-kilogram pot?"

"We have a pot, but I don't know how big it is."

I invited her in, observing her closely.

"My husband, his other wife, his mother, and the relatives are coming up here today."

"It won't be easy to receive so many guests with Badry sick."

"What can I do, *Khānom?* The other wife has gotten this craving into her head. She wants vermicelli soup."

I handed her the pot.

"It's too small," she said, "But there's no alternative. I'll have Badry bring it back."

"Then Badry's up and around, no?" I asked happily.

Her whole face turned red. "The truth is, there was nothing much wrong with Badry." Embarrassed, she added, "I thought you knew all along. . . ."

Then she set the pot on the floor and said, "Dear lady, children make life worthwhile for a mother and father. Why don't you have children?"

"I don't know."

"You must be afflicted by a curse. Is anyone in your family due to have a baby soon? Do you know the bathhouse masseuses?"

"No."

"Dear lady, I have some problems to work out today, but let's go to the mortuary together one day when I'm not so preoccupied."

"The mortuary?"

"Yes, dear lady, yes. Don't you know that going to the mortuary has an exorcising effect? It's very strange. You have to pass next to a corpse for your curse to be lifted."

She laughed, picked up the pot, and left.

Translated by John Green

Sīmīn Dānishvar

Perhaps the best-known of Iran's women writers, and the author of Savushūn [Mourning], *the best-selling Persian novel of all time, Dānishvar "was born in Shiraz, the third of six children, on April 28, 1921. She grew up in her native city and moved to the capital* *in 1942 to attend Tehran University. There she studied Persian literature, wrote her dissertation on 'Beauty as Treated in Persian Literature,' and received her doctorate in 1949. Dānishvar and a fellow student, Jalāl Āl-i Aḥmad (1923–1969), whom she had first met on a bus traveling from Shiraz to Tehran, were married in 1950. Two years later, she went to America on a Fulbright Fellowship to study creative writing at Stanford University. Upon returning to Iran, she first taught in the Tehran conservatory and later joined the Department of Archaeology, Faculty of Letters and Humanities, at Tehran University."* In addition to the writings listed here, she translated several books, including Chekhov's* The Cherry Orchard *and* The Enemies, *Hawthorne's* The Scarlet Letter, *Paton's* Cry, the Beloved Country, *Saroyan's* Human Comedy, *Arthur Schnitzler's* Beatrice, *Shaw's* Arms and the Man, *and two collections of international short stories.*

Dānishvar held a number of positions in government service, serving as principal of several Tehran elementary schools, editor of the magazine Naqsh va Nigār *in the National Fine Arts Administration, and instructor at Tehran University. In addition, she was a collaborator and contributor on the journals* 'Ilm va Zindagī *and* Kayhān-i Māh, *with which her husband was also actively involved.***

---

*Farzaneh Milani, "Power, Prudence and Print: Censorship and Simin Danashvar", *Iranian Studies* 18.2–4 (1985): 325–347.

**Fakhrī Qavīmī, *Kārnāmah-'i Zanān-i Mashhūr-i Īrān* (Tehran: Vizārāt-i Āmuzish va Parvarish, 1352/1973 or 1974), pp. 228–229. See also Farzaneh Milani, "Power, Prudence, and Print: Censorship and Simin Daneshvar," *Iranian Studies* 18.2–4 (Spring-Autumn 1985): 325–347, and Hūshang Gulshīrī, "Jadāl-i Naqsh bā Naqqāsh" [The Struggle of Painting with the Painter], *Naqd-i Āgāh* (Tehran: Āgāh, 1984).

❧ Congratulations and Condolences

MAHDUKHT KASHKŪLĪ

A thin ray of sunlight was shining into the room through the window, where it settled on the shelf. Black cloth had been spread all around the frame holding Ali's picture. The picture was leaning against the wall in the center of the shelf.

There, in the middle of the frame, sat Ali in the dark, distant background, all alone, frowning, his head tilted to the side. To the right of the frame stood a glass vase filled with plastic red flowers, which had been pushed back up against the wall so it would not tip over. On the other side of the shelf, a small mirror was anxiously soaking up the light. Abbas Aqa was leaning against the wall, arms folded, his lips pressed together at the corners by some hidden pain. His eyes, half-opened, were fixed on Fati. Fati was sitting next to the doorway. The neighborhood kids had told her that the radio reporter was on his way to convey his congratulations and condolences. You could hear the noise of the children playing in the distance.

On the way to their house, Gelin Khanum found an opportunity to question the reporter. "Did you come to give

This story is translated from the story *Tabrīk va Taslīyat,* published in *Ārash* 6, Shahrīvar, 1360 (1981):108–117.

them a house?"* She heaved a sigh and said, "It's a pity I wasn't able to have children . . ." The neighbor women, like loving sisters, were trying non-stop to console Fati. Zari, who had found a piece of cardboard, was fanning her with it. The reporter waded through the hands and legs of the children. He calmly took out a pen and paper and set up the tape recorder in front of him on the ground. He tried to look sad, but a smile appeared on his lips, the sort of smile that comes with the exercise of one's profession. He looked about himself and then at Fati Khanum, who with a puffy face, puffy eyes, and a meaningless smile, was sitting on her knees, lost in a memory.

The reporter, his voice hoarse, said, "Dear Mother, you must be proud of the fact that your son was martyred." Fati opened her eyes and stared at the reporter. "Huh?"

The neighbor women gestured with their eyes in the direction of the reporter. The reporter paused for a moment and then repeated his question with a smile. Fati, still staring at him, placed her hand on her breast right where the strange hole in Ali's chest had been seen. Her cry of despair echoed through the room, drawing all the children, terrified, to their mothers' sides. The reporter angrily picked up his tape recorder and left.

One year and four months previous, just as the sun began to yawn over the tops of the Cypress trees, Ali was sitting on the balcony overlooking the coffeehouse peeling onions. His nose and eyes had started to water. His eyes were almost closed. The breeze wafted upwards over the balcony, bringing with it a fresh scent of earth and trees, but, upon encountering the smell of onions, it would back up and die away.

To the right of the balcony, in the yard of the coffeehouse, there was a wooden bed frame, which served as a bench, over which had been thrown a faded old rug. On it were

---

*The Iranian government gives financial compensation to the families of "martyrs" killed fighting for the revolutionary cause.

sitting a handful of people—it looked, through his swollen eyelids, to be a few men and women—talking. Ali couldn't quite make out the words; they reached his ears as a faint hum. When the onions were finished, he tossed the knife in the basin and came down the ladder.

Tears were still running from his eyes. He took hold of his nose with the hem of his shirt and blew. He wiped the tears away with the back of his hand. As he reached the bed frame, he stopped, his twinkling eyes fixed upon them. They were all talking together, shouting even, though not in anger. One of the men glanced at Ali and said to his friends, "Take this one for example. Look at him. How old are you, son?"

Ali looked at him.

"Well, son, tell me. Do you know they're exploiting you here?"

"They're doing what?"

"I said, they're exploiting you. It means they've made you into a servant, a slave. It means they're forcing you to work." Ali looked at them. The man turned victoriously back to his friends and said with a smile, "You see, in a capitalist system wages are the price of manual labor which the workers sell to the exploiters." From within the cool darkness of the coffeehouse, Jafar Aqa's voice called out to him, "Hey, son! Ali! Hurry up for godssake. Run and bus the tea glasses." Ali was still thinking about the group of people there. He ran to grab a tin tray and rushed off in the direction of the tea glasses. The fatter man turned his head. He had thick, black hair and the hairs of his mustache concealed the movement of his lips. His belly hung out like a soccer ball. His short legs were swinging back and forth between the bed frame and the ground. His boot laces were untied and his red socks were protruding out from his boot tops above his ankles. He wetted the tip of his cigarette in his mouth, lit it, and began puffing deeply and vigorously.

Ali looked at him surreptitiously. All at once the man

began speaking, his fat white fingers opening and closing into a fist all the while. "You see, as long as there is no consciousness, how is a worker supposed to know what his rights are? A clever leader is needed to awake the masses from their heedless dream. I haven't got much faith, though. The masses have been fast asleep for thousands of years. I'm beginning to think this country fully deserves the tyranny it's got. They've grown accustomed to this system. It's my own damned fault I came to this dump in the first place. Absolutely nothing is done right here!"

The words seemed to assault Ali, flying right in his face, though he did not really understand what they were saying. He just stood there, tray in hand, mouth agape, staring at them. At this point the thin man with the clipped red beard and yellowing eyes lost control of his emotions and jumped up, knocking the burning end of his cigarette onto the rug, though he paid no attention to it. He threw his hands into the air, shouting, "The thing is, you know, that the entire country is stupid! Their beliefs are all wrong, their way of life is all wrong! They're just a bunch of degenerates and beasts of burden, to say nothing of their women, who, instead of training their children, spend their lives window shopping. They do more harm than good!" Then he turned to the girl who was with them. "Of course, I'm not talking about ladies like yourself."

The girl was well made-up and perfumed. She seemed to be very well rested. She thanked him with a bright smile. He continued, "The men, on the other hand, act like nothing's going on. They're all either making the rounds from one cafe to the other or lusting after some unlawful wealth or somebody's daughter. I say they must be guided or beaten to their senses. A guy like Hitler doesn't look so bad! What's wrong with seeing people lined up against the wall when you're out for a walk?! I'm telling you, it wouldn't make me bat an eye to see the streets filled with the corpses of these degenerates.

Let them all be exterminated and a new society brought into being! A society based on correct beliefs and principles. A real, thorough purification! Anyone who's left should be beaten to his senses—of course, you've gotta bring them up from childhood with the right principles. It should be done all over the world. I'm in favor of just annihilating the whole world!"

The girl, looking very civilized, said, "Good grief! Whatever for?" The man wheeled around and shouted, "For the sake of progress! Progress!" Then, exhausted, he hopped up like a grasshopper onto a corner of the bed frame and, taking a seat, yelled toward the coffeehouse, "Tea here!"

Ali was frightened and stepped back several paces. Then he ran into the coffeehouse. That night Ali spread his bedroll on the balcony and pulled the covers over his head. The cotton stuffing had gathered together in separate clumps, but, between them he could see the twinkling stars. He tried to recall their conversation, but could only remember a few words.

"What's wrong with them?" thought Ali. "What were they talking about? That man really felt sorry for me; he called me a slave and a servant. Why did he say that? I'm not a servant! I'm an assistant to the owner of a coffeehouse. I've gone through the fourth grade—I wish I remembered all those words. I would have told him a thing or two right then. How is a worker supposed to know his rights!?"

"How is a worker supposed to know his rights?!" Ali said aloud. He laughed and, drawing up his knees, placed his arms underneath his head like a pillow. "So what do they know about the rights of Ous* Abdollah's son? God bless Ous Abdollah. He used to drag his son to work, but in the end, he turned out to be a crook. What a lucky guy—they put his picture in the newspapers and Ous Abdollah's wife

---

Ous is a substandard pronunciation of Ostad, which here refers to the master of a trade (such as Master Carpenter, etc.)

showed it to everybody. She used to say that Ous Abdollah
cut it out of the paper and gave it to her himself. But he had
chewed her out, 'Take it, woman! Take the picture of your
darling boy! After all the trouble we took, he turns into a
thief! Now they've gone and put his picture in the papers
and now I can't hold my head up to a single soul. It's your
fault, you spoiled him!'"

Ous Abdollah's wife had taken the picture and stuck it on
her prayer carpet. She would take it with her whenever she
went on pilgrimage, and rub it on all four walls of the
shrines. But she wasn't allowed to talk about her son in front
of Ous Abdollah.

Ali rolled over and yawned. His eyes were burning. He
remembered the last of the men, and said to himself, "He
was carrying on like a madman at the end. They should all
be killed or beaten up . . . they're just a bunch of degenerate
coolies. Why degenerate? So he's a coolie! It doesn't mean
he's degenerate. What is a degenerate anyway? If a guy is
good, then he shouldn't be killed. What about dad? So he's a
coolie, that doesn't mean he's bad! He's a good hard-working
man; he never sets his burden down. Everybody'll know he's
a coolie and he'll be the first to be done in." Ali's heavy
eyelids fell shut.

In the morning Qoli nudged him in the side with the tip
of his foot. "Come on, get up, lazy bones. You sleep like a
bump on a log. Get up, Jafar Aqa's on his way."

Ali rolled over and after a few minutes was bent over the
basin on the balcony peeling onions, his eyes and nose watering. Through his sniffling he could once again make out
the voices of those people. He turned to look. The fat man
waved to him and laughed. "How are you, my friend?"

Ali laughed, but Qoli gave him a stern look and said,
"What are you looking at?"

"Some customers have come. They'll be wanting tea."

"Don't worry, Jafar Aqa is there, he knows how to take care of business better than you."

Ali looked down and continued working, but his thoughts were on the group of people.

The smell of fried eggs and fresh bread mingled with the smell of onions. As they ate, the group talked. The thinner man tried to put his fried egg on his bread with the tip of his fork while addressing the question of the Third World. The voice of the girl suddenly said, "They don't wash the plates too well here."

Ali thought to himself, "If I was down there, he'd say 'How old are you? Do you know they're exploiting you here?'" He broke out laughing.

Qoli looked at him sternly again. "What are you laughing about?! Keep your mind on your work. I can't work with you if you're not going to pay attention."

Ali gathered himself together and tried to think only of the onions and the basin. When he came down the ladder Jafar Aqa called him. "Ali, Ali! Run and get the tray."

Ali passed by the bed frame. The fat man, his short, fat legs swinging more quickly now, said with a noisy laugh, "Hey son, what's your name?"

As Ali ran by he said, "Ali, at your service."

The man got up and followed after him a few steps. "Wait a second." Ali stopped.

The man clasped his shoulders and looked him straight in the eyes. "You are not a servant. You're our friend. Come, have a glass of tea on us."

Ali shook loose. "No sir, we've got our own way of looking at things here."

Ali was used to them being around. Sometimes just two of them would come. Usually they would come before the sun had warmed up, staying till around noon, drinking tea, smoking, and reading the paper. The wind would blow their paper this way and that. Ali would gather up the sections and read them out loud for Qoli at night. He'd leave out the hard words.

"Enough, enough!" Qoli would say. "If you want a parrot to talk, you put a sugarcube in its mouth," and Ali would fall silent.

Whenever this group of people would come, Ali would hover nearby. He couldn't make heads or tails of what they were saying, but he liked it. Whatever they were saying, it was different than the things that Qoli and Jafar Aqa and his father talked about. It made Jafar Aqa cross. Qoli would nag. Ali smiled mockingly.

It was always the fat man who would strike up conversation. He'd shake his head and say, "How are you, my friend?"

"I'm fine."

The man would repeat Ali's answer with a long laugh. "I'm fine!? How can you be fine in your situation, huh?"

Ali would stop laughing and fall silent. "What situation?" he would think. The man put his hand on Ali's shoulder. Ali tried to shake free.

"You're a good kid," the man would say.

Jafar Aqa would call out to him. "Ali! Don't stand there doing nothing! Whaddaya think this is?! You've got a job to do!" This would annoy Ali. He'd frown and bang the cups and glasses together, which only made Jafar Aqa angrier.

Qoli would step in and counsel Ali. "You shouldn't hang around those guys." Ali shrugged his shoulders.

Jafar Aqa would badger Ali even more. Ali would frown. Jafar Aqa would threaten to fire Ali. Ali would turn a deaf ear to him. As soon as Jafar Aqa and Qoli took their eyes off him, Ali'd go sit next to the group and listen, open-mouthed, to their words.

When he was alone with Qoli he'd repeat what he had heard. It all went right over Qoli's head, who'd grumble,

"Look, Ali, it's all talk. These guys have nothing to do. If they had a job, they wouldn't be sitting around here in the middle of the week. Don't hang around them. They don't feel sorry for us. You think they're friends with you. No way! They're not, I tell you. They're just thinking about themselves, they say work is good and the worker is noble. For God's sake, if it's so good, why don't they become workers themselves? Let them toil like asses from morning till night so that they don't even have time to go to the toilet! If you die tomorrow they won't even ask what happened to you."

Ali stared at him and said, "Well, somebody's gotta save the downtrodden. I mean, if you think about it, we're really miserable."

Qoli would yell, "Who says we're miserable? You're miserable, I'm quite happy. I work. Is it right that a body should eat for free?"

Ali looked to be deep in thought. "I don't know. Actually, everybody is downtrodden."

Qoli swore at him, "Get off of it, don't wallow in self-pity, for godssake." When he'd get angry, he'd throw whatever was handy at Ali. Ali would duck.

Jafar Aqa, hearing the ruckus, would enter the battlefield. The veins on his neck sticking out, his face flushed with anger, he'd run up shouting: "Have you no shame, Ali? Respect your elders. This is the last time I'm telling you. I'll fire you."

Ali would crawl off in a corner and try to avoid Qoli the rest of the day. He'd stay busy until late at night so that Qoli would already be asleep. Then he'd quietly climb the ladder and spread his bedroll on the balcony. He would stretch out there and think. His thoughts twirled around and around like the spirals of a conch shell. He understood some things, but not others; he'd feel some things, but not be able to make them out. He'd toss and turn until he fell asleep.

Saturday evenings, Ali would get time off. From noon

onward he'd be on pins and needles, looking at the sun every other minute, anxiously awaiting sunset. The last rays of sunlight would still be lingering on when Ali ran out of the coffeehouse. On that day he ran into the fat man just as he turned the corner. He smiled and said hello. The man nodded and extended his hand. Ali had been taken unawares and didn't know what to do for a moment, but he caught hold of himself and took the man's hand, shaking it vigorously two or three times.

They set off together. Ali's breath was short and the silence made him uncomfortable. The words he had heard them saying were swimming before his eyes. Finally he screwed up his courage and said, "You feel sorry for people who are downtrodden, don't you?"

The loud laughter of the man shook him. He stood still. The man said, "That's right, yeah."

Ali asked doubtfully, "So are you gonna help them?"

"No."

"Why not?"

"You must be joking."

"You all are always talking about them."

"Well, yeah, we talk. We can't talk about ordinary stuff, we have to talk about important things."

"Are the downtrodden important?"

"I don't know if they're important in themselves, but it's important to talk about it."

Ali cleaned the edges of his mouth with his tongue. "So . . ." The crowd separated them. When they found each other again, Ali asked, "Do you think I can help them?" Ali looked at him imploringly. He wanted to hear him say, "Yes, of course," but the man laughed and shrugged his shoulders.

"What can I say? You should just forget all about such things, Ali. It's just to keep the mind occupied, it's all talk. We have to have something to talk about when we're together." He yawned.

Ali swallowed hard. He wasn't expecting this. He frowned. He walked the rest of the way in silence. They had come to the bus stop and had to split up. Ali got on the bus. Face pressed against the window, he stared outside the whole trip and felt like crying. So it was all talk. So what were they yelling and shouting so passionately for? What if Qoli was right? The hell with it.

Ali didn't know how he got from the bus stop to his own street. At the head of his street he saw the neighborhood kids gathered together and he decided to tell them that he would save them some day, but Ahmad, showing his joy at Ali's arrival, tripped him up from behind. Ali was forced to grab him by the collar and wrestle. They rolled around over the dirt and the trash, and when they were finally separated, Ali had forgotten about saving the downtrodden. But when he opened the door of his house and the smell of the Indian oils that his mother rubbed on her swollen legs reached his nose, and when he saw his father, hands folded, staring off into the distance, he sank once again into thought.

In the morning he had to go back to work, but he couldn't stop thinking about the downtrodden. He ran to get back to the coffeehouse, the sun was already all warmed up and he was worried about being late. Several times his ankles turned as he ran. When he reached the door of the coffeehouse, Jafar Aqa was standing there and handed him his bedroll. "Ali, let's part on good terms. We just can't get along. Whenever you've come to your senses, come back to me."

Ali had never dreamed it was possible. He turned pale, but he kept control of himself. For a few moments he stood there in the street, fists clenched, grinding his teeth. He didn't want to beg. For an instant he saw Qoli's face behind the window, but he turned away, picked up the bedroll and set off.

On the way he stopped at the shop of Ous Reza, the carpenter. Ous Reza was measuring planks of wood and putting them in stacks. His mouth full of nails, he answered Ali's greeting with a nod. Ali set the bedroll down near the door of the shop and went in. He waited for a moment. Ous Reza was bent over measuring the planks, and didn't pay any attention to him.

Ali ran out. After a short while he sat down on a step and hid his face in his hands. He sat there motionless, transfixed. An unknown, unexplainable desire had taken root in him. He wanted to press his cheeks to the warm stones of the wall and cry out "I want to die," but he was afraid to give voice to these thoughts. He was so afraid, in fact, that as he walked away he looked behind himself to make sure that death had not heard his words and come after him.

He walked on for a while. All at once he was conscious of himself, wandering around confused, oppressed between the low sky, crowded with buildings, and the grey of the asphalt. The walls were plastered with posters and lines of graffiti in red and black, scribbled crookedly this way and that. There was one poster showing a soldier smiling drowsily, a carnation stuck in the end of his rifle and a ring of flowers around his neck.

On the bridge on Shahreza street, an army officer was yelling into a bullhorn. "Break it up! This time we fired into the air, next time we won't be responsible for the consequences."

The crowd didn't budge. For a second Ali thought to himself that the people must be demonstrating in the street to save the downtrodden and he joyfully thrust himself into the crowd. He didn't ask anybody what was happening though, because he was afraid they might, like the fat man, say, "Well, it's just talk, just to pass the time."

Ali turned onto a side street and rushed into the open door of a building. He could hear the sound of gunfire, but he was even more afraid of the dark, winding corridor in front of him. Two men with briefcases came down the stairs and went outside, closing the door behind them. Ali opened the door after them and ran out onto the sidewalk. On the far side of the intersection the people were shouting slogans. They kept coming onto the side street and returning once again to the intersection. Some were running. Ali took a deep breath and ran with them.

He couldn't smell onions, but there was something else choking him and bringing tears to his eyes. He returned to the intersection, the mob returned with him. The soldiers were slowly advancing towards them. The people moved backward.

Ali was confused, he just stood there motionless. The soldier's lips were dry, his dark eyes flashing. His lips moved slightly, muttering, "Beat it." Ali stood there. His lips, like the lips of the soldier, were all dry. There was something familiar about him. The soldier was a sad imitation of himself.

The people behind Ali were cheering and mimicking the soldier. The soldier shouted, "Go on, beat it, all of you." The people hooted.

Ali wanted to turn back and run, but the people were shouting, "We're not afraid, shoot, shoot." The soldier, his face flushed, bit his lower lip. Suddenly he shouted, "Step aside, Boy, or else."

Ali moved.

The people cried, "No, no, don't budge." "Don't pay any attention to him, let him shoot. He doesn't dare."

The soldier took aim. The look in his eyes was no longer familiar.

Ali ran towards the sidewalk. He didn't know what to do. He was getting hot under the collar over the way the people kept shouting at him, "Don't move, don't move, he won't dare pull the trigger."

He stopped and stood his ground. He turned around to see the soldier. He wanted to say to him, "Let's save the downtrodden," but all of a sudden he felt a burning in his chest and a loud noise assaulted his ears. His hands grasped at the dirt, plunging into the moist soil of a flowerbed.

He closed his left eye and squinted with his right, sizing up the soldier. The stupefied soldier was standing in his place like a statue, staring at his rifle.

Ali could hear the clatter of footsteps running away. He could hear Ous Reza's hammer banging on the nails. The sound of his hammering inched back and forth through his skull like a worm. It entered his skull like the buzzing of a fly and exited through his ears. The sound of a musical instrument and drum from a distant, dubious party reached his ears.

Qoli was bent over, his lips forming a rhomboid grimace of contentment. He had bunched up his shirt into a ball and was wringing the frothy, grimy water from it onto the face and head of Ali. Ali was trying to pull himself away, but his path was blocked by the deep muck in the gutters. He wanted to curse, but fountains of blood were gushing painfully from his mouth. He tried to lift up his head.

He saw feet fleeing past him, hands burrowed into pockets, untied bootlaces. Not one of them was thinking about the downtrodden. Ali closed his left eye. He squinted with the other to see better, but both eyes fell shut and his head sank back onto the warm, malodorous asphalt.

Translated by Frank Lewis

MAHDUKHT KASHKŪLĪ

Kashkūlī was born in 1950 in Tehran. She holds a Ph.D. in culture, language, and religion from Tehran University. She worked for Iranian educational television from 1975 to 1985 and then as a member of the faculty at Tehran University's College of Arts.

This is from *Stories by Iranian Women Since the Revolution,* translated by Soraya Sullivan. Austin, TX: Center for Middle Eastern Studies, 1991: 50.

❧ Gowhar

ẒAHRĀ KHĀNLARĪ

Ḥavvā's daughter Gowhar was twelve years old. Her delicate and beautiful face set her apart from the other village
girls. Her black, beguiling eyes were especially attractive
against the pale skin of her slender face. Her delicate and
well-proportioned body, which deserved to be dressed in
thousands of colorful and expensive garments, was always
concealed behind a chador, so men could never enjoy the
sight of it. On the first encounter with a strange man she hid
herself so well that only the pupil of one of her eyes was
visible. After several meetings, however, like the moon coming from behind a mountain, Gowhar's face gradually
emerged from its veil. Gradually her white, high forehead,
her big black eyes, her red cheeks and lips, her lovely chin,
and her slender neck were displayed.

Gowhar was one of Damavand's literate girls. This was
because her mother and father had wanted at least one of
their children to learn to read so she could recite the Qor'an
during the nights of mourning for them, and to read its
opening verse for their departed souls. Gowhar was proud of
this and whenever she was given the job of doing the books

This story was first published in *Sukhan* 2:4, Farvardin 1324 [21 April–21 May 1945],
pp. 296–303.

for her father's store she gave herself wholly to the task with pride and praises to God. She was so intensely absorbed that no one dared interrupt her.

Despite all her hopes, however, Gowhar could not attend primary school because of her poverty and the high costs at the school. She had to stay home to take care of her younger brothers and sisters.

Gowhar's mother Ḥavvā was a young woman with seven daughters and a son. Because of this she was ashamed before her husband and friends. Giving birth to daughters was not a good thing in their eyes and made a woman an embarrassment to her husband.

Ḥavvā had a child every year. Always during delivery her husband Mohammad Ali waited outside the room with great impatience waiting for information about the baby. He didn't want to know how much his wife suffered or screamed, nor was he even concerned about this. This was a woman's responsibility, for which she had been created by God. He was waiting to see if it was a boy or a girl. When they brought the good news of Gowhar's arrival, he said, "Ok, if she had the baby she had the baby. Tell me if it's a bread-eater or a bread-winner." When they told him it was a bread-eater, meaning a girl, he wrinkled his brow and left without looking at his new daughter. For her part, Ḥavvā was no sooner relieved of the pain of childbirth than she had a new worry, the dread of her husband's anger. After a time, of course, both of them resigned themselves to the situation. They thought God had ordained it so and that there was no alternative but to submit.

Each of Ḥavvā's daughters, the young ones and the old ones, took on part of the task of earning a livelihood for the family. All summer they picked fruit with their thin, delicate hands, herded the sheep, reaped the crops, milked the goats, and carried water from the spring. They even did the cooking sometimes, but they still bore the shame of being girls.

Although they breathed clean air, drank clear water, and never knew the wilting heat of summers in the city, they never grew much because of poor nutrition, and as a result of this were all shy and withdrawn, especially Gowhar, who was boundlessly silent and shy.

Gowhar's mother Ḥavvā's only hope was to give her daughters to husbands and reduce the number of bread-eaters. She was fortunate in that her daughters were famous for their beauty. Anyone with a son had his eye on Ḥavvā's daughters, and would pick one to be his bride when she was old enough. Even the people in town got these ideas at times.

It is not necessary to wait a long time to marry off the girls in Damavand. None of them are subject to formal legal restrictions, and as soon as a girl is ten years old they have an engagement ceremony for her. In Damavand, a seventeen- or eighteen-year-old girl is no longer marriageable. She is a disgraced and embarrassed old maid.

Gowhar had come of age and was no longer welcome to live at home. Her mother and father were afraid to give her to someone in the city and have her married to an utter stranger who might turn out to be a bad Muslim, so they promised her to a young villager with a one-year engagement. She still wasn't allowed to wear new and clean clothing, she still went around barefoot, she still did chores for her mother, but she was no longer that simple, thoughtless girl who worked like a machine and kept things in order for her mother. Now there were thousands of hopes and thoughts in her mind, and sometimes she secretly looked at herself in the mirror. She didn't know who her husband was or what he did, nor did she dare ask. Sometimes when her mother would get into a discussion about this with the neighbors, she would find an excuse to send Gowhar out of the room, because, as they said, "It would open her eyes and ears."

At night Gowhar would envision thousands of men,

choosing one for her husband and then thinking of him constantly. Of course she imagined her husband the way she wanted him to be, with a plump ruddy face, a large, powerful frame, and large, muscular legs and arms. But what difference did appearance make? Her husband could be any way he wished, and no matter how he looked would be fine. What was clear was that he would bring her bridal gown. He would bring lace shoes and colorful stockings, he would bring a mirror and a lamp, and he was preparing a home and a life for her. And how beautiful! To put on new clothes to show to friends and neighbors was such a great honor! She would no longer have to look after her sisters and brother, she could cook any kind of food she wished. She would keep her room tidy and the door to the cupboard always locked. When friends would come to see her, she'd open it to bring out food for her dear friends. He'd give her money and she'd bake his bread, wash his clothes, and keep things tidy all the time while she waited for her husband. She'd be a lady and her cousins would be jealous.

Sometimes, however, these thoughts led Gowhar to a vision of a broken dish and an angry husband who made an excuse of it to knock her down and stomp on her back with his cotton shoes. This vision would bring her back to reality with a start. She'd find herself panting heavily and trying to put this out of her mind. She would think "They aren't all like my father, using excuses like this to beat their wives. And even if they do, it's nothing. There's nothing to be afraid of. Beating is a husband's duty. The more a man beats his wife, the more he likes her."

This is how Gowhar would calm herself and go to sleep.

Sometimes Gowhar, Mohtaram, Fakhri, and Zinat would go to the spring to share secrets. They would gradually get into a discussion about their fiancés and their hopes.

Mohtaram, who had secretly seen her husband once, expressed dissatisfaction. "My husband is bald," she said.

The others would console her. "The bald ones have a lot of luck!" they'd say.

Fakhri, who had never seen her fiancé at all, said, "I've heard he's a forty-year-old cobbler. What can I do? He's as old as my father."

"Don't be sad," the girls would say. "He's got money, and he'll appreciate you, so he'll make you good shoes."

Zinat's fiancé was from the city. He was planning to come to Damavand the next summer to marry her and take her there. The girls were jealous of her. "You're so lucky, Zinat," they said. "You'll see the city, go to the cinema, wear pretty clothes, and go sightseeing. Remember us when you're having a good time."

But these three girls knew Gowhar's fiancé and praised him constantly. "Your husband isn't rich," they'd say, "but that doesn't matter. He's young, good-looking, and one day he'll have things."

Gowhar spent that year immersed in many hopes until the long-awaited day arrived. First two pretty young bridesmaids were chosen for Gowhar. They did her hair and sang:

> Oh Bride with the braided hair
> With one corner of your mouth
> Kiss me
> God knows a mescal
> Of those kisses is worth plenty

They took her to the public bath. Her husband had bought admissions for her friends and family. They stayed in the bath from early morning until noon. They burned rue* and put a red dress on her while the bridesmaids sang:

> The moon and her stars are taken to the bath
> Outside they beat the drums and played the pipes

*Wild rue is burned as a counter-potion to the evil effects of the evil eye of envy, whose gaze is dreaded on happy occasions in the lore of the rural popular culture of Iran.

> Oh bride, you will be my brother's wife
> You will be the light of my old mother's eyes
> You will kneel before my brother
> Speak to him word by word
> I am your husband's sister

The next day was whey-making day. They prepared yoghurt soup and sent it out to friends. The next night they held Gowhar's marriage ceremony and put henna on her. At midnight they placed a large tray of henna in the bride's hands. Members of the groom's family came and each one took a fingerful of this sacred henna. They all sang:

> Henna, henna, it is henna
> How beautiful is the henna
> Don't cover the bride's hands
> Before the groom can come and see

The next day was the day for putting collyrium on the bride's eyes and having the bridal shower. There was a tray in the middle of the room where they had placed the bride's jewelry and makeup. First they made Gowhar's black eyes even blacker and drew arched eyebrows above her eyes.

> The little bridelet is skinny and long
> Her forehead has a place between the eyebrows to
>   touch for prayer
> The groom does ablutions for prayer at that altar

The guests then began playing their parts, each tossing as much money into the tray as he could afford. Someone sitting next to the tray called each donor by name and everyone clapped and chanted, "He is too generous," "May God give her son a good marriage," and "May we feast on rice together when her baby is born."

Everyone sang in unison:

A thousand bravos for her mother
Who has such a jewel in her house

Another night they took the groom to the public bath and thirty or forty of his friends stayed there with him all night, feasting and drinking.

The next night was the night for taking the bride to the home of the groom. At sunset they undressed the bride in the open air and poured sacred water that had been prayed over on her head. The guests were given dinner and generous hospitality. The bridesmaids sat at the *sofreh* and beat tambourines, singing:

I am the host, the host
At the *sofreh* is a pomegranate flower
Bring the bowl and ewer
Bring the water pipe with the silver mouthpiece

After dinner they came from the groom's house to get the bride. A girl with a small tray on her head holding a chador and a pair of shoes turned around in a circle in the center of the room singing:

Dear mother, let's go get the bride
Mother of our sister, let's go get the bride

Then she put the tray on the floor and they made preparations to deliver the bride. They put a chador over Gowhar's head, and the bridesmaids sang:

Little bride like a china doll
Where is the garden to take you to pick flowers
Where's the garden that will shade you
A garden full of parsley and lilies

They slowly walked her to the groom's house, holding lanterns and mirrors and beating tambourines without singing. Near the groom's house he came out to meet her. From a distance he tossed a pomegranate* at the bride's breast, then fled.

Throughout these ceremonies the bride kept her head lowered, considering it her duty to perform them one by one. She sighed with relief when each one ended, and then waited to perform the next one.

The bride's family was proud that their daughter was beautiful and a source of dignity for them. They therefore did not provide her with an elaborate dowry. They had prepared a box with a prayer carpet and a belt for each of the men and women in the groom's family and sent it along with Gowhar. There was also a box containing necessities, halvah, and various foods so there would be something in her house for guests, since she wouldn't be leaving it for awhile.

The seventh day was the groom's day to receive the bride. They delivered the tray of gifts and collected the money.

The excitement died down after these seven days passed, and silence prevailed in the household of the bride and the groom. Gowhar was not allowed to leave the house for a year or two, because according to custom a bride could not even visit her mother and father before having a child, and since Gowhar was still a child herself she did not become a mother soon.

During this period she became thinner every day. She was not unhappy with her life, and claimed that her husband liked her, but so what! A good husband with a bad mother-in-law wasn't worth much. After Gowhar had worn out her new, expensive clothes it was a long time before she got any new ones. Her husband was poor and unable to keep his wife dressed in new cloth shoes and chadors all the time.

One day Gowhar grew up and got pregnant. She had the

---

*The pomegranate has long been a ritual symbol of union between man and woman. In the Greek myth of Persephone, the daughter of Zeus and Demeter, a pomegranate she had accepted from Hades became the basis for his claim to rights as her husband.

first, second, and third children, and each time the problems and difficulties of having children became worse. All of her children were thin and sickly, and wandered around in the gardens and fell down on the wet ground. The first one nursed the second one and the second one nursed the third, and Gowhar didn't know why her children were ailing and afflicted. She complained about her smallest child's illness and sometimes wished it was dead. In her own opinion she had given it every kind of medical treatment possible; it was its fate to be sick. The child had had diarrhea for several months, but it refused to stop eating green fruit or get up from the cold, wet ground. It had a protruding belly and its spidery legs dragged its weak body along, but Gowhar thought it would survive. Gowhar herself was becoming thinner, nursing her children and becoming weaker. Every year during the Ramadan feast she fainted near sunset every day from weakness and broke the fast with a bite of bread and some tea. She would fast again the next day. If she tried to skip the fast she would be lectured and scolded by her mother-in-law, who threw the sin in her face every second. Gowhar's mother-in-law held absolute dominion over the household. Her husband Gholam'ali had no discretion concerning his wife when his mother was around. If the mother-in-law provided food, the bride ate; if she dressed her, she was clothed; otherwise, she remained hungry and naked.

Every time the mother-in-law looked angrily at Gowhar it frightened the girl out of her wits, but this domination did not last long. The mother-in-law died, Gowhar breathed more easily, and even began to flourish in time. Gholam'ali was not a bad man. He went about his business honorably and quietly and left Gowhar alone. Because Gowhar was given control of the finances, with a small amount of savings and the help of her husband she was able to put a new and improved face on their situation.

Gholam'ali, who had grown up with Gowhar, came of

age for military service and refused to fulfill this heavy obligation for a year or two. Finally, however, the military conscription official, who had no hopes that he would volunteer, took him. Although his family tried to convince the military that he was responsible for a wife, three children, and an old father, no one could get anywhere with them. Finally the military officials took Gholam'ali away to the city and Gowhar became responsible for the family. She was not a useless or incompetent woman, but in the end the man of the family is the breadwinner.

Gowhar did odd jobs around the village whenever she could, but her children and their illnesses did not allow her time to work as much as her husband had done. Their garden and their farmland were thus taken away from them by the landlord and turned over to somebody else. Gowhar lost all of her work and sold everything she had. Her mother helped as much as she could, but their belongings weren't worth enough to feed a family for long. Gowhar was driven to beggary. Her clothing was worn out and her children were sick and barefoot. She shuddered to think of another cold and hard Damavand winter, when everyone crawled into his cottage and never left the fireside. The desire to survive the two years of her husband's absence kept her alive and gave her strength, however. Sometimes she got letters from Gholam'ali in which there were nothing but complaints. His letters complained of poverty and said he was fed up with the cruelty of the officers, until one day he wrote to Gowhar that he had become an orderly in the colonel's house and that his work had become somewhat easier. He had no complaints about being a servant, but because his boss was a thief he considered himself in hell.

Sometimes, when she got some little gift like a pair of stockings or a scarf from her husband, Gowhar thanked God and felt proud because Gholam'ali was thinking of her and still loved her. She told her friends about this and made them all envious. During the last year, however, Gowhar gradually lost contact with her husband. No more gifts came, nor even a letter. Gowhar could write, and she sent reproachful letters to her husband, but the answers were dry and unkind. She never worried about this. She thought her husband's work and hardships kept him from writing letters. She therefore kept waiting for the end of this torturous duty so she could resume life with her husband. She counted the days, each of which seemed like a year to her, but she was normally calm and smiling. The sadness never showed in her face.

Gholam'ali's period of service ended. His friends came to Damavand and told Gowhar that Gholam'ali would be arriving Thursday night, and Gowhar told her mother. Thursday night she washed and swept the house. She got some money together, put on a broth, and sat waiting for him. Night fell. She kept the children up, promising them that their father was coming with gifts for them. Around midnight someone knocked at the door. They all jumped up. The children clapped their hands and shouted. It really was Gholam'ali, plumper and more handsome than before. The hardships of the army and the separation from his wife and children had in no way caused him to suffer or lose weight. He was smiling and happy, but he was not alone. A woman and a ten-year-old girl were with him. Gowhar was somewhat astonished at first, but she brought them in and served them, waiting for a chance to discover the status of this woman and child. In the course of conversation Gholam'ali said that they were the wife and child of a friend. Gowhar was satisfied the rest of the evening. The next morning her mother, friends, and neighbors came to see Gholam'ali, but they were all surprised to see a strange woman and child and whispered things to each other. Gowhar was too busy to watch her guests, but sometimes she heard them say "The poor thing still doesn't know. If she knew she'd die."

One or two days passed. Gowhar saw that these guests,

this woman and child, didn't go anywhere. They stayed in that same room. She gradually took to complaining and whining about serving these evil newcomers who had become a barrier between her and her husband. One day she went to the bazaar wearing her chador. She overheard a shopkeeper telling someone:

"Friend, did you hear about the souvenir our friend Gholam'ali brought back from Tehran? He's taken a Tehran woman for his wife who has a ten-year-old child by her other husband. He's turned out to be quite a rascal. What kind of behavior is that, bringing home someone else's child, and undoubtedly an illegitimate one at that, and keeping them in front of your wife and children?"

When Gowhar heard this the world went black before her eyes. Stumbling and crawling, she dragged herself to her mother's house and started crying. She beat herself against the floor so much that she passed out. Everyone gathered around her, splashed her face and head with water, steeped borage, made an herbal tea with it, and fed her until she came around somewhat.

She got better. She stayed at her mother's house for a week or two to display her anger, but they all convinced her that the children would die under the care of that other woman. She was persuaded to make the sacrifice of going back to her husband's house and starting over.

After much investigation, the neighborhood women learned that Kolsum was the Tehran wife of a man named Gholam'ali. She had been employed in the colonel's house and had fallen in love with Gholam'ali. She had given him whatever she earned, fed him whatever she stole, fattened him, and attached herself to him, along with a child she had had elsewhere. She had made him love her with smooth and gentle speech, and had come with him to Damavand to become a thorn in poor Gowhar's side.

Gowhar suffered, and moaned constantly about her husband's unkindness. Gholam'ali no longer paid her any attention nor considered himself responsible for her children. There was just him and his forty-year-old wife. He gave her whatever he earned, and all his kindness and affection. Gowhar and her children were deprived of every kind of affection and supervision. The basis for the warm and kindly life they had known for several years was gone. Nothing remained in that house except poverty, stinginess, unkindness, and frustration. Gowhar constantly burned with jealousy, because she loved Gholam'ali and longed to spend a night at his side. However, although she knew she had lost this precious treasure, she was afraid of seeming ungrateful. She usually told herself, "A man can't get along with only one woman, but he ought to take care of them. This man can't even afford to buy himself a couple of shirts, but he wants to feed two wives and four children. God, my children are going to bed at night without supper and this fellow doesn't give a damn."

Everyone thought that Kolsum had cast a spell to make Gholam'ali forget Gowhar and put herself in Gowhar's place. On the advice of various other people, Gowhar would eat certain things, and even feed things to her rival wife that might make him forget her so she could regain her original place. Gowhar's neighbors, however, seeing that these measures had no effect, finally decided that Kolsum's magic was better than hers and that there was no point in trying to cast spells on her.

Gowhar no longer had any desire to stay at home and look at the face of her rival wife from Tehran. She spent most of her time visiting her mother and friends, staying with them until night. She cried every time it was time to leave them and go back home.

Gowhar made people weary with her complaining, and they all gradually took to ignoring her without following up on what she said. This heedlessness angered her, and she

accused them all of collaborating with her husband and sup-
porting her rival wife. She turned away from everyone, even
cursing her mother.

If the people saw someone in the shadows of the willow
trees along the dark alleys at sunset, crying loudly

> Little bride like a china doll
> Where is the garden to take you to pick flowers
> They take the moon and star to the bath
> They beat the drums and gongs outside
> Oh bride, who are you, my master
> Give me a kiss from that corner of your lips

they knew right away it was Gowhar, who was now a
vagrant in the alleys. Gowhar laughed sometimes, so loudly
that the others were stopped cold, and sometimes she cried
so much that people felt sorry for her. Thursday evenings she
would light a candle and read the Qor'an, asking God to
drive away this evil. She would go to the fortune teller, have
her fortune told, and make covenants with the descendants
of the imams.*

Like most villagers living in nature, Gowhar knew nothing
of its grandeur and beauty. She could comprehend nothing of
the dancing of the trees in the wind, the majesty of the
mountains, the silence of rivers, and the purity of the sky.
Sometimes, however, she could be seen sitting by the riverside, taking up fistfuls of sand and angrily tossing them into
the water. She would mumble:

> Oh bride with the braided hair
> With one end of your mouth please kiss me

---

*It is a common practice among the Shi'i Muslims of Iran and elsewhere to ask one of
the twelve imams of the faith in their prayers to intercede with God on their behalf to help
them solve a problem, and the request is usually accompanied with a promised good deed,
such as a feast for poor people, if the problem is solved. Such covenants are particularly
popular as a part of a pilgrimage to the grave of an imam.

God knows that a mescal
Of those kisses is worth plenty

Sometimes she would see a city woman and curse her. She often beat her children to death. Others stepped in and saved them from her clutches.

Gowhar would say, "One day soon I'll be rid of this rival wife. I had a dream where someone saved me. In another week Gholam'ali will divorce her and send her back to Tehran. Then he'll come to me. He'll buy me a blouse and stockings, and kiss my children. I'll be his favorite. Then I'll take his hand and I won't let them draft him again. I had a dream. Next Thursday night."

The next week the people of Damavand were telling each other with pity and concern that Gowhar had gone insane. The poor thing was only twenty years old.

Translated by John Green

ẒAHRĀ KHĀNLARĪ

Born in 1294 [21 March 1915–20 March 1916—Gregorian equivalent dates for Iranian solar year 1294] in Tehran, Khānlarī went to high school at Dār al-Mu'alimāt and began teaching at government elementary schools at age seventeen. She took college entrance examinations with male students by special permission from the Ministry of Education, and entered the Tehran University College of Literature in 1934, the first year this institution was open to women. She received a bachelor's degree in 1937, a doctorate in Persian language and literature in 1942. She served as principal of Nurbakhsh Middle School, then as Professor at the Tehran University College of Literature. In 1941, she married Parvīz Nātil Khānlarī, a classmate in her doctoral program. Beginning in 1943 she was a frequent contributor to Sukhan, *the important literary journal which she and her husband founded. In 1960, she went to France* and England to study textbooks as an employee of the Ministry of Education. When she returned she and her colleagues made extensive changes to the country's elementary school textbooks, replacing traditional textbook formats with more Western ones, using Iranian contextual material, adding material for teachers on new instructional techniques. In addition to literary writings, she is the author of a number of textbooks and literary adaptations for students, including books on language and adaptations of literary classics for children such as Bayhaqi's story of Ḥasanak the Vazir and the legend of the mythical bird, the Sīmurgh. One of the most popular such works is her book Dāstān'hā-yi Dilangīz, written as a vernacularized reader of the Persian literary classics for young students.

Khānlārī has written very little fiction. Gowhar is included here because it was the first short story by an Iranian woman to appear in a major literary publication.

[Fakhrī Qavīmī, Kārnāmah-'i Zanān-i Mashhūr-i Irān (Tehran: Vizārāt-i Āmuzish va Parvarish, 1352/1973 or 1974), pp. 228–229.]

❧ *The Starling Spring*

SHOKOUH MIRZADEGI

The sun was fading in the sky, setting over the village. The livestock were returning from the fields and the polyhedral village square was covered with dust. A bent old man was pitching water out in front of a coffee shop located at the southern corner of the square. He was holding a pail in one hand, dipping out water with a small bowl, and tossing it into the air in a lazy arc. Like thin muslin, the water trembled in midair in the dying golden light, then flattened out and settled on the ground. The earth was soaked wherever the water landed, the dust settled, and those sitting in front of the coffee shop could suddenly see much farther.

Mohammad was struck by the smell of the damp earth as he came out into the dust. He took a deep breath, said hello to the old man, and passed him as he was dipping the little bowl into the pail a final time to get out the last of the water. Mohammad's tall body and broad shoulders, enlarged next to the old man, were conspicuous. In one hand he was carrying two large empty buckets, and they wobbled like struggling birds dangling by their feet.

This story is from the collection *Āghāz-i Duvvum [A Second Beginning]* (Tehran: Intishārāt-i Tūs, 1970), pp. 5–27.

As Mohammad approached the door of the coffee shop the men in front of it stood up part way in deference to him, continuing to talk loudly. The older ones kept their seats and said "Yā Allāh." Mohammad protested humbly and shyly. He put the buckets down to one side and sat on the edge of one of the benches. The men continued their conversations. They were talking about the locust plague. As the waiter was pouring tea for Mohammad, Sheikh Mahdi called him. He was sitting inside the coffee shop. Only his shadow was visible. Mohammad got up and went in. He said hello again. Sheikh Mahdi was sitting on a little carpet alongside the *jū* that passed through the middle of the coffee shop. He stood up part way for Mohammad. Mohammad, quick to restrain him with a hand on the shoulder, sat next to him. Sheikh Mahdi ordered two teas in a loud voice. He then said immediately, "The plague has hit."

"Yeah, when I was washing tripe down by the river at sunset I saw it had hit the lower fields."

"We'll lose everything if we don't move quickly."

"Sepahi said the crop sprayers from the city would be here tomorrow."

"Come on, man. Sprayers can't deal with this plague."

"Sepahi said if they couldn't they would spray from an airplane the way they did in the village of Qasem Abad."

Sheikh Mahdi removed his skullcap and laughed as he rubbed his short stubbly hair.

"From an airplane? Qasem Abad is up high. We're surrounded by mountains. Is the plane going to turn into a sparrow so it can get down between all these mountains? Anyway, this plague won't be so easy to beat. In all my long life I've only seen one other plague like this."

The waiter sat two teas down in front of Mohammad and Sheikh Mahdi and left. Sheikh Mahdi continued, placing a sugar cube in his mouth.

"I was no more than seventeen or eighteen years old when a plague just like this one came and devoured everything in two weeks. In those days there were no crop dusters and things of this nature, so no one ever thought of such things. When the plague would come, Mulla Abulqasemu, may God have mercy on him, used to go up personally and bring water down from the Starling Spring. That would finish off the plague.* Now the plague has taken the whole village, and all they can say is 'The crop dusters are coming, the crop dusters are coming.'"

Sheikh Mahdi fell silent, and they drank tea without speaking.

Mohammad broke the silence.

"What should we do now, Sheikh?"

"Last night the *Kadkhoda* and Sheikh Ramazan came to my house. There is no alternative. Someone must go to the Starling Spring."

"Good idea, Sheikh. There's no alternative. No sacrifice is too great. In the dead of Winter there won't be anything to eat."

Sheikh Mahdi toyed with his teacup. Abruptly, he said, "You must take on this job, Mohammad."

---

*There is a mountain in East Azarbaijan called Chashmah-'i Sārān (the Starling Spring). For several centuries the villages around this mountain have had a special ritual for purging locust plagues. In years when the locust swarms descend on a village's farms, the old men choose a man and send him on a mission to the mountain. The person selected must be strong, above reproach morally, and physically healthy. Before sunrise on the appointed day he goes to the mountain which has the Starling Spring at its peak. He takes a flask of water from the spring and returns. (While returning, he must think only of sacred things, and never look back, speak, or allow the flask to touch the ground.) On the previous day the village people will have dug out several small holes at the level of the village near the fields, and the emissary fills these holes with water from the Starling Spring.

The villagers say the spring water has characteristics that attract the starlings. By sunrise the starlings fill the village sky, and attack the locusts. The starlings feed on the locusts for several days and drink the water in the holes. At the same time the villagers believe that if the emissary is not morally pure or if he fails to perform the ritual precisely, the water will have no effect whatsoever.

Author's footnote.

Mohammad reeled.

"Me? Sheikh!"

"Yes. You're the most honorable man in the village."

Mohammad lowered his head.

"As you like, Sheikh, but no one's perfect."

"Don't be modest. You're more upright than any of the rest of us, and you can do it."

Mohammad turned red to his ears, lowering his eyes. He was afraid the Sheikh would see the color of shame in them in the glow of the sunset.

About a year had gone by, it seemed to Mohammad, since he had begun sinning in secret by harboring a love for Javaher,* the young wife of the old village *Kadkhodā*. His eyes and heart yearned for her. A day never went by when he did not think of Javaher. He never passed a night without going to bed thinking of her, and. . . .

Sheikh Mahdi put his hand on Mohammad's shoulder. "Eh? What do you say?"

"Sheikh. Come on. I'm not even from this village."

It was the only excuse that came to mind.

Sheikh Mahdi laughed. "You've worked in this village for two years. You've eaten its wheat and drank its water for two years, and slept on its soil. These things, after all, are what constitute residency."

"Come on. . . ."

Sheikh Mahdi figeted impatiently. "Why are you making excuses Mohammad? This is a service. Only you can help the people of this village. In a few more days there won't be a kernel of grain to be found here. Come Winter, our children will starve to death."

Mohammad lowered his head in silence.

---

*This female proper name also means "jewels" in Persian.

Sheikh Mahdi, laughing with self-assurance and satisfaction, ordered more tea.

Mohammad was a butcher, but he lacked the crudeness and harshness of his profession. He had a rudeness that was all his own. He was coarse in a polite and tranquil way. He had come to Zia Abad two years ago. He had been unable to remain in Qasem Abad after the scandal that had taken place there. His wife had run away with a boy from the city, and as soon as he had heard about it he had gone to the local mulla, divorced her, sold his house, property, and store, and moved to Zia Abad.

The people of Zia Abad had disliked him at first. They had said he was spineless. "He should have killed her instead of divorcing her. How could he let his wife go free to enjoy her paramour?" And "The women will get ideas because of the way he acts. . . ."

They accepted him quickly, however. They became his customers, and took a liking to him. He was quiet, worked hard at his business for a minimal profit, and was generous with this minimal profit.

Every week he went into the mountains and bought several sheep, which he released in the pasture behind his house. Every morning he culled out two sheep and took them to the riverside. He would kill the sheep, remove the skin carefully, cut up the meat, put it in a bucket, and go to the shop. He ate lunch there. He would take out a portion for himself from the meat he sent every day to Nanny Belqays.

Every day at sunset he would go to the coffee shop, drink a few cups of tea, and go directly home. He averted his eyes when he talked, rarely looked at anyone, and if he happened to do so by chance, he seemed not to see them. He didn't seem to see anything or anyone. He seemed to revolve within his own thoughts and his own world.

He was the envy of everyone because he was so much at peace. He actually had been at peace before seeing Javaher. After that scandal and his move to Zia Abad, he had thought of nothing.

He simply lived, with no joy and no sadness. But the sight of Javaher had ruined his life. He was afire inside, burning and trying to keep others from reading the fire in his face. There was never a moment when Javaher's face was not before him. The thought of her colored his life with sweetness and ecstasy, and when this idea merged with the concept of sin it tormented him like an evil nightmare. Even so, no one imagined for a moment that he was interested in Javaher, or that he was even capable of being interested in a woman. Once or twice the old women of the village had undertaken to find him a wife, but the way he reacted convinced everyone that Mohammad found women and marriage disgusting and abhorrent. They all saw all of this as a characteristic feature of his life.

Even Javaher, the gay and witty wife of Zia Abad's *Kadkhodā,* could not comprehend the trouble she had caused in Mohammad's heart. She would put herself in his path on every pretext, and even went to his shop once a day to buy meat, although there was no need for her to leave home to buy things since there was always a flurry of activity around the *Kadkhodā,* and they were all ready to do anything for her. Javaher, however, was not a woman to sit idly, and from the moment her heart had conceived a desire for Mohammad, she had used every womanly trick she knew to attract his attention. Yet when Mohammad calmly and quietly passed her by and it seemed to her that she had not yet found the way into the heart of the stone, Mohammad was actually passing himself by. On the inside, he was really full of Javaher.

Mohammad wanted Javaher. He wanted her with all his being. At first he had tried to drive her out of his thoughts.

He had cursed himself, stayed busy, and performed his prayers, sometimes pleadingly, sometimes angrily, asking God to remove her from his mind and heart. Javaher did not leave, however, and in fact she became firmly established within him.

His resistance collapsed one summer night when he unexpectedly saw Javaher from the roof of his house in the five-door room in her house. From then on, every night when he returned from the coffee shop, Mohammad went up on his roof. Stealthily he would creep to the edge of the roof, stretch out between the two large earthenware crocks there, and stare at the five-door room in the *Kadkhodā*'s house. Javaher moved about in this room, bareheaded and ruder than she ever was out in the streets.

She would comb her hair and change clothes in front of a little mirror hanging on the wall, standing and stooping. When the *Kadkhodā* came home, she would tease him riotously and gaily. After witnessing these things and going back down, overcome with dizziness, Mohammad would have fantasies based on what he had seen: He had watched Javaher, he had talked with her, feuded with her, caressed her, professed his love to her, gone to the brink of sin with her, and. . . .

When he got home, the words "You are the most honest, upright man in this village" throbbed relentlessly and distressingly in his head like a drum beat. He had not thought of sin for months, had not thought of God to make sin occur to him. It had also been months since he had last prayed. As soon as he had seen that Javaher was also present when he prayed, and that his words of praise and worship were reaching her before they reached God, he had given up praying. Yet the moment Sheikh Mahdi had uttered those words, seeming to draw him to the brink of a chasm, he had become terrified. He now remembered that in the minds of the village people, to look at another man's woman was the greatest of sins. He remembered that to look at a completely naked woman secretly who is also the wife of another man is to walk hand-in-hand with Satan.

He was disgusted with himself, like someone caught red-handed: Is this the most upright and honest man, who must go and deliver the people from famine and plague? Is this the breast that must harbor faith and pure thoughts, this breast full of satanic and sinful love? Are these the hands that must bring the people a gift from the sacred Starling Spring? These hands that for many nights have sinfully imagined caressing and embracing a woman and. . . .

"Oh, no. I must repent. I will not go to the roof again tonight. I will pray until dawn, I will repent. I will cleanse my spirit and soul of Javaher, who has darkened my life like a black cloud. I will pour her out. Tomorrow, tomorrow all the people will be watching me. Famine, hunger, winter, the children."

Mohammad paced in his room like a wounded animal. He talked to himself, whined and grumbled, pounded the wall with his fists. He was so lost in himself that when he heard the sound of knocking at the door he stood in the middle of the room in a daze for several moments. Then he drew a deep breath and left the room. He passed through the dark narrow passage between the room and the door to the house, and opened the door. It was one of the *Kadkhodā*'s servants.

"Sheikh Mahdi and Mash Rahim are at the *Kadkhodā*'s house. They want you to come too."

He was about to say, "I'm tired; I have to go to the field early in the morning and. . . ."

He was about to say, "I'm in the middle of a complete reading of the Qor'an; I need to do the two *ḥājat* prostrations, to ask God for what I need, and. . . ."

The same things he always said whenever he evaded invitations to gatherings, weddings, or funerals, but he could not. After several months, since the time he had generously opened the doors of his being to Javaher, this was the first time he had been invited to someone's home.

Before that, he had always turned town invitations on some pretext, and the people had not repeated the invitations. It wasn't that they didn't like him. They respected his self-absorbtion and assumed he was busy praying.

After the *Kadkhodā*'s man left, he stood in front of the door a few minutes and then set out for the *Kadkhodā*'s house, not to see what was new there, but to see Javaher. He thought only of that.

The moon had appeared when Mohammad reached the *Kadkhoda*'s house. It was a full moon. Javaher was on the porch beating clothes hanging on a wire with a scythe.* Mohammad said "Yā Allāh" loudly as he passed under the grapevine trellis. Javaher stopped where she was when she heard the sound of his voice. Her hand fell heavily on her side, still holding the scythe. She watched Mohammad a moment as he walked past the tomato bushes, then suddenly came to herself. She smiled and said "Salām" loudly, then, "Welcome, Mohammad Agha. You must have forgotten the way here," gazing intently at him with her large dark eyes as he ascended the steps to the porch. Mohammad came up the steps with a firm stride, though his knees were trembling.

"At your service, madam."

For the first time Javaher sensed a gentle kindness resonating in this heavy, deep voice that was always harsh and severe. She took a step in his direction just as the *Kadkhodā* came out and embraced Mohammad excitedly.

---

*In some of the villages of Azarbaijan the people believe that if there are washed clothes hanging on the line on the eve of the fourteenth day of the lunar cycle, the moon will afflict them with sickness and misfortune unless the clothes on the line are beaten with a scythe several times when the moon rises. [Author's footnote.]

"Welcome, Mohammad Agha. You have illuminated our home, and God knows a visit with a friend and a neighbor is also a form of worship."

He went inside arm-in-arm with Mohammad. Sheikh Mahdi and several others sitting in the room rose in deference to Mohammad, who motioned them all down with haste and embarrassment. He was about to sit in a corner when Sheikh Mahdi and the *Kadkhodā* took him to the front of the room. His face turned red as he stammered responses to their cordialities, while at the same time his mind was on a window that opened on the porch. Without looking at the porch, he could see Javaher's shadow moving along the clothes line and the moonlight reflecting on her pink chador. His heart pounded.

He did not understand what they said and what he heard. Only when they were making plans and laying strategy did he realize that he would have to go to the Starling Spring the following day.

They said: "Tomorrow, at the time of the morning prayer, Mohammad Agha will start out and we will begin digging pits. He ought to be back by sunrise. . . . Praise God that he has this strength. He will have gone up the mountain and returned before the sun rises."

They said, "By the time the sun rises the starlings will appear."

They said, "Before the noon prayers have been said, the plague will be routed."

They said, "God willing, we will have a good winter and the children will not go hungry."

They said, "Thank God the fields and the trees are fruitful this year. If the wicked plague is cut short, we will make a good profit. Praise God."

Javaher came in with a tray of tea. Her chador was loose on her head and her white scarf cast a bright halo over her face.

"Praise God," said Mohammad.

Javaher set the tray of tea on the floor and said innocently: "May God grant you success, Mohammad Agha. I have heard you are going to the Starling Spring?"

Only Mohammad perceived a hint of that typical impishness in this voice and these words. He lowered his head and said: "If God grants success."

"God always grants success to his pure devotees," said Sheikh Mahdi.

"With all due respect," said Mohammad, "no one is pure."

As Javaher set the tea down in front of Mohammad, she looked at his face.

"As you like, Mohammad Agha, but God knows you're just like the blessed saints."

Her musical voice, among all those male voices praising Mohammad, rang like a bell. Only Mohammad perceived the cunning persistence in this voice. He burned from head to toe.

Again it was Javaher, and the delicious ecstasy of the thought of her. No people, no winter, no famine, no plague, no God, and no sin.

Again they said, "It's a good thing the plague has only just begun."

Again they said, "If we had waited too long, the plague would have devoured everything. The children would have gone hungry and it would have been a hard winter."

Mohammad stood up in a crazed state.

"With your permission, I'll be leaving."

The *Kadkhodā* jumped up, taken by surprise. "Where are you going, Mohammad Agha? We have a bit of bread and cheese to eat together."

Mohammad lowered his head.

"Thanks anyway, *Kadkhodā*. Let's make it another night. It's better if I leave early. I have to get ready for tomorrow."

Sheikh Mahdi, who had stood up, put his hand on Mohammad's shoulder kindly and said, "Mohammad Agha, night is the time for prayers, and this night needs more of them. God willing, after the plague ends, we'll have many evenings like this."

The others said things Mohammad did not hear. The *Kadkhodā* left the room with Mohammad, and Javaher appeared in the doorway in a state of confusion.

"What, you're leaving? Dinner is ready, Mohammad Agha. Why don't you stay for dinner? This is your house."

For the first time, Mohammad looked into her eyes, and said in a halting voice, "It's been the house of my dreams for a long time, madam. Another time, God willing."

Javaher was so overwhelmed by the impact of this gaze, a fiery reflection of love, that after Mohammad went down the steps of the porch she hurried into the kitchen and sat on a bench in a corner.

Baji, a servant who had come to help her, said with alarm, "What's happened to you, madam? Why has your color changed this way?"

Javaher did not hear her. She was thinking. "Mohammad was really in love, and I didn't realize it. What an imbecile I was. I was an idiot. . . an idiot. . . and. . . ."

She spoke the last sentence aloud.

Baji approached her, even more anxious.

"Madam, God forbid, has anything happened?"

Javaher noticed Baji for the first time. "Huh? No. . . . My stomach, my stomach's upset. I don't feel well. I was foolish to walk to the upper village this morning."

Baji thought for a moment and then said happily, "Yes! Madam, this was surely a sign. Didn't I tell you it wasn't too late? Didn't I tell you that a lot of women get pregnant after two years?"

Dumfounded, Javaher looked at her, then laughed. Her color came back and the usual mischievousness was back in her eyes.

"Baji dear, what are you talking about? Pregnant by who? The *Kadkhodā* can't father children anymore."

"Nonsense, madam. A one hundred-year-old man can still father children. Women are the ones who become barren. A man, who. . . ."

Javaher said to herself, "Tomorrow, when he's returned from the Starling Spring, when the starlings have come down, I'll go to his house. The whole village will be preoccupied with the starlings then. He won't be able to resist there. He can't."

Mohammad stretched out in the middle of the room when he got home. His body felt hot. Something was burning in his chest, like a piece of dry wood that had caught fire.

He had felt this way two other times in his life. He had been no more than six years old the first time, when he had heard the news of his mother's death. He had gone with his father to put the sheep out to pasture. Around noon, just when his father was opening the cloth bundle that contained their food, his uncle arrived. He was out of breath, redfaced, and there was white froth around his lips.

He said something in his father's ear, and his father leaped up with great agitation and ran down the mountain. Not knowing what had happened, Mohammad ran after his father. There was a crowd bustling in front of the house. Almost all the residents of the village were on the long street where their house was. There Mohammad heard that a snake had bitten his mother.

"It's all over. She's turned black. The poor woman's done for."

No one paid any attention to Mohammad, and instead of going home, Mohammad ran away. He went up the stairway leading to the public bath near the house and sat in a corner, fixing his eyes on the house from above. An hour later, perhaps longer, they brought his mother's coffin out the door in the midst of the crying and wailing of the women.

The coffin rode on the men's shoulders like a feather. The wind ruffled the white sheet draped over his mother, exactly as it had done the time Mohammad had watched his mother's white chador flapping in the breeze as he ran after her. Mohammad wanted to scream, to cry, to throw himself down the bathhouse steps, but he only felt his chest burning, and a piece of dry wood aflame in his heart. He sat down where he was. The coffin passed through the street, and the people ran behind it leaving the street empty behind them. But Mohammad did not move. He sat right there for hours, until the piece of wood burned itself out completely.

The other time was when they brought the news of his wife running away. He had been dazed for a few moments, then he had felt the same piece of wood burning in his chest. He had left the shop and gone home, holding his head down to avoid eye contact with anyone else. The piece of wood burned, burned, and. . . .

And now. . . . Now, again that familiar piece of wood had caught fire in his chest. Had he lost something again?

"No, I will repent. I have the whole night. God is generous. I will repent and evict Javaher from my heart. In the morning I will go purified and clean to the Starling Spring."

"No, Javaher won't go away, and you can't go to the mountain with her inside you. She will taint the Starling Spring water. She won't go away. You can't get away from Javaher, and this piece of wood is not burning in your chest because you lost Javaher. It's because you lost your own self. Yes, your own self, Mohammad. You must go, forget about yourself. Forget yourself."

Mohammad jumped up suddenly and nearly screamed, "I'm going, I'm going!"

He hastily approached a little chest in a corner of the room and in a single instant all the turmoil and anxiety cleared from his face. His face now looked pale and tired.

He mumbled under his breath, "I'm going. Now that Javaher won't go, I'll go. I'm leaving this place. Let Javaher be with me, let her eat up my soul, let my soul burn."

The piece of wood burned, without going out.

At dawn, right when the men and women, young and old, were milling around near the fields with spades in hand, when Sheikh Mahdi and the *Kadkhodā* were designating places for pits, and right when Mohammad had reached the beginning of the highway, suitcase in hand, waving down a truck headed for the city, a flock of starlings appeared in the village sky. The starlings came down toward the wheat fields in horizontal formations, where the plague undulated like green silk in the light of the dawn.

Translated by John Green

SHOKOUH MIRZADEGI

Shokouh Mirzadegi (Shukūh Mīrzādah'gī in the Library of Congress spelling) has the distinction of being the first Iranian to write a science fiction short story, 'Dar Ān Sū-yi Fanā' (On the Other Side of Annihilation), in her 1979 collection Āghāz-i Duvvum *(Second Beginning). The story was neither an inspired effort nor a stimulation to further development of such a Persian genre, but it was an interesting milestone.*

A Visit with the Children in the Upper Village

HUMĀ NĀṬIQ

The upper village is a rural settlement at the foot of the high mountains. Its crops are rice and citrus fruits. Until recently, the thickest jungles in Mazandaran were in this area. Today they have cut down the old trees. They have stripped and mutilated the young saplings. The saws are never silent. Kiln smoke rises into the sky on all sides. Every donkey is carrying a load of wood. I say to myself: "This is the work of those same people. People who cut off ears, hands, and feet. People who mutilate corpses. Do you expect them to let the trees live?"

Anger and loathing rage within me. I go along the winding, uneven road to the upper village with my daughter. An old man squats alongside the road smoking a pipe. I want to ask him something, but I might as well have been invisible; he doesn't raise his head. A few steps higher, several ten- to twelve-year-old village boys are standing and talking. I don't know whether to approach them or not. They begin whispering and laughing when they see us, but they stay where they are.

"Hello children," I say boldly.

One or two of them lift their heads. "Hello."

This is from *Kitāb-i Jum'ah* 32 (April 24, 1980), pp. 64–74.

I don't know whether to continue on my way or stop. Their faces are not particularly warm or kind, and they don't seem friendly. The whispering and laughing begin again. My daughter feels very uncomfortable. She wants us to go back. There are village houses and several city-style villas on both sides of the road at intervals. They have flooded the rice fields. I am still determined, and I think I would like to try to manage a little visit in the village.

I stop and say to the children, "Children, your village is very green and pleasant." I wanted to add, "Too bad they've cut down the forest," but I didn't have the nerve.

"Where are you going?" one of them asks.

"I was taking a walk."

"Are you going to the spring?"

"I don't know where the spring is. I came to walk around."

"Very well, then, go straight ahead. There's a river too."

"Go straight up this road. You won't come to a spring, though. You'll come to a river."

"All right, that's what I'll do."

My daughter and I set out again. I turn and look behind me. The children have begun following us at a distance, talking. Three or four other people from the neighborhood have joined them. We are in a regrettable state, however. No position could be more artificial than ours. I resolve inwardly to find a pretext for asking them why they have stripped these forests. I can think of nothing but the trees. The children have come closer. I stop and wait for them to catch up.

"Children, does your village have a school too?"

The biggest boy says, "Yeah, it's got one. I've finished the fifth grade myself." He laughs. "What's a school? Who gets a chance to study?"

We begin talking to each other. The children talk among themselves in a local language that I don't understand. I ask the older ones their names one by one.

Rajab'ali, Mahdi, Hossein, Qorban'ali, 'Ali . . .

Hossein, who is just a young child, says, "Learn Mahdi's brother's name too."

"Rajab'ali," I say, "Why did you say 'What is study?'"

"Studying is for city people. It doesn't do anything for us. Isn't that so, Mahdi? I've finished the fifth grade now, for example. What have I learned to do? Nothing! I didn't even finish school. Every day my father pulls me out of class and says 'Go get firewood. Come load the donkey.' As long as we live in our fathers' houses we won't be able to study."

"What does your father do?"

"He's a shepherd. When he goes to the flock, I have to do the chores around the house. We are all in this situation. Isn't that so, Mahdi?"

Mahdi, who appears to be the leader of the children, affirms what he says. "Rajab'ali is telling the truth. Village work doesn't go with study and training. There's a lot of work to do. They don't let us rest. Morning and night we either have to load firewood or cut trees."

I don't know what to say. My tongue is tied. I wish I had heard him wrong.

I ask anxiously, "Children, do you cut trees too?" I don't give them a chance to answer. I quickly begin pontificating. "You've been to school. You know that once these trees die they will never live again. The forest must not be killed, it must not be destroyed. Rainfall will diminish. The humidity will decrease. The air will become polluted. The earth will be barren. Then the village of Chalandar will be gone." I string words together one after another. I can see from their faces that what I have said has absolutely no relevance. If I continue, I will alienate myself entirely from the children.

Qorban'ali answers me. "We know these things ourselves. We've grown up among trees and in the forest. Is it possible that we don't realize that a good tree ought not to be cut down? Of course we know. But if we don't cut the trees, where will we get fuel? How will we live in the winter? Since the revolution they've only given us heating oil twice. It's been two and a half months since anybody saw a drop of oil around here. Haven't you seen the way they chain and rope the oil drums together in the city? Every motor is silent. We can't farm. Only the landlords and city people have oil in their houses, which they buy at a high price in the city and bring here. Do you understand? Myself, every time I go to cut trees, I don't care if they live or die."

"I thought someone else cut the trees."

Rajab'ali says, "What would someone who has fuel and a house want with a tree?"

I am at a loss for words. I ask mechanically, "Children, is it all right if I make notes on this? May I write down what you are saying?"

"Go ahead. Write anything you want."

"What about your names? May I write down your names too?"

"No problem. Write them."

Hossein reminds me, "Don't forget Mahdi's brother's name. He's not here himself. He's finished the twelfth grade and gone to the thirteenth!* Write his name so you'll have a note of it."

Embarrassed, I say, "I don't have a pad and pen with me, and I have very little paper."

They consult in the local language, speaking very rapidly. Several little girls have also joined us.

Rajab'ali says, "We'll go to Fatimah's house and get pen and paper. She has a note pad. Her house is nearby."

We set out for Fatimah's house. They point to it from a distance. It is an ordinary village house. It even has a little portico. The children tumultuously call out to Fatimah. A

---

*Meaning he has left school.

twelve- or thirteen-year-old girl appears on the porch; her face shows that she doesn't approve of all the noise in front of her house. I am in the most ridiculous position of all. I consider myself responsible for the disturbance to a certain extent and I am not sure what to do. Mahdi comes to my aid. "Fatimah, bring us your note pad. We'll return it soon."

"What are you going to do with my note pad? I've written my lessons in it. You'll take it and lose it."

The children all talked to each other, "We'll take out two or three pages and return it soon. Give us the note pad, Fatimah!"

My daughter looks at me; her look is reproachful. I know what she wants to say, but it is late and there is no way to go back.

I say, "I promise I'll return the note pad in good condition. I won't take more than two pages out of it. I have some paper myself. I just wanted to write a few lines of notes."

Little Hossein reminds us, "Give us the note pad, Fatimah. She wants to write down Mahdi's brother's name in order to remember it."

Fatimah laughs. She finally brings out the note pad and entrusts it to me, with orders and recommendations. I have some other scraps of crumpled paper in my coat pocket. If there isn't enough I'll compensate somehow. But it is a good writing pad.

Again we set out with the gang.

"Ok, children," I say, "so much for the note pad. Now what shall I write?"

Mahdi, more serious than usual, says, "Write what we say, but be accurate!"

"You children tell me some worthwhile things as well."

A little boy asks Mahdi, "Should we say funny things too?"

The answer is decisive. "No! First Rajab'ali, Qorban'ali, and I will talk."

All of them have quieted down. Actually, the children are arranging a program for us that we hadn't anticipated. I came to walk around and ask the children some questions about trees and decimated forests; now the story is taking a different turn.

Mahdi continues. "Write that we object and we have objected."

"Where have you objected?"

"To the *comité*."

"What did you say?"

Qorban'ali says, "What difference will it make in our situation whether you write these things or not?"

Rajab'ali doesn't agree. "Well, she'll take it to the city and talk to the others about it. Anyway, she's asking us to talk to her and we ought to give her proper answers. Isn't that so, Mahdi?"

"Rajab'ali's right. Why shouldn't we tell our side of this?"

I say, "Ok children, I'll write it. Maybe we can publish it too. Then maybe older people will read it. I agree with Mahdi."

Mahdi reminds me, "Write that we have no oil or motor fuel."

"You already said that. Tell me about how you protested."

"We said 'These big landowners don't let us own property, there is no land left for us to cultivate. We are out of work. Now we're cutting down trees to build houses for ourselves.'"

"Do you mean the villagers don't own any land?"

"Some do, some don't."

"What did the *comité* say?"

"The *comité* says 'You are villagers, not oppressed people.* There are no plans to give land to villagers. We are here to

---

*'Oppressed people' [*mostaz'afin*] are often mentioned in the rhetoric of revolutionary Iran. They are the poor, the uneducated, and the dispossessed of the world, who are regarded by the Islamic Republic as its true constituency, both in Iran and elsewhere.

help the oppressed people.' The *comité* is bad with the villagers. They don't like us."

Qorban'ali says, "Go to the foot of the mountain and you'll see. We have cut and cleared the forest. These people came, fenced off the land, and took it for themselves. But they don't cultivate it themselves or allow us to cultivate it or build houses."

My daughter, who has been quiet until now, reacting to the influence of television, asks, "Don't you have a *Reconstruction Crusade?*"

Rajab'ali says, "A handful of incompetents came up here to live off us. We threw them out. They haven't had the nerve since then to set foot in Chalandar."

"What about the oppressed?"

"The oppressed aren't villagers. They come from the outside. They're another sort of human being; they aren't our people."

A very young boy arrives and joins us. The children say "Rahmat is here, Rahmat is here."

"Who's Rahmat?"

"Rahmat is the top student in the fourth grade. He knows a world of poetry and songs."

"Hello Rahmat. The children talk about you a lot."

Rahmat laughs and asks, "what are you doing?"

"I'm writing down what the children are saying."

"Then write good stories for good children,* like Samad."

Hossein laughs. "He means the television Samad.**"

"No, you fool! I'm talking about Samad Behrangi."

I say, "Rahmat! A person must live like Samad in order to be able to write stories like him. His stories come out of his struggles; they are the product of his life among you. How can I write stories like Samad when I haven't lived like him,

---

*A reference to a book of children's stories by Samad Behrangi.

**Referring to a village yokel character on an Iranian children's television program played by Parviz Sayyad.

when I haven't struggled like him. You can see that today in this place there is nothing, but his name is here."

Not satisfied, he asks, "So what do you do?"

I change the subject. "I had come here to take a walk, when I saw the children."

An old man holding a rosary passes us. The children start whispering. When he is some distance away they say, "He's from Churan."

We reach the foot of the mountain and the riverbank. The children show me the empty lands and the barbed wire.

Qorban'ali says, "We cut down the trees and they took the land."

The girls go up the hill, squat down, and pick mountain violets. Hossein explains, "They're for the side of the road." I had guessed myself. We have to wait. We sit on rocks. I'm tired but ashamed to admit it. In front of me up on the heights are standing half-alive trees; several of their corpses are still lying on the ground. Donkeys will carry the wood into the village tomorrow. I look and say nothing. Qorban'ali has read my thoughts.

"These trees are old and rotten," he says. "They may even come to life a second time."

This feeling of empathy and friendship depresses me. I am sick of myself; poetic emotions and delicate sensitivities are sometimes ugly and inappropriate. My little friend is trying to sympathize with me in this exchange of friendship, even though my discomfort is no concern of his, while I am thinking about cedars, pine trees, and the peace of nature. I am still thinking of the hatchet that was a stumbling block for me, and how my heart clung to it like a vine.

"You're right, Qorban'ali," I say, head in the air. "These trees are old and rotten, and, as you say, maybe they will grow again someday. Who knows? Anyway, there isn't any choice, is there?"

"If we had fuel and houses, we wouldn't cut down the trees."

Rajab'ali also repeats "No, we wouldn't cut them down, would we Mahdi?"

Mahdi furrows his brow. "We told her once already. She knows it herself. Don't talk about trees so much. Write that we told the *comité* 'This road is ruined. Getting in and out of here in the winter is difficult. Asphalt it.' They gave no answer. We said 'Most of the houses in this village don't have toilets. Loan us money so we can build them.' They didn't agree to it. We said many things like this. Why do we need the Reconstruction Crusade? If they give us the means we'll do everything ourselves, and we'll solve the unemployment problem too."

One child, whose name I don't know, says, "We want work to be created for us, not for the Reconstruction Crusade. We want to work for ourselves, not our fathers. They don't pay us. They could open a couple of shops, for example, like a cobbler's shop, a carpenter's shop, a plumber's shop, and things like that where we could go and work and learn a trade at the same time."

Hossein also agrees with all these things. Evidently he has heard them a number of times. He repeats it, saying "We must think of tomorrow. Soon our fathers will be saying 'When you're grown you must marry, take a wife, make a life for yourself, and build a separate house.'"

I laugh loudly. Mahdi protests "It's no laughing matter. He's right. The older children are already collecting wood to use later on to build something for themselves. Even now their fathers are telling them 'You must get married.' There are always weddings in this village. The boys are afraid to take a wife."

In spite of Mahdi's protests, it is impossible not to laugh. It is unbelievable. The violet picking is over. Now we must retrace our steps over this entire road. We set out; the road keeps winding down. The little girls are running, holding up bouquets of violets. The older ones laugh at them and ridicule them behind their backs, saying,

> These crazy kids
> In the Middle East
> Ought to be shot

"What song is this, anyway?"

"We made it up ourselves."

"Why?"

"Because every kid who puts up with life in this village is crazy. A sane person leaves this place to find work. He works in a store somewhere."

Mahdi says to Rahmat, "Very well Rahmat, you sing a better song. Sing one from Mazandaran."

"I don't know any. I don't sing them."

Hossein insists. "Come on, sing one. She'll write it down."

Insisting is fruitless. Rahmat says, "She doesn't know our language; it's pointless." Then he turns to me slowly and says, "There are tape recordings of them if you're interested. We can go to Ali Kilid Dar's house and hear them."

The children affirm this. "Ali's father has a radio. He has tapes too."

Mahdi says "But I'll teach you a song."

Again they speak in the local language and then two or three of them recite these lyrics:

> Churan is not far from here
> Too bad the road there is arduous

"Children, where is this Churan that you talk about so much?" I ask.

"Don't you know?"

"No, we don't know. I admit I don't know anything about Churan."

The children are surprised by my ignorance. Little Rahmat

is uneasy. "Not so loud, kids! Someone from Churan may pass, hear what we are saying, and be disturbed. We have a lot of Churanis. They know all of us."

"Ok, what finally happened to Churan?"

Rajab'ali starts. "Churan is a village behind the mountain." He gives a location, but I can't make heads or tails of it. "The people of Churan are really ignorant. They don't know anything about anyplace. The people of the villages around here have made a lot of jokes about the Churanis. For example, a Churani found a radio. When he turned the dial, he heard it say 'This is Tehran.' He angrily threw the radio on the ground and said 'Son of a bitch! This is Tehran? No way. This is Churan!' The radio lay in the road and the battery finally went dead. The next day when the Churani was on his way to work he passed the radio again and heard that there was still a weak moan audible from it. Happily, he said 'See what I did? I've cut these Tehrani jerks down to size so they won't lie to us anymore. Sir, this is not Tehran; this is Churan.'"

This story had a lot of significance. It was evident that the Churanis are not as ignorant as they are reputed to be.

Rahmat is still anxious. "Don't write about the Churanis by name now. Don't write those names we gave you. We have a lot of Churanis here who will be upset."

I promise not to write the names of the Churanis. We eventually arrive at Fatimah's house.

She comes out when she hears the children's voices. Mahdi takes the note pad from me and returns it to her.

Fatimah offers us tea, we say we have to go back. For the first time the children ask me to stay, openly and kindly.

"Don't go tonight. If you're really a friend then stay here tonight. We'll go to Kilid Dar's house. He has room for you and your daughter."

"I have to go back. Perhaps I'll return another time."

"So what will happen to our discussion?"

"Perhaps it will be published."

"In a newspaper?"

"Do you read newspapers too?"

"No, we don't have the patience for it."

"Then perhaps in a magazine."

"Ok, if you come in the summer, we'll be here. This year we won't be going to summer quarters."

"Where are your summer quarters, anyway?"

"Every year we go to Kajur or Alam Kola."

"Ok, then maybe I'll come. This time I'll bring my own note pad. I promise I'll bring Samad's books too."

"If you come there's room in Ali Kilid Dar's house."

"I'll come. If they still haven't given you oil by that time or built any shops, then maybe I'll even come with you and we'll cut trees together. Who knows?"

Translated by John Green

HUMĀ NĀṬIQ

A French-educated historian sympathetic to leftist political thinking, Humā Nāṭiq was one of forty prominent intellectuals who helped revive the Iranian Writers Association in 1977 after more than a decade of suppression by sending an open letter to Prime Minister Hoveyda denouncing the regime for censorship and violation of the Constitution. Nāṭiq was kidnapped soon thereafter and badly beaten by SAVAK, the Shah's secret police organization, as a part of a series of reprisals.

[*Ervand Abrahamian*, Iran Between Two Revolutions *(Princeton: Princeton University Press, 1982), pp. 502, 508.*]

The Tale of the Rabbit and the Tomatoes

GĪTĪ NĪKZĀD

Every day I say to myself, "I am going to write a story." But at the end of the day after dinner as I put the last washed plate in the kitchen cabinet, I yawn and say to myself again: "I will surely write it tomorrow."

I am done with washing the dishes and cleaning the kitchen. I sit down to watch TV. I say to myself, "It is better to write a summary of the story that I have in mind on a piece of paper and stick it to the mirror in the bathroom. It will catch my eye tomorrow when I go to the bathroom to wash my face." Tomorrow after making lunch and before the kids come back from school and my husband comes back from work, I will have time to write the story. Tomorrow I will make steamed rice and tomatoes which is easy to make and doesn't take too much time. The kids like steamed rice and tomatoes, but my husband . . . I can imagine his face. He will stare at his plate, eat his food, and leave the kitchen table without saying even a word. I know that he doesn't like steamed rice and tomatoes, but he doesn't complain. He doesn't talk about it. To make up for it, I will make his favorite food the day after tomorrow. I will go to the market

This is from the story "Qiṣṣah-'i Khargush va Gawjah-Farangi" in *Adīnah* 35: June 1989, pp. 54–55.

and buy fresh vegetables. I will make Khoresht-e *Qormeh-Sabzi.* The day after tomorrow, when I will have no story to write, I will have enough time to clean the vegetables and go to the grocery store and complain of dirty and muddy vegetables to the grocer. I will fill the kitchen sink with water and soak the vegetables in it. I wash them once and change the water and wash them again and change the water one more time and repeat this for the third and fourth time. I will put my glasses on and examine the vegetables carefully to see whether they are completely clean. Then, I will cut them up. This time I am careful not to cut my fingers. I always cut my fingers when I cut up vegetables. My husband laughs and jokingly says, "You are still clumsy after having done this for fifteen years." I laugh too. I know that he is teasing me. I cut the vegetables up into small pieces. My mother always says, "The vegetables prepared for *Qormeh-Sabzi* must be cut up into small pieces." She is extraordinarily skillful in cutting up vegetables. She does it fast and never cuts her fingers. One should get the knack of frying vegetables. I have done this for fifteen years and now I can claim that I have learned it. Vegetables should be stirred constantly over a low flame. They shouldn't be burned. I should remember to soak the beans. The last time I made *Qormeh-Sabzi,* I forgot to soak the beans. The meat was cooked and became mushy, but the beans had not been cooked yet. My husband didn't say anything, but when I was taking the dirty dishes and plates away, I saw that he had not eaten the beans and had put them aside. That night my daughter said that she had a stomachache. My husband set his newspaper down and looked at me. Then, he smiled and pointed at the kitchen. That night my thirteen-year-old daughter had her period for the first time. Tomorrow I will make steamed rice and tomatoes and it won't take too much time. I will have time to write my story. The story I am going to write is for kids. This story is about a rabbit who falls into a hole dug by a hunter.

The hole is very deep and the rabbit is unable to get out of it. His friends finally find him, but they can't help him either. They bring him food and water to keep him alive. He stays in the hole for days. He has food to eat and is warm and comfortable, but he wants to get out. Down there, he can see only part of the sky which is either clear and blue or cloudy and grey. He can see birds flying in the daytime and stars blinking at night. I still don't know how to get the rabbit out of the hole. I will think about it tomorrow. I have to write it down in a few sentences. I don't want to forget it. I yawn. I have to go to bed and sleep. I want to be fresh when I wake up in the morning. Tomorrow I will have to help a small rabbit get out of a deep hole. I am thirsty. I go to the kitchen and open the refrigerator to take the pitcher of water. I see only two tomatoes there. This is not enough to make steamed rice and tomatoes. I will have to buy tomatoes tomorrow. I drink a glass of water. I am sleepy. I set the glass down, turn off the light and leave the kitchen. I was going to write something. What was it? I tear a piece of paper out of my notebook and write "Tomatoes." I have to stick this piece of paper to the mirror in the bathroom so that tomorrow I won't forget. . . .

February, 1988, Germany

Translated by Farzin Yazdanfar

GĪTĪ NĪKZĀD

Gītī Nīkzād started her writing career with the publication of three short stories, published in the literary journal Chishmandāz *(No. 5, Fall 1988).*

❧ *Sara*

SHAHRNŪSH PĀRSĪPŪR

Whenever the doctor came, and he used to come very often, he would stand in the vestibule and throw his cigarette butt towards the flower-bed. He would look around and spit in the direction of the cigarette butt. He was forty-five years old and had fallen too soon into the habit of spitting like an old man. He was feeling old for no reason.

Mr. Bahari's house looked like a museum with all those statues and paintings, skillfully copied from European masterpieces. They had been brought home by his father on his many journeys to Czarist Russia and by Mr. Bahari himself on his numerous trips to Europe and the Far East. Some of the rugs in the house were fifty years old. They were in the habit of drinking tea in genuine china cups. Now that Mr. Bahari was old and his older sons had left the house, he was thinking about buying a piece of land for his grave in Haifa, and establishing a family foundation somewhere. And his youngest son, Firuz, who had resigned himself to study in one of the local universities, loved to sit on the porch in the summer afternoons after three o'clock. Every afternoon at one o'clock the sun turned away from the porch. Mr. Bahari

This story is from the collection *Āvīzah'hā-yi Bulūr* (Tehran: Intishārāt-i Rāz), 1974, pp. 51–57.

would wait for his son to come back home at five o'clock when they would sit on the porch and drink tea. The doctor would probably show up around five or six o'clock. The three men would chat and expose everything to argument: communists; green monkeys in Africa; distinct, clear handwriting; the tropic of cancer; the equator; Marziyeh, the modulation of Banan's voice; the comparison between the ships made in England and those made in Japan; and the secrets of NATO.

Once, their argument turned to earthworms.

The doctor was saying: "Earthworms are truly interesting creatures. The fertility of soil and the growth of plants are greatly affected by the movement of earthworms from underground to the surface. They bring up nourishing materials from the lower levels of the soil to the higher ones." Then, he sipped the last drop of tea from his third cup and set it on the table carefully. Catching a moment when he was not being observed, he looked at the window to Sara's room. This was the eighth year that he had been doing this.

Firuz took advantage of the doctor's silence:

"Nonetheless, earthworms are dirty creatures, doctor. Their shape is quite sickening."

Mr. Bahari was listening in silence and seemed to be in agreement with his son. The doctor patiently shook his head in disagreement. "No, no," he said. "This is the very point that is always overlooked; the fact is that animals are not in any way responsible for their own shape and looks. Nobody asked the earthworm's permission to create him this way."

"Of course, if somebody has indeed created them," Firuz said.

The doctor paid no attention and continued, "Nevertheless, the earthworm is a useful creature."

The topic of discussion shifted to grafted cherries, and the servant brought a plate full of grafted cherries from Mr. Bahari's garden. The cherries were brittle, large, and had two colors: some were red and some were yellow.

The sound of music could be heard from the room of Mr. Bahari's twenty-nine-year-old daughter. She was listening to a hit record with the English title, "My Friends, My Friends." It had a sad theme. The sun was setting and the remaining redness of the summer sun mixed with the singer's sad voice. The three men remained silent for a moment.

Mr. Bahari was carefully looking at the window of his daughter's room through his farsighted glasses. The window of her room was opposite the porch. Mr. Bahari could see the awkward shadow of his daughter who was leaning against the window. She looked like a pumpkin from a distance. Finally, Mr. Bahari's feeble voice broke the silence, "My father had an expert gardener; one of those matchless gardeners who come along only once every hundred years. He used to produce big cherries! This big!"

Firuz called out the servant and told him to ask his sister to turn the record player down. After the servant left, the doctor asked Firuz whether he disliked the music. He, irritable and restless, made a vague gesture of impatience. Silence prevailed once again. Both the doctor and Firuz thought how much they disliked each other. The sound of music had stopped. Mr. Bahari's daughter was walking in the garden. The men could see her from a distance. The doctor looked at her strange body which looked like the body of pregnant women—women who would be giving birth to twins or triplets. The doctor knew such women very well. They all had thin moustaches on their upper lips, covered by beads of perspiration, and they all smelled of milk and dirty woolly clothing. He wished to get a closer look at Mr. Bahari's daughter.

Mr. Bahari's daughter was dragging her heavy body under the trees. A gentle breeze was playing with her black hair.

Her hair hung down to her shoulders. If it had still been daylight, the doctor might have been able to see her face, but the approaching darkness concealed everything about the girl but her belly.

The doctor said, "It is said that women with black hair are horny." He blushed because of the word he had used. Mr. Bahari was listening carefully. "They say this about women with red hair." Firuz said. He was sitting in the dark and his nervous voice could hardly be heard, as if he was talking from the bottom of a well.

Mr. Bahari asked the servant to turn on the light. When the light came on, the garden faded into darkness. Mr. Bahari thought that he would never let anyone light a lamp on his grave. Perhaps he would see or touch something through the particles of dust even if it was pitch-dark, and he regretted that he had not become a poet. For the first time this acute longing was bringing tears to his eyes.

Once again music came heard from Sara's room, this time quite softly. The doctor had no desire to talk. He wanted to listen to the music and surrender to the pleasant coolness of the evening breeze.

"They say women with red hair are very horny. They are the type of women who send their lovers to an early sexual retirement." Again this was Firuz. The doctor did not answer.

"This is the case even in the world of movie stars. The redheads are horny and high-strung."

The doctor was thinking about Rita Hayworth. He was wondering whether she was a blonde or a redhead. He couldn't remember.

"Doctor, why did you say that black-haired women were horny?"

"Huh?"

"Why do you say that women with black hair are horny?"

"I don't know. It came to my mind for no reason. I remembered that I had read somewhere that these women were nervous, jealous, hateful, and naturally horny."

Firuz was leaning forward in his chair, his face bright and attentive.

"You said it for no reason, but you were looking at the garden." Firuz said.

The doctor was tired. He said that he was looking at the grafted cherries.

"No, you weren't looking at them. You were looking at something else."

The doctor said that he was looking at something else too, but he didn't know what Firuz meant. He meant "Sara."

Firuz rose up to stand as he looked angrily at his father. Mr. Bahari was not as excited as his son. To him what the doctor had done could easily be justified. The thought of his grave hadn't left his mind yet. "Maybe the doctor was looking at the garden, but it isn't important anyway. Sara has been like this for years. I see no connection between Sara and the doctor," said he.

Then, all of a sudden, he discovered that there might be a connection. Sitting on his chair, he bent forward and beat on the arms of the chair with his fists. He thought he was dying and leaving all of his good and bad fortune to his survivors, and he would leave his closely-spaced greedy-looking eyes (although he was not greedy), to his daughter Sara.

"You see no connection! Of course, you see no connection." Firuz said. He sat back calmly in his chair. What fault was it of his that his father was so irresponsible, he who would inherit most of the chinaware and paintings in the house? The doctor felt that it was time to go, but the smell of the soup coming from the kitchen weakened his will. Nonetheless, he got up to leave, but Mr. Bahari asked him to stay for dinner. He sank into his chair and his thoughts. Was it really worth struggling for something and not being able to get it after all these years of schooling, only to end up with a mere bowl of soup and perhaps a piece of *kutlit*? What hope did he have after all these years? What hope?

The music coming from Sara's room stopped and she turned off her light. Mr. Bahari said, "Is there any harm in Sara joining us for dinner?" He faced his son as he spoke. Then, he turned towards the doctor and said, "Doctor, my daughter has been pregnant for nine years. Don't you think it is strange?"

The doctor felt that an old frozen thought was melting and evaporating in the back of his mind. He answered,

"Maybe she is sick. Maybe it is a tumor . . ."

"No, it can't be a tumor. The baby moves."

"Maybe it is the tumor which is moving."

"It isn't unlikely."

The doctor was angry at his own curiosity, even though he had not seemed inquisitive and had come by information unintentionally—information that would distract him from his tiresome thoughts and would give him the opportunity to live again. Forty-five years old? It doesn't matter. When he was young, he had dreams; now he was forty-five years old and was facing reality. It had always been like this. If they asked him to examine her, he would become quite upset. But the soup smelled good and was appetizing.

"This is a very strange case. If it is revealed, it will cause quite a stir in the world of medicine," the doctor said.

"But it shouldn't be revealed," said Mr. Bahari hastily and fearfully.

"Ok, I'll examine her if you like."

"Examination! What for?" Mr. Bahari asked.

Then the doctor was greatly relieved. He had lost his sense of curiosity a thousand years ago. He had been staring at the flowers painted on the china cup for so long that he had memorized the colors.

"Ok, if you don't want me to . . ." he said.

"The problem is that she wants to give birth to a martyr."

148

The doctor thought: My God! This damned soup! How nice it smells . . . The problem is one cannot simply want to do something, one must have possibilities . . . You know, as always, possibilities. . . .

"That's right. The possibilities! Does it mean that it isn't possible. . . ?"

"Well, everything is possible, but you should see what the conditions are. To give birth to a martyr requires the proper conditions. Perhaps it requires certain conditions; for example, certain kinds of things . . . they say things, for instance, the role of a historical figure. But the questions are: What history? What role? What figure? For instance, Sara. How is she going to . . ." He wondered, oh God, what else to say.

"Well, it isn't possible then."

"Why doesn't the baby want to be born? Why is it delaying so long?" Mr. Bahari regretfully said.

"I don't know. It is strange, but I swear by God that I don't know," the doctor answered.

"It seems to me that this is the first time you haven't known something," Firuz said.

"I have seldom not known something. But, you know, the problem is I am simply not curious. Well, what is to be done, each person is a certain way. Since I am not curious, my ignorance is justified. No doubt it must be justified . . . Besides, the only thing I want is to have some kind of life with a bowl of soup, one or two pieces of *kutlit*, and a wife."

Sara. After eight years, Mr. Bahari breathed a sigh of relief.

"That's right," said the doctor. "I can easily get along with her. Somehow, we'll manage to get along with each other. Ah, it took so long," the doctor said.

Mr. Bahari told the servant to ask Sara to join them for dinner.

Translated by Farzin Yazdanfar

Shahrnūsh Pārsīpūr

Shahrnūsh Pārsīpūr was born in 1946. Her father is a Shiraz lawyer. She has a son from a former marriage. Shahrnūsh holds a B.A. in social science from Tehran University, and studied Indian language and culture for two years in France. She was imprisoned after the 1979 revolution, was later released and continues to live in Iran. In addition to her literary works, she has translated four books.

❧ *There Is No Truth*

ZHĪLĀ SĀZGĀR

The sun had warmed the waters of the sea. The fish was satiated and calm. He watched the school of fish going this way and that in search of bait.

Most of the fish in this part of the ocean knew him and liked him. The color of his scales was white, with a red spot on his right side. Above and beyond his physical beauty, he was a hero. He was bold and fearless. He loved to challenge the hooks of the fishermen. The bait had to be stolen without getting hooked. In that part of the ocean, every fish who had tried to imitate him had been caught and had disappeared.

He always traveled with the school, except on certain rare days when he stopped in one spot without the slightest movement like a stone on the ocean floor, and with a dignity and presence that no one had the courage to disrupt by approaching him.

For the fish, the whole world consisted of this very free and unbounded ocean, and all of life was play: play among the other fish, among the stones and plants at the bottom of the sea, and with the hooks that would hang waiting above

This story is from the collection *Pas az Marg-i Māhīhā* [After the Fish Die] ([Tehran]: Amīr Kabīr, 1349 [1970]).

their heads for hours. Play with everything and everyone, free and fearless play.

They had had no experience with the bitterness of captivity, dryness, fear, and death. Clearly, that which had not been experienced was not real; it aroused no fear and was not even foreseen.

Who can tell what will happen? The fish thought nothing would happen. He thought life was a stream of peaceful identical moments and days, but fishhooks are not always pulled out of the sea broken and empty, and finally one day the fish was caught. The heroic fish, the white fish with a red spot, was caught by a fisherman. It was unbelievable. All the fish lifted their heads and watched his hopeless struggle on the fisherman's pole. A bitter feeling swept over that part of the ocean. A hero had been captured, a hero had been lost, the sun hid behind clouds. The fish were choked with tears It was as if they were not on speaking terms with one another.

The fisherman tossed the fish into a bucket of water. Why didn't he let him die? No one knew.

The fish was agitated and uneasy. He beat his head against the sides of the bucket until they got home. He leaped up and fell down again. He was not afraid of death. He was full of desire to rebel, to return to the free ocean and the other fish.

When they got home the fisherman threw him into the *howz*. The sides of the *howz* were hard and dirty. There was no sign of the soft sands of the open sea. The walls seemed to press in on the fish, crushing him. He had never seen a wall in his life. He stood in a corner, face to the wall. What could he do? Surrounded by high, hard walls? In standing water? What could he do?

The days passed one after another. The fish became accustomed to the *howz*. His fear and struggling ceased. Now they were feeding the heroic fish. Every day they tossed his ration into the water of the *howz*. In the first days he hid in a corner of the *howz* with a hungry stomach and endured the hunger. He wouldn't touch any food; he thought only of the open sea. But how long could he endure hunger? The fish quietly got used to eating fish food. He came to resemble the *howz* itself, in a torpor, with no ambition, motionless.

He thought less now. A day must pass, and a night must come and go behind it. There was nothing to fear from larger fish in the *howz,* nor from the hooks of fishermen. The *howz* had devoured him. The *howz* gave him shelter.

Every day the fish saw the shadow of his owner, who would stand above the *howz* and look at him with a crooked, haughty grin. He always fled from his gaze to the bottom of the *howz,* but there was a black shadow there too. It was there that the fish remembered the ocean, its clean, pure water, the waves, and the fish. The fish thought and thought.

He didn't know why his owner took him out of the *howz* one day and put him in a large clear container. The clear container was in a room where the fish saw no light, other than a strip of it that shone between the curtains in the morning. The sky, with all its vastness, was no more than a thin blue line there.

Swimming was impossible; it was impossible to move. If the fish tried to move, his head instantly struck the side of the container. The ocean—may its memory never die—never ended. Here, however, tightness, captivity, listlessness, weakness, and weariness were everything. Here, even the light of the sun and the sky was rationed.

A life without struggle, without effort, and without loss or gain had tired the fish. Heroic deeds of the past were no more than colorless memories. Now the fish was always fed by others. He had become lazy. He had become a piece of stone.

Short, fruitless periods of stalking from one wall to the other, banging his head against them, had gradually turned the fish into a living corpse, a corpse that sometimes moved, but only sometimes . . .

It was not clear what the fish's owner had in mind. One day he took him out of the clear container and dropped him into a small bowl. The bowl's diameter was only perhaps the length of the fish's body. He wriggled in place with difficulty. They changed the water in the bowl every day and his ration was provided, but the fish did not forget the immensity of the bounteous sea, and it was difficult to endure such cramped conditions. Now the fish had to bend his head to make a move and his whole body was pressed together. So he stayed calmly in place and thought.

It was sweet, thinking about the beauties of the past, of the freedoms, the heroic deeds, and the joys . . . It was very sweet, but it did not diminish the pressure of today's confinement.

Then one day the fish's owner grabbed him by the tail, took him out of the bowl, and dropped him into a cup that was even smaller. The poor fish's head was all that was in the water; the rest of his body was left dangling out of the cup, inert and dry.

Sometimes his tail moved. From this one could tell that he was still alive. This was life—a kind of continually worsening suffocation between walls that grew tighter and blacker every day. A little water, a bit of food. The fish endured it however, got used to it, and did his best to breathe.

The past no longer seemed real. All was forgetfulness, weakness, and sad resignation to fate.

There was so little water in the small cup that it was there in the morning and gone in the afternoon. The fish didn't panic; he didn't complain. It no longer made any difference. It was even possible to live with dehydration. His owner also sensed this. One day he grabbed the fish by the tail and tossed him into the middle of the room.

The fish flopped. After a long silence in the open space

of the room, a feeling of panic came over him. His body seemed to have gone to sleep. He looked all around. He tried to move, but remained in place. He looked at the room's high, hard walls. What difference did it make if one went from this side of the room to the other side? From this wall to that wall? No, it no longer really mattered. And nothing changed as the days went by. There was also no hope of a miracle. The fish no longer thought of the ocean. This was also a kind of a life. Who could tell? Perhaps it was even a better life. His owner had bought him several little colored balls that he played with. It wasn't bad. Sometimes he even played. Who said life in the sea was better? What did "better" really mean? What was the meaning of "worse?" Why should one live in fear of nets and be preoccupied with stealing bait from fish hooks? Why should one take shield in hand and go to war when there was peace, rations, the security of a room with closed doors, and colored balls?

One day, just before noon, the fish woke up. His rations had come. He ate his food and went around the room. His owner had closed the door and left. The fish was despondent. He approached the colored balls and looked at them; he was even tired of playing.

He glanced at the window. Why had his owner forgotten to close it? He must have forgotten.

The fish returned to the colored balls, but the half-opened window tempted him. "You can go out, you can go . . ."

The clear blue of the sky and a cool breeze that was blowing in seemed to awaken the fish from a long, deep sleep. "Go out, go see what's going on . . ."

His owner would surely be angry with him for doing this. He would never forgive him. But . . . The world would not end. He would go and come back. He would come back quickly.

The fish heaved itself up on the windowsill with a leap and looked outside. What was he waiting for? He crawled out the half-open window and landed on the cobblestones in the yard. He looked around. Beautiful flowers were blooming in the garden; the sun had a soothing warmth, the breeze carried the smell of perfume.

The fish went around the garden. The stones on the floor of the yard were warm. His whole body twinged when he saw the *howz*. He became sad. One after another his scales felt the sensation of thirst. The water was pulling him. The water was calling him. Every cell of his body cried "Water . . . Water . . . Water."

Tears filled the fish's eyes. Who said fish don't cry?

He leaped and leaped again. He no longer saw anything except the water of the *howz*. He no longer felt anything. He reached the *howz*. He leaped off the footbath and did a belly flop in the water.

When the fish's owner returned at noon, first he went into the room to get him, but the fish wasn't there. He looked around for him. So where had he gone? He noticed the half-open window and ran into the yard; the fish wasn't there either. He looked around in the garden and then the *howz* caught his eye, stopping him where he stood. The white corpse of the fish was floating on top of the water.

The water had drowned the fish!

Translated by John Green

ZHĪLĀ SĀZGĀR

Zhīlā Sāzgār holds a bachelor's degree in journalism from an American university and has completed a two-year course in journalism at Tehran University. She has contributed short stories to Iṭṭilā'āt-i Bānuvān *and* Tamāshā. *While living in the United States she did editorial work. (Chihrah-'i Maṭbū'āt-i Mu'āṣir, p. 92.)*

❧ *The Great Lady of My Soul*

GOLI TARAGHI

Kashan. I have arrived. And I am tired. I head out of town. I am unfamiliar with the surrounding area and I lose my way. The air is cool and light, replete with invisible damp and fragrant particles.

"What is your contribution to this revolution, Mr. Haydari?" I asked. Mr. Haydari was tremulous and sleepless in fear of impending famine and pillage. My wife said, "I am suspicious of the landlord. He is in contact with Israel." She was sitting by the window polishing her silverware. She was jubilant and under her breath hummed a revolutionary jingle.

Overhead, the sky is tangible and within reach. The plain, stretching all the way to the foothills, is tinged with green, spotted with thorn bushes and red poppies. In the steep ravines pomegranate trees grow in abundance. The far mountains are purple, blue, and vermilion. They look naked in a feminine sort of way, with the contours of timeless

The story translated here, called "Buzurgbānu-yi Rūḥ-i Man" (The Great Lady of My Soul), was written in the summer of 1979 and published in the important, but short-lived, post-Pahlavi journal *Kitāb-i Jum'ah* 1, no. 5 (8 Shahrivar 1358/30 August 1979, pp. 38–50). Taraghi herself describes this story as "a memento of a trip to Kashan with Sohrab Sepehri" and considers it her best work, more suitable than her other stories for translation.

womanhood. The horizon plunges to infinity, to nothingness. In the distance, under the shade of the aspens, a policeman is standing in prayer. At my feet has grown the world's smallest flower.

I address my friend, the poet, "Where is your historical conscience?"

"I am still in amazement over this flower," he replies.

The air is so fresh, so mild. The breeze is redolent with the smell of pastures, trees still damp from a recent rain, flowers freshly blooming. It is as if it has blown from a forested sky and has mixed with perfumed breath. The policeman is still there, now prostrate, with his forehead pressed to the ground.

My father is opposed to the execution of policemen. He does not understand the meaning of "waging war against God." My wife says, "Islam approves of vengeance," and stares in morbid awe at the newspaper photographs of corpses of those recently executed.

Some friends say it is time to pack and go. Some friends say it is best to take a stand, to proclaim, to enlighten, to fight. Friends are hastily publishing newspapers, forming groups, establishing syndicates. Mr. Haydari has stocked his cellar with flour, rice, fuel, and grains. He has moved his silk carpets to our house and his gold coins now hang around his neck in a sack.

All of a sudden my wife has discovered God. She is ecstatic. At night she attends classes in canonical law. Every morning she rushes off to the Ladies' Guidance and Religious Instruction sessions. She has clipped her nails and has wiped the green shade off her eyelids. She has sworn an oath of abstinence. She does not play cards anymore and covers her hair, making sure that the ear lobes are not exposed to public view. She often sits by my side, eyes me ruefully, and tells me of the divine grace of Imam Reza, God's mercifulness, the evils of imperialism, and the viciousness of communism.

"Don't you believe in God?" she asks. I am reminded of a man who killed himself to prove that there is no such thing as divine will, that man is in control of his own destiny. "Don't you believe in heaven and hell?" she wants to know. She holds my hand. Her skin feels hot and burning against mine, her breath feverish. She is not like herself anymore; she is not like anyone I know. Sometimes she stays awake at night. Every time I look, her eyes are open. I get a queasy feeling.

The university is in turmoil. Someone is addressing the crowd, which responds by shouting religious slogans. Outside the university walls peddlers are selling baked potatoes, boiled sugar beets, and beans. Pictures of the Imam hang from the trees. I am stopped by an old woman who shows me the picture of her slain son. She is here to seek restitution and is looking for an obscure ayatollah.

The street is blocked. I detour.

Sidewalks are paved with books, cassette tapes of religious chants, and sermons. There are sneakers, blue jeans, and likenesses of the Holy Martyrs on the sidewalks, all for sale. Nearby, a militiaman is teaching a group of bystanders the operation of an Uzi submachine gun. Under a tree, a man and a woman have spread a rug and are having lunch with their children.

I am accosted by one of my students. He inquires after my health. I don't even remember his name. He has smeared his face with a dark substance and is wearing a black and white plaid headdress. His overcoat is several sizes too big for him; so are his boots.

My class has been called off. There is a student meeting in progress. They are holding *in absentia* trials of faculty members. They beat angrily on the walls with clenched fists.

They want to make known their protest. In the university halls they search for the essence of liberty. They ask, "Sir, which is valid, matter or spirit? Where is the truth, in history or in God?" My students are reading *The Ruzbeh* Trials, Marxist Discourses,* and *Guide to Religious Regulations.* They are confused.

In the dead of night there is heavy pounding on the door. My wife jumps out of bed. My father hurriedly conceals his vodka bottles. But it is only Mr. Haydari, who has brought us powdered milk, cheese, and Indian cod-liver oil. He is fraught with alarm. "Fuel has practically run out," he says. "There is an epidemic of cholera, even smallpox. Soon people will have to eat one another. We will all freeze to death."

My wife is whimpering. "The Imam will provide," she says. My son snickers bitterly and kicks the flour sacks. He believes the true revolution will come later and victory will be to the suffering masses. He goes to the factory every day. But he does not know how to relate to the laborers. He wears soiled shirts and sleeps with his boots on.

The wilderness is so far from all this, so uncomplicated, so pristine. I don't know why I took the trip to Kashan. One morning I got up and hit the road. My wife was in the middle of her morning prayer. She has only recently learned the ritual and is reading the litany off a piece of paper stuck on the wall. The landlord was already in the yard. He stood up when he saw me. He was visibly agitated and seemed to be waiting for someone. He eyed my briefcase.

"Are you running away?"

"No."

"Is your name on the list?"

---

*Khusraw Ruzbeh was a captain in the Iranian army who was tried secretly and executed by a firing squad on 11 May, 1958 on charges of spying for the Soviet Union, murder, and membership in the Communist party. He is admired by some Iranians for his early and forthright stance in opposition to the Pahlavi regime.

I shook my head.

"They are going to arrest me," he said. "Either today or tomorrow. They'll arrest you, too. They're arresting everyone."

My father, too, was up. He was seated behind the window tuning his *tar*. He had recently laid his hands on a large sack of raisins and a pressure cooker and was busy extracting alcohol for his domestic vodka. Formerly, he used to teach music. But now his students had stopped coming. Most evenings Monsieur Ardavaz, the Armenian, would come over to have a drink with him. Ardavaz had closed down his small tavern after it was burned and had converted one of the rooms of his house into a small shop from which he dispensed dry toast, canned fruit, and a few miscellaneous items. Monsieur Ardavaz is frightened of imperialism and has voted for the Islamic republic.

Mr. Haydari is looking for a job in the *comité*. At night, with the sack of gold coins under his arm, he stands watch in the neighborhood.

I halt. The narrow path has come to a sudden end. Just ahead is a stretch of wheat fields dotted by an occasional cucumber patch. There are multicolored flowers on the borders of the fields. In the distance, at the foot of the mountains, there is a hamlet, peaceful in the shade of tall cedars. Downhill, leading to the hamlet, there are deserted flour mills, a busy, swelling stream, and, under some rocks, a bubbling spring.

A sense of lightness pervades me, and I feel as if I am floating in the air. A song forms at my lips:

> What fragrance in the meadow,
> In this oasis
> I searched,
> Perhaps for a dream,

For light, a grain of sand,
A smile.

Farther ahead, on a small raised plateau, is a pond, an adobe hut with no doors and windows overlooking it. I am thirsty. The water tastes stagnant and there are swarms of minnows darting about and swaying algae on the bottom. I sprinkle water on my face. I can hear a bird far away. I light a cigarette. The striking of the match startles a lizard. I keep walking. There is a vague rustling in the grass. A snake? An old man and his burro pass me by. The rustling is directly behind me now. I walk faster, more purposefully, as I am to meet someone somewhere.

The landlord said, "They are going to arrest me for sure. They are going to arrest you, too."

My son says we should kill everyone. He has compunctions about stepping on a roach. In his room he practices a revolutionary oration. With red paint he writes slogans on the walls. From the dark green welt under his eye I can tell he has been beaten up.

An old woman is sitting near a grass patch with a handle at her side. The sunlight settles under my skin. I feel feverish in a pleasant, sensuous sort of way. The old woman is interminably chewing on something.

My father is flustered and abusive and desperately looking for good-quality raisins. The recent batch of his domestic vodka has an unpleasant odor. Monsieur Ardavaz has been given twenty lashes of the whip.

I think of my daughter: fifteen years old and in love. She paces under the trees barefoot, talking to herself. Her mouth is always stuffed. She has gotten fat, obese in fact. She hides snacks under her bed and munches on them at night. She eats uncontrollably. As a child, she chewed on paper, erasers, and crayons. She also ate clay, leaves, and chalk. And now she is in love. In love with someone we don't know. She is always tearful and forlorn.

Thousands have lined up for the communal prayer. Thousands go down on their hands and knees in a gesture of submission to God. A woman is standing next to me, trembling, reciting prayers. Women, clad in black cover all veils, crowd the alleys and passageways.

My friend the poet is ill and in bed. They say he has gone mad. He raves and throws himself against the walls of his room. I go to pay him a visit. I am depressed and heavy-hearted. He is asleep and half-conscious. His hair is plastered to his sweaty forehead. His mother is sitting in the hall near the door of his room mumbling to herself, inattentive to my presence. I look at the figure lying on the bed. There are dark patches under the eyes and at the corners of the mouth.

His wife does not understand. She is confused and distracted. When she sees me, she bursts out crying. "I have no idea what he wants," she tells me between sobs. "He is always begging God's forgiveness. He prays two hundred times a day and thinks everything is unclean. He climbs on the roof every night and disturbs the neighbors with shouts of *Allaho Akbar*. He cries every night and cannot sleep for fear of God."

I can hardly believe this. He used to be so quiet and withdrawn, so level-headed and imperturbable. During the month of Moharram, he would come to our house and together we would listen to the sounds of the revolution, the strange cacophony of voices rising to the night sky, to the sporadic small-arms fire from distant streets. We could hear the shriek of a woman in the neighborhood exhorting all to rise in revolt and the sounds of hundreds of doors and windows in our general vicinity bursting open and disgorging countless women, children, and old men into the streets.

During all this my friend would remain calm and undis-
turbed.

The sky now has a green hue as if it is a vegetable substance. The fields come to a sudden end and what I see
before me now is the desert with its dry, lifeless sands creeping toward a dark, mysterious infinity. My sensitized eyes
and ears see and hear a tumult in the immeasurable distance.
The desert sand at my feet frightens and fascinates, like an
aroused and devouring woman radiating a bewitching odor
and breathing febrile nocturnal breasts.

I am lost and there is no one in sight to guide me. Fatigue
and darkness are setting in but I keep going. I know the
desert is alluring and relentless. But I go on, uncontrolled,
compulsive.

"I wish we knew where the Absent Imam is!" says my wife.

The far distance is the bastion of demons and lost souls.

The policeman on our neighborhood beat has been executed. His wife, distraught and demented, is pregnant. Every
day with her several children she waddles to the top of the
street where she throws stones at passing cars. My wife has
a dream in which the sky is on fire. She is obsessed and
frightened.

My hand smells of blood, the fresh, warm blood of a
youth whose name I don't even know. We were side by side,
talking and running. He was shaking his small delicate fist in
the air, challenging the troops. Then I lost sight of him
around the corner. There was a fire raging somewhere
nearby. The street was filled with smoke and flames. Women
were running pell-mell and shopkeepers were closing up in
haste. Shooting had started. Moments later I saw the youth
again. He was bent over with his arm around the trunk of a

tree. His face was turned toward me as if he were about to tell me something. He seemed around fourteen or fifteen, the same age as my son. I was losing my mind. The ambulance sirens were driving me crazy. I lifted him and he felt heavy and lifeless. I called for help, dragging him frantically with me. I tried to stop a man. I called after a soldier. No one seemed to heed me. The youth's head was pressed against my chest and his eyes were open. I searched his pockets and found nothing. Someone's lost, unidentified child. There was a soft growth of hair over his lip. His hand was in mine.

I am awakened by my wife gently dabbing my sweaty brow with a damp cloth. My mouth feels dry. I breathe heavily. I open the window and shuffle onto the balcony. It is snowing. I clutch at the snow and rub some of it on my burning neck and face. My hand smells of blood, warm, innocent blood.

My father believes that the Age of Darkness is nearing its end and a cataclysm is imminent. The landlord has now been arrested. My son believes he and his like should be exterminated. My son opposes the capitalistic order. He is for the masses.

My daughter is still in love. She has a collection of dried flowers and butterflies. She also collects pictures of foreign film stars. She is glad schools are closed. Every day she lies in bed until noon. She ties her hair in silk ribbons and paints her nails green, orange, and purple.

My wife is a believer in the Reconstruction Crusade. On the National Clean-up Day she swept the alley and cleaned the irrigation ditches in the neighborhood. She is also concerned about housing for the poor. She has donated her silver bracelet to the local mosque.

It is as if someone is calling me from the far end of the desert, as if in each step I am accompanied by an invisible being. I can hear him breathing, disturbing the air as he moves at my side. My heart is throbbing and I am permeated with an obscure fear. I look up and the wilderness stares back at me. I am engulfed by the desert. A strange sensation is in the air and I feel the presence of tormented spirits around me.

"Mr. Haydari, what is the secret of your success?" I inquire. My wife pontificates, "The infidel, in all his corporeal entity, even his hair, fingernails, and all the secretions of his body, is unclean."

The desert floor is gently rising and falling. Around me, the sand dunes seem imposingly tall. I find I am talking to myself, singing, laughing. I am shouting, running.

"Death to philosophy! Death to the reactionaries!" shout my students. They love social sciences.

I suddenly stop. All the commotion has ceased. The desert appears familiar and friendly. What is in front of me is something out of a dream. Vivid, urgent, and yet unbelievable. There is a grove bordered by tall green trees. From among the branches I catch a glimpse of a rustic house sitting in the middle of an enclosure, a courtyard. The scene is so unreal, so visionary, as if it has been conjured up from thin air. I advance cautiously, afraid that the scene may dissolve if I take my eyes off, or it may blow away if I breathe. There is a small gate ajar on the south fence. I enter a courtyard, empty, deserted, quiet. Ancient, thriving cedars line the low walls. In the flower beds there is greenery spotted with clusters of small white flowers. There is a reflecting pool to the front. The water is clear and calm. The flagstone walkways are covered with a thin layer of fine dust. I see no footprints, no tracks anywhere. There is no movement in the leaves, no breeze, and time itself is frozen and immobile here. The sight is wondrous, dream-like, the relic of a bygone magical epoch. And the house, with its porch, clear crystal window panes, and slender collonade, is set against the turquoise sky. It is so delicate, so fragile that it seems to float, unanchored, unattached to the ground.

I lean on the wall. The cool air rising from the reflecting pool is refreshing beyond belief. I sit at the edge of the pool, wash my face, and in my cupped hands take a drink of water. An unfathomable pleasure permeates my whole being.

The house casts a deep reflection in the waters and the trees seem to sway on the surface. The pool is brimming with the azure of the sky. I look around and see no one. I undress and slowly slip in the water. The cool sensation cuts through my skin and settles in my bones. I sink lower and lower but cannot touch bottom. Under water, the light reacts playfully. I twist and turn and float to the surface gasping for air. The cool and wetness are in every particle of my body.

The sunlight is now creeping up the length of the tall cedars. I see the house and a mute yearning grips my heart. In all its charm, the house is so simple, so intimate, so inviting. It seems curiously weightless and immaterial, aged and yet untouched by time. It looks like a vaporous formation hanging in the sky. It is strangely reminiscent of people and places. Involuntarily, I associate it with someone once close but now forgotten, someone remembered from a distant dream, someone whose memory has been cleansed and purified by the baptism of time. I recollect an ethereal woman with body celestial and eyes fluid, as I recall my mother in her wedding portrait, looking diffident and virginal, pale and ghost-like behind the white veil, holding a four-petaled, solitary flower between her fingers. I remember a woman who once, late in a snowy night, came to visit, a distant relative, according to my father. I can see a woman even more distant than she, a woman of my ancient ancestry, flowing through the continuum of time.

I step out of the pool. The desert air is cool and moist

against my wet skin. I put my clothes on, pick up my shoes
and walk barefoot toward the house. I count twelve steps up
to the porch. Someone has stood in prayer here, sometime
in the distant past: I see the paraphernalia lying about. The
porch is open and spacious. It is covered with a rug of white
background adorned with a delicate blue floral pattern. I
walk inside and step in a hall, airy and well-lighted, with
white, unadorned walls. There is an alcove on each side. The
ceiling, where it meets the walls, has exquisite plaster reliefs
of small flowers and tiny inlaid mirrors. The windows are
simple, unpretentious, chaste. There are two doors, each
leading to a room. Each room in turn leads to other rooms.
Everywhere I go there are intimate, private nooks. The cor-
ridors are long and narrow, like a labyrinth. There is a spiral
staircase in semi-darkness leading up to the roof.

I am breathless at the top of the stairs. The view is phe-
nomenal. From here the line of vision travels unobstructed to
the four corners of the world. The sky is no more than a few
feet above my head. Below, the desert stretches to the horizon, to the brink of infinity. I lower myself to my knees.
Slowly, I begin to lose track of time. I feel dazed and sleepy.
But the sleep is perched on my eyelids and does not affect
the brain. I lied down for a time that seems like hours. One
by one, the stars have appeared in the sky. I feel incapable of
thought. My glance strays through the space. Thoughts, as
circles radiating from where a rock has hit the surface of
calm water, reverberate on the surface of my consciousness.
I am losing sensation in my limbs. My body is relieved of its
material weight and is bursting out of its contours. I merge
with the trees and the porch and become an extension of the
desert. My eyes are suspended from the stars. All the logical
bond of causalities and the count of moments have drained
from my head. I feel distant from all and everything, from
the geometrical conjunction of forms and figures, the interre-
lation of objects and absolute values of digits. I am far from

established connections and organized thoughts, from the massive tablet of human laws and the colossal tome of ethics. I feel further and further removed from the dicta of exhortation to acceptable deeds and discouragement of prohibited conduct, and care not for the principles of wholesome living and exemplary existence. I lose sight of the tyranny of matter, the validity of history, the absolute righteousness of ideologies, the rules governing coitus and menstrual cycle, the emanations of primary intelligence, and the metaphoric medium. As moments pass, the struggle between East and West, rich and poor, the rites of ablution and burial concern me less and less. Even the one who said "God is dead," and those who live in mortal fear of death anxiously awaiting the Savior are of no consequence to me.

It is dawn before I emerge from this trance-like euphoria. I look around me, dazed, disoriented. I stagger to my feet and feel a healthy appetite. I have a sensation of lightheadedness and well-being. The breeze feels good on my face. The small hamlet at the foot of the mountain has now awakened and I can hear a cock's crow. I put my shoes on and descend. Somehow, I am not surprised to see an old man sitting at the edge of the pool washing his hands in preparation for the morning prayer. He has a thick white beard. I greet him and he acknowledges me with a nod of the head. He seems to be praying under his breath.

The ancient dust on the stairs and walkways shows my tracks. At the gate I stop and look back. I know this is the last glance. I am saddened at the thought. In the twilight the house looks so serene, so perfect. It is so genuine and wholesome. I understand this inherently and inherently I am exhilarated for this understanding. The house watches me as I walk away.

On the way, the road is no longer unfamiliar. The desert is calm and serene, devoid of demonic beguiling. I cross the fields and arrive at the road. A truck picks me up. The driver is a young man, bearded and swarthy. Pictures of a hundred ayatollahs decorate every inch inside the cab. I get off at a roadside tea house. By now, I am overwhelmingly hungry. The sun is up; it is a bright, warm summer morning.

The tea is hot and aromatic. There are eggs, cream, and toasted bread. My daughter loves unleavened bread. Since the start of her romance, she has been eating more.

I am worried about my son. My wife often weeps and prays for him. She is convinced he has been subverted. She wishes for the annihilation of the material world and the demise of imperialism so we can all live in God's grace.

"Anything else?" asks the young waiter. I look up and shake my head. He is so alive, so real, so healthy.

I return to my room at the town guest house. There have been several calls from Tehran. The friend with whom I was supposed to meet the night before has left me a note. I must hasten back. Something important has come up. There is a message on the night stand. Students are on strike. Professors are staging a sit-in. I pack and get in the car. Service stations are all closed, but I have enough fuel. I head for Qom, the first stage of my journey. There is heavy traffic on the road: cars, trucks, horse carts, donkey trains.

In Qom a funeral procession has blocked the street. There are chants, hymns, prayers as black-clad women press against one another in the march. The air is full of dust, the odor of stagnant water and decomposing bodies. The heat is overwhelming. I get out of the car for a while and stand in the shade of a high wall waiting for the road to clear. Eventually, I get back on the road. I am stopped near the shrine where the car is searched and I am frisked. I feel dizzy and frustrated; I chew on my cigarette butt, I spit, curse, and honk the horn at pedestrians. A woman bangs on the hood of my car and utters obscenities. The child in her arms is crying his head off.

I speed up when I get to the highway. Trucks hurtle down the road at breakneck speeds, trying to run me off the road. I think it will be a miracle if I get to Tehran in one piece. The reflection of my face in the rearview mirror is depressing. I roll down the window. Everything looks dead and gray, and the rocky hills are rough and charmless.

My wife wants to know the whereabouts of the Absent Imam. My father in a drunken stupor is following the late landlord's wife around. He has smashed his *tar* and has taken to singing revolutionary anthems. I ask Mr. Haydari if he has exported his silk carpets. I have a meeting early tomorrow morning. The article I had promised is not yet ready. I must attend the memorial service for my recently deceased poet friend. "Watch out," my wife warns, "counterrevolutionaries are sitting in ambush."

The brick kilns near Tehran are now in view. Someone is blowing his horn behind me urging me to go faster or let him pass. I can hear him shouting, threatening. I have an urge to get out and start a fight. There is soot and stench of diesel fuel everywhere. I long for a breath of fresh air.

The sky looks asphalt-gray and the horizon seems bleak. Concrete clouds are overhead, and the thick abrasive air clashes with my vision. I feel sad and heavy at heart at the thought of hard times ahead. Then, in a flash, a divine casement in the solid horizon of concrete opens and I see an apparition of the house in the desert. It is a miracle, a blessing approaching me in all its fresh, untainted glory. I have a primal awareness that it is there, where it will always remain. I know that it will brighten for me many sad, sultry dusks and dark, desperate nights. I know deep in my heart that it will remain with me, the great lady of my soul, giving me succor and solace till the day I die.

Translation by Faridoun Farrokh, first published in Iranian Studies
Vol. XV, 1982, pp. 221–225.

GOLI TARAGHI

Born and raised in Tehran, Goli Taraghi (Gulī Taraqqī in the Library of Congress spelling) is the daughter of the late Lotfollah Taraqqi, publisher and editor of Taraqqī and Āsiyā-yi Javān. She attended elementary and high school in Tehran, college in the United States. She holds a bachelor's degree in philosopy from Drake University and a master's degree from Tehran University. During the 1960s, Taraghi was employed at the Plan Organization and also wrote a number of short stories. Prior to the closing of Iranian universities in 1980, she had taught philosophy at the Faculty of letters of the University of Tehran for six years. In addition to her short stories and her novel Khvāb-i Zimistānī (Winter Sleep), she wrote the script for the commercial feature-length motion picture Bita, directed by her ex-husband Hazhir Daryush. Taraghi currently lives with her two children in Paris, where she continues to write. She is currently working on a narrative called 'Ādat'hā-yi Gharīb-i Āqā-yi 'Alif' dar Ghurbat (The Strange Behavior of Mr. 'A.' in a Strange Land). It is the story of an Iranian expatriate living unhappily in Paris.* A high school history teacher in Tehran who truly cared for his students, Mr. "A." left Iran in 1980 after being struck on the head by a stone in the school courtyard. That day he had learned that he and the other teachers were perceived as traitors in the context of the new Islamic Republic of Iran.

*Faridoun Farrokh, introduction to "The Great Lady of My Soul," is a translation of Taraghi's *Buzurg Bānū-yi Rūh-i Man* in *Iranian Studies* 15.1–4 (1982): 211–212. Additional biographical notes on Taraghi are found in Francine Mahak, *Critical Analysis and Translation of Winter Sleep*, by Guli Taraghi (Ph.D. Dissertation, the University of Utah, August 1986), pp. 2–5.

❧ *Someday*

GOLI TARAGHI

Mr. Haydari takes good care of his hands. Mr. Haydari looks at his shiny shoes and says "I am responsible for myself; I am proud of this blood running through my veins; I'm counting the days waiting to see them; I'm alive."

It is 5:03. I remove the wilted flowers from their vases and toss them into the street. I stop. I look at my shadow on the ground, at the fringes on the carpet, at the particles of dust in the air, at my socks, at the tiles and the moisture on the wall. That stubborn, exasperating lost feeling has filled the room again. I sit down. What are the people like, anyway? Do they think this much about dying, the way I do? I get up. I walk. They will be here in two and one-half hours. Tuesday is the thirtieth of *Khurdād*, finally. After tomorrow, I will be a lucky person. After tomorrow, I will laugh like other people, and I won't think of anything.

"How old are you, madam?" asks Mr. Haydari.

"Forty-two."

He is washing his hands. "What difference does it make if they are here or not? They justify everything."

I bend over and knock breadcrumbs off the bedsheet. No one is in the street. The Yosuf Abad Bus has stopped in the

This story is from "Yak Ruz," *Jahān-e Naw* 2:8–10 (1347/1968), pp. 83–90.

shadow, empty. Tomorrow it will be my turn. Tomorrow I will take my children by the hand and tell myself this is what I am living for. For them. I am responsible for them. They see everything.

Mr. Haydari clips his ingrown fingernails; he rests one hand on top of the other. "How much do you make in a month?" he asks.

"1,100 Tomans."

He shakes his head. His teeth are white and clean. "That's plenty," he says. "For a mere typist, that's really plenty."

I go on the balcony. Above I hear the sounds of talking and footsteps, the sounds of doors closing, the sound of rapid breathing, the sound of laughter, the sounds of knives and forks, the sounds of a radio, and children yelling and screaming. I walk through empty rooms. The table by the wall is covered with dirty dishes. Mosquitoes crawl on my face. It is hot. My Haydari likes the heat, and he carefully picks the mosquitoes; his fingers glisten.

"Why do you need them?" he says. "To hell with them; let each person look out for himself."

At the end of the street, at the curve, the blind ticket seller stands silently and motionlessly in the shadow. He is right there all day, his hands on his white cane, staring straight ahead. The neighbor across the street waters his flowers with a ewer, whistling and wiping his face. On the floor above I hear a spinning wheel, a refrigator door, and I can smell fried onions.

No, Mr. Haydari doesn't understand. Mr. Haydari doesn't know. I need a reason to live. I look at my hands. Someday I will no longer feel them. No, I need a reason to wash my hands. Two hours and fifteen minutes to go. Is it really too late? No, forty-two years old is nothing. Tomorrow I will start all over again. Mehri *Khānom* says hello from a distance and buttons her blouse. What is my daughter's name? I bend over and pick up the cherry seeds on the balcony floor. I laugh. Manizheh. Of course, Manizheh. I repeat this name to myself one hundred times a day. I talk about Manizheh from morning to night. She's in the twelfth grade. Her letter came; she sent her picture, she has a cold, she has lost weight, she has grown up, walked, laughed. My daughter has made a woman of herself. Yes, yes. This is my son. I told you I have two children. Today is Tuesday the thirtieth of *Khurdād*—I told you.

I change clothes, wash my face, comb my hair. If only I were younger. If only my stomach weren't so large. But it doesn't matter, it doesn't matter at all. What difference will it make to them? I lie on the bed. I wait. I'm like someone who is about to die and doesn't believe it. What am I afraid of? They are my children, of course I love them. No, seven years is nothing. Of course I haven't forgotten them. I'll get a bigger house, a one-story house with a courtyard, big windows, and geraniums. I'm tired of these two rooms, of this street, of this sunken single bed, of this Mehri *Khānom* with her grey blouse and rubber sandals, of this ticket seller at the end of the street, of this anonymous, forgotten neighborhood. . . . I will live with my children from now on. I'll sit with them on the balcony and greet the neighbors from a distance. No, Mr. Haydari, you are mistaken. Their presence will change everything. I will no longer beat my head against the wall. I will no longer be afraid. They will give me a new lease on life. I have a reason to be, a reliable justification.

I rearrange everything again; I open the windows, pull back the curtains, dust the chairs. I go and borrow several plates from my neighbor. I stop and laugh. I listen and don't know what to do. I hear voices, car doors slamming. My heart races. I quickly change shoes, toss old newspapers under the bed and close the door to the privy. I hear a bell. The lamp in the hallway is burned out. I smell old paint and dampness. All I have to do is open this door; just another moment. How simple it is to be with one's family.

My daughter smiles and looks at me from a distance with her small eyes. She slowly reaches out and says something incomprehensible. Her hair is tied back with a yellow ribbon. Her arms are white and hairy. She is wearing a white blouse and her dress is covered with tiny flowers resembling watermelon seeds. I look at her hands, her protruding chest, her nose, her face, her bushy eyebrows, her dark lips, her small pink ears, the curvature of her neck, her long eyelashes, her white high-heel shoes. She is short and fat, eighteen years old, grown up. So quickly. I thought she was still the same little girl who used to sit on my knee and play with my hair. She holds her purse carefully against her stomach and stands uneasily at the door. I take her hands quickly, kiss her, hug her hard. She is too big for my arms. I laugh, she breathes rapidly and looks around. My son is tall, thin, and pale. His face is covered with pimples and he has a slight growth of stubble. He stands to one side and watches his sister. He wears his hair parted on the side and a large watch is on his slender wrist. I hug him with difficulty; his skin is rough and his body smells like oil.

"We got here a bit early," my daughter says. "I was afraid you wouldn't be here." My son is silent and embarrassed. He sets his suitcases along the wall and looks around without curiosity with his grey, petrified eyes. I insist that he to sit down. I take his hand and try with difficulty to kiss his face again. They've changed so much. Their hands and faces have gotten so big. Their voices have changed so much; their eyes have gotten smaller and their faces have changed color. They don't resemble me in the slightest. Not even their father. Why are they standing by the wall? What are they thinking of? Perhaps they are tired; perhaps they are hungry. "Why are you standing?" I ask. "Why don't you sit down?"

My son hastily sits down and rubs his knees with his hands.

"Are you tired?" I ask. "Did you have a good flight?" My son nods, opening his mouth only with reluctance.

My daughter says "The weather was bad all the way to Esfahan, but the flight was fine after that." Oh God, what a wonderful day this is, I say to myself. What a good day. I have waited seven years for this day. I have calculated, counted, and waited patiently for seven years. If only Mr. Haydari were here to see this. If only he could realize that I was right. How simple it is to bring everything to life again. How easy it is to say that none of those years were wasted. I remember our house on Farvardin Street: myself, Naneh Gowhar, my husband, my children. No, nothing has changed.

No one speaks. I don't know where to begin. "Well, how is your father?" I ask.

"He's fine," my son says, nodding. "He's not bad."

"How about your brothers?"

"Very well."

"Haven't you seen them?" asks my daughter.

"How is your father's wife?"

"She's fine."

"How are Grandmother, Grandfather, and the rest of the family?"

My son nods and rubs his palms. "You don't look at all like your pictures," he says.

I go into the kitchen. I take containers of sweets and fruits from the refrigerator. I stop and lean against the wall. My heart has become mountainous. I tell myself, "No, it doesn't matter, it isn't important." They are surely tired. The poor kids have been traveling. They're excited, away from home, and hungry.

"Let me help you madam," my daughter says. I remember the nights when Naneh Gowhar and I carried the two of them in our arms to the *Shahrdārī* coffee house. We would buy walnuts and ice cream on the way and ride the merry-go-round.

"No, I don't want anything to eat," My son says. "I have a stomachache and it's bad for me." The whole time he presses his hands together and looks at the flowers on the carpet. I have so much to say; there are so many things I must ask. Where to begin? My daughter slowly cracks apricot seeds with her teeth. She restlessly turns her head this way and that.

"Shiraz is a beautiful city, isn't it?" I ask. My daughter leans over and picks out a few cherries with the tips of her fingers, puts them on a plate, and plays with their stems.

"No, it isn't a beautiful place," says my son.

The entire room, the whole wall, is covered with pictures of them. On the table by the bed I have placed a photograph of my daughter at six years of age. Her hair is braided and her arms are around my neck. How she has changed. How she has grown. If only she would put her arms around my neck and laugh, like she did then. If only she didn't call me "madam." If only she didn't restlessly turn her head this way and that.

I bring them tea. My son doesn't want any, my daughter takes some and sets it on the table without drinking it.

"Well, we're finally together," I say, "Just like old times."

"I have to go back soon," says my daugher. "I have work to do. I can't stay long."

My son talks about military obligation, of foreign study qualifying exams, of mechanical and electrical engineering. I show him a picture of Naneh Gowhar. I take his hand and try to smile. He doesn't remember anything—nothing. I talk to them about Bizhan street, of the Shukufeh elementary school. No, Mr. Haydari was mistaken. Their presence changes everything. I give them my place and I'm happy. I stand. I smile.

"What did you say?" asks my daughter.

No, I will no longer count the days. I have the day off tomorrow and I'll be with my children. I won't think of the office and being tired at my desk. Tomorrow I won't be just another weary and lonely typist. Tomorrow I'll walk out and yell "Look, people! I'm not alone anymore, I'm talking, I'm walking, I'm living with them. Now it's my turn, get out of my way, go on . . ."

"Aren't you well?" my daughter asks.

I try to smile. Of course it's good, it's wonderful, it's deliriously happy.

"We're very happy too," my son says.

"Yes, we're very happy," says my daughter.

I pick up plates and turn on the light. Still that darkness, that blackness, that stagnation made of old and ancient things remains in the hallway and in the corners of of the room. My daughter fans herself and breathes deeply. Her face is perspiring, and her bangs are fluffed up. I turn on the fan. "Would you like to see your childhood photos dear?" I take two dusty albums from under the bed. My hair gets caught in the bedsprings and my shirt clings to my body. I wipe the dust from my face and smile.

"No, I don't like pictures from those times."

I look around. No one has anything to say. I take out report cards from their childhood and place them beside them.

"Excuse me," says my son, "Where's the ice water?"

I gather up my little treasures, empty my suitcase in the middle of the room. I have tucked the first composition my daughter wrote in one corner. I gather up the papers. I see my son watching me out of the corner of his eye; I hurry and get him a glass of water. Oh God, what has happened, I ask myself? Why doesn't anyone say anything? Isn't this Tuesday the thirtieth of *Khurdād*? Weren't we all waiting for this day? No, it doesn't matter, it doesn't matter. Everything will gradually work out. They'll gradually start talking, be happy, clap their hands.

I go in my room, look for a cigarette in my purse. I put my hand on the edge of the bed and breathe heavily. I think I'll feel better if I eat something. If I wash my hands, splash water on my face, or turn on the radio, I'll feel better. I go back.

"Would you like to go out?" I ask. My son nods his head and gets up immediately. I'm tired and my feet are aching. I wish I were alone and asleep. My daughter combs her hair and powders her face, washes her hands and puts lipstick on her lips. I feel old and tired. I look at my hands, at the wrinkles on my face, at the skin hanging from my cheeks. Watching my daughter, I tell myself, this is the young me, come back again. I hug her and kiss her hair.

"What time does the movie start?" asks my son.

They talk and whisper to one another. What are they thinking of? Maybe they thought their mother was young and pretty. Maybe they thought I live in a big well-decorated house. I'm a common typist. I'm forty-two years old and my body aches with illness and fatigue. Yes, yes, I live here, in these two rooms. The sun doesn't shine here and the roof leaks in winter. I'm wearing the best outfit I have. Perhaps they're glad they don't live with me? To hell with them. Damn them. What do they know about life? I look at my daughter's hands. They are smooth, white, and shiny. Her clothes smell like flowers, like a laundry. Her shoes are new and polished. No, they have nothing to do with me. They won't carry on for me. They've taken care of themselves and that's all. My daughter slowly opens and closes her mouth like someone in a dream. She doesn't even seem to realize herself what she's saying. She's like a wind-up doll with a pre-recorded tape in its stomach. My son is thinking of traveling to America, of the future. They no longer remember the house on Farvardin Street, near the municipal coffee house, nor Naneh Gowhar—nothing.

I stand waiting for a taxi. The streets are crowded. They

walk faster than I do. They stand in front of store windows and talk. I quicken my pace, breathe rapidly, to catch up with them. My daughter is thinking of going back. No, she's thinking of buying presents to take back. She buys little things for people I don't know.

"What did you say?" I ask. My son laughs and shrugs his shoulders.

"We've really made a lot of trouble for you," my daughter says. I quicken my pace again, walk beside my son. I try to take his hand. They stop, they go, they turn around, go in stores, come out, laugh. I change positions and walk by my daughter. I attempt to start a conversation.

It is hot and sticky. My daughter holds a corner of her purse and fans herself. "Are you tired dear?" I ask. She nods. She's ill-tempered and listless. I tell them about the old days, the things they did as children, of the nights we were to-gether, of our old house. They don't remember anything. You'd think they were born just this way with no past. I stop at the intersection, put my hand on my son's shoulder, and lead them across the street. They run in front of the cars, laughing.

"Are you hungry?" I ask. They talk, point out other boys and girls to each other, read signs, look at stores. They are alive, healthy, and happy. No, they haven't sensed the strange, lost feeling in my room. They know nothing of those absolute "musts," those loathesome, unwanted "musts."

We walk all the way up the street. I want them to see me with my children, to look at me. "How good it is to be with one's children," I tell myself. I look at the rental houses. I take note of the real estate dealers; I'm thinking of our new house, a big house with a yard and a *howz*. I'll find someone like Naneh Gowhar. We'll go to the municipal coffee house again in the evenings and buy walnuts at the corner.

"So where is this taxi?" asks my son. I'm exhausted and

my shoes are hurting my feet. I want to stop and sit. I want
to go back. We cross the street. We turn and walk all the way
down the next street. We reach the movie theater.

The movie has started already and the lights are out. My
daughter laughs in the dark, finding her own way. They hold
hands and run ahead. I can't see anything. I reach out and try
to take their hands. I do a spin; I'm dizzy and don't know
where to go. People frown at me, mumble and gesture with
their hands. I go up and down, stepping on feet, going back
the other way. Someone stops me and shows me to a seat
with a flashlight. They've found their own seats and started
watching.

"Did you get left behind?" my daughter asks. I sit and take
off my shoes.

My eyes gradually become accustomed to the darkness.
The doors are closed and the room is full of heavy breathing
and the smell of bodies. Things are moving around on the
screen. I didn't bring my glasses and I can't see well. The
room is full of heads, full of incomprehensible whispering,
full of a nondescript crowd. Out of the corner of my eye I
look at my son and daughter. My daughter is bent forward,
her head to one side, watching intently. Her eyelashes are
black and bushy. My son has stretched out his feet and
slumped in his seat. I can't see his face. He's eating something he bought along the way. Someone is sitting on my
right who seems familiar. His shoulder is touching my arm
and I can hear his breathing. I turn and look at him. He's
holding a large sandwich and eating it meticulously. He's
looking straight ahead and chuckling to himself. No one is
paying any attention to us. No one realizes I'm with my
children; no one realizes I'm no longer alone. "Excuse me sir,
do you have a match?" I ask. He shakes his head and takes
another bite of his sandwich.

I try to watch the film. Yes, Mr. Haydari is right. To hell
with them; I am the only one that matters. My son and

daughter talk softly. I lean over and say "What did you say?" They look at me and shake their heads. They don't care if I live or die. They don't even remember I am here, that I am with them, that today is Tuesday the thirtieth of *Khurdād*, and that we're finally together. So why did they come at all? Why did they wait so long for this day? I have a lump in my throat. I squirm in my place and don't know what to do with my hands. I look at my watch in the dark. I'm getting sleepy and have to separate my eyelids by force. The man next to me moves. The sandwich is finished. He cleans his mouth and tosses the wrapper under the seat. I press my arm against his shoulder. I put my hand on the arm of the seat and ask, "Excuse me, what time is it?" He shakes his head without looking at me and withdraws. I want to get up and go. I want to get up on the stage and shout "You fools, look at me instead of these artificial people. I'm with my children. I'm alive and not afraid of dying."

I put my hand on my daughter's shoulder. "Are you all right dear?" I ask. She looks at me with surprise.

"Yes, of course," she says.

No, these are not my children. There has definitely been a mistake; they've tricked me and sent someone else's children. Someday my real children will come and then everything will be different. I'll come laugh at Mr. Haydari that day. I'll stick out my tongue and say "Look, you've made a mistake, you didn't know, you didn't realize." Someday, some other thirtieth of *Khurdād*, my children will come and everything will start over.

We get in a taxi. I give the address and roll down the window. The air seems to be filled with something heavy and inert—full of heat, dust, and dryness. Both of them gradually doze off. The streets are empty. I know this taxi driver. I think I've been in this taxi before.

"Please slow down a little sir," I say. I look at my daughter. Her eyes are swollen, and she is tired and sleepy. Tomorrow, the next day, and the next. We turn. A red light. We start again. The drug store, the grocery store, the dry cleaner, a ruin, trees spaced far apart. What an ugly place this city is. My son yawns and lays his head against the back of the seat. Dogs are lying on the asphalt in the street. We arrive. We stop. The blind ticket-seller with his white cane sits in the gutter and stares straight ahead.

My daughter rubs her eyes and straightens her skirt. "What a good film that was," she says.

Translated by John Green

✣ Glossary

'Āshurā. The tenth day of the Muslim lunar month of Moharram, when Imam Hoseyn and his followers were martyred at Karbala.

Comité. Muslim organization established throughout Iran after the revolution for coordinating local affairs with central authorities. All have now been disbanded or absorbed into police organizations.

Emāmzādeh. A shrine dedicated to and named for a descendant of an Iman.

Homāyun. One of twelve Persian musical modes, or scales, usually played in the key of C. The notes in C are: G, A half-flat, B, C, E-flat, F, and G.

Howz. A Persian architectural pond, a standard feature in the courtyard of a traditional Iranian home.

Jū. A type of open gutter, usually with a rectangular concrete or tile lining. Often, it is used as a channel for water from village water supply canals.

Kadkhodā. A village head man.

Khānom. A polite form of address for women, variously meaning Ms., Madame, or Ma'am.

Khoresht-e fesenjān. A braised poultry dish with a sauce made from walnuts and pomegranate.

Khorsht-e qormeh-sabzi. A Persian dish made of sauteed onion, meat, scallion, coriander, fenugreek, beans, and dried lemon and is served over rice.

Khurdād. The third month of the Persian solar calendar corresponding to late spring.

Korsi. A low wood frame covered with quilts and blankets. A fire—usually from a kerosene burner—burns beneath. In the cold months of winter, it is used both to warm feet and as a gathering spot.

Kutlit. A popular Iranian food made of ground meat, onion, and potatoes.

Mash. A title given to someone who has been on a pilgrimage to Mashhad, Iran, the burial place of the eighth Shi'i Imam, 'Alī al-Rezā.

Reconstruction crusade. A program, now a ministry, instituted by the government of the Islamic Republic to utilize Iran's vast pool of unemployed and undereducated 'oppressed people' to undertake public works projects using labor-intensive methods. Similar programs were carried out in Maoist China.

Sharbat. A sweet drink made from the extract of fruit or blossoms.

Sofreh. Literally: *tablecloth*, but often refers to the display of food and decoration at a feast.

Tār. A six-stringed instrument similar in appearance to a guitar, but with a small rounded box. It has a resonating face made of skin, and the six strings are hung in pairs and tuned in octaves.

Ta'ziyeh. A dramatic performance that is part of the traditional Shi'ite ritual mourning for the death of Imam Hoseyn at Karbala in 680 A.D. In the time of the Qajar monarchs, plays such as this one at the Tekiyah-ye Huseyn were huge productions and a regular feature of court life, sometimes attended by thousands.

Tekkeh or Tekiyeh. The name of the theater where the ta'ziyeh is performed.

❧ Translators

MICHAEL BEARD

Michael Beard teaches in the English Department at the University of North Dakota. He is coeditor of *Edebiyat: A Journal of Middle Eastern Literatures.* He is the author of *Hedayat's "Blind Owl" as Western Novel* and has edited (with Adnan Haydar) a study of the Egyptian Nobel laureate Naguib Mahfuz.

FARIDDOUN FARROKH

Fariddoun Farrokh is associate professor of English and chairman of the Division of Arts and Sciences at Laredo State University. His research interests are Restoration and Eighteenth-Century English Literature and contemporary Iranian fiction, translation.

M.R. GHANOONPARVAR

M.R. Ghanoonparvar teaches Persian and comparative literature at the University of Texas at Austin. He has translated numerous works from Persian, including four major novels.

His books include *Prophets of Doom: Literature as a Socio-political Phenomenon in Modern Iran* (1984) and *Iranian Drama: An Anthology* (coedited with John Green). His latest book is *In a Persian Mirror: Images of the West and Westerners in Iranian Fiction* (1993).

JOHN GREEN

John Green is procedures analyst at *Mathematical Reviews*, the review journal of the American Mathematical Society. He holds a Ph.D. in Persian Literature from the University of Michigan, and has translated and published numerous works of Persian literature. He lives in Ann Arbor, Michigan.

FRANKLIN LEWIS

Franklin Lewis is a Ph.D. candidate in Persian Literature at the University of Chicago, completing his dissertation on the lyric poetry of the twelfth century poet Sāna'ī. He has translated several short stories by contemporary Iranian writers, including Sīmīn Dānishvar, Hūshang Gulshīrī, Gulī Taraqqī, Shahrnūsh Pārsīpūr, Ahmad Shāmlū, and published a number of scholarly articles. He lives at present in the Chicago area with his wife and daughter.

FARZIN YAZDANFAR

Farzin Yazdanfar holds Master's degrees from the University of Michigan in applied economics and Near Eastern Studies. He has contributed translations to *Iran: Chicago Anthology 1921–1991*, and is a contributing writer to the journals *Rackham Journal of the Arts and Humanities*, the *Chicago Review*, and the Persian journal *Iran Nameh*. He lives in Chicago.

❧ Selected Bibliography of Iranian Women's Short Stories

COMPILED BY JOHN GREEN

ABṬAḤĪ, FĀTIMAH

1979 [1358]. "Nihāl-i Girdū'ī bar Gūr-i Masīḥ" [A Walnut Sapling on Masih's Grave] *Kitāb-i Jum'ah* 9 (Shahrīvar, 1979 [1358]): 21–30.

AFKHAM RASŪLĪ, MAHĪN

1978–79. *Chahārdah Dāstān* [Fourteen Stories]. 1st ed. Tehran: Tābish.
    Rawzanah'ī bih Bāgh-i Bihisht [A Window on the Heavenly Garden]
    Mār va Pūnah [The Snake and the Mint]
    Vaqtī Chirāgh'hā Khāmūsh Mīshavad [When the Lights Go Out]
    Dīdār dar Qaṭār [A Meeting on the Train]
    Ṭulū'-i Āftābī Dīgar [Another Sunrise]
    Khānah-i Shumārah-i 5 [House Number 5]
    'Arūs [The Bride]
    Laḥzah'hā-yi Zindagī [The Moments of Life]
    Must'ajir [The Tenant]
    Janjāl dar 'Arūsī [The Brawl at the Wedding Party]
    Haftah-i Shāns [The Week of Fortune]
    Dāgh-i Havas [The Pain of Capriciousness]
    Dar Sāyah-i Tafāhum [In the Context of Mutual Understanding]
    Saṭḥ-i Bālā [The Upper Level]

'ALĪZĀDAH, GHAZĀLAH

1977 [1356]. *Safar-i Nāguzashtanī* [The Endless Journey]. 1st ed. [s.l.]: Naqsh-i Jahān. 111 pp. Short Stories.

Shajarah-yi Ṭayyibah [The Good Tree]

Pāndārā [Pandora]

Bā Anār va bā Turanj az Shākh-i Sīb [With the Pomegranate and the Citron from the Apple Branch]

AMĪRSHĀHĪ, MAHSHĪD

1969 [1348]. *Ba'd az Rūz-i Ākhar* [After the Last Day]. 1st ed. Tehran: Amīr Kabīr. 164 pp. Republished by Amīr Kabīr in 1976.

Ba'd az Rūz-i Ākhar [After the Last Day]

Majlis-i Khatm-i Zanānah [Women's Mourning]

Āghā Sulṭān-i Kirmānshāhī [Agha Soltan from Kirmanshah]

Ākhar-i Ta'zīyah [The End of the Passion Play]

Ismguzarī-yi Bachah-'i Sīmīn [Naming Simin's Child]

Mih-i Ḍarrah va Gard-i Rāh [The Mist of the Valley and the Dust of the Road]

Intirviyū [The Interview]

Dar īn Makān va dar īn Zamān [In this Place and at this time]

1973 [1351]. *Muntakhab-i Dāstan-i Mahshīd Amīrshāhī* [Selected Stories from Mahshid Amirshahi]. 1st ed. Dāstān'hā-yi Mu'āṣir-i Īrān. Tehran: Intishārāt-i Tūs.

Ism Nivīsī [Writing the Name]

Garmā [The Heat]

Ālbūm [The Album]

Sūsk-i Ḥanā'ī [The Red Beetle]

Bārān va Tanhā'ī [Rain and Loneliness]

Ya'qūb-i Lays 'Ayyār

Bū-yi Pūst-i Līmū, Bū-yi Shīr-i Tāzah [The Smell of Lemon Rind, the Smell of Fresh Milk]

Ba'd az Rūz-i Ākhar [After the Last Day]

Ākhar-i Ta'zīyah [The End of the Passion Play]

Dar īn Makān va dar īn Zamān [At this Time and at this Place]

Mih-i Darrah va Gard-i Rāh [The Mist of the Valley and the Dust of the Road]

Khvurshīd zīr-i Pūstīn-i Āqājān [The Sun Under Āqā Jān's Coat]

Lābirīnt [The Labyrinth]

1971 [1350]. *Bih Sīghah-yi Avval Shakṣ-i Mufrad* [In the First Person Singular]. 1st ed. Tehran: Intishārāt-i Būf. 112 pp.

Lābīrint [The Labyrinth]

Paytūn Plays [Peyton Place]

Nām, Shuhrat, Shumārah-'i Shināsnāmah [Name, Fame, ID Number]

Paykān-i Pulīs [The Police Car]

Khvurshīd-i Zīr-i Pūstīn-i Āqājān [The Sun Under Āqā Jān's Coat]

1966 [1345]. *Kuchah-'i Bun Bast* [Dead End Alley]. Tehran: [s.n.]. 151 pp. A collection of 11 short stories.

1968 [1347]. *Sār-i Bībī Khānum* [Bibi's Starling]. 1st ed. Tehran : [s.n.]. 247 pp.

    Sār Bībī Khānum [Bibi's Starling]

    Khānivādah-i Āyandah-i Dādāsh [My Brother's Future Family]

    Ya'qūb-i Lays̲-i 'Ayyār [The Bandit Philanthropist]

    Sūsk-i Ḥanā'ī [The Henna-Colored Beetle]

    Khurram'shahr Tehran [Khorramshahr Tehran]

    Bārān va Tanhā'ī [Rain and Loneliness]

    Pidar Buzurg-i Man [My Grandfather]

    Jūjah'hā-yi Ākhar-i Pā'īz [The Chickens Will Come Home to Roost Later]

    Pārtī [The Party]

    Bū-yi Pūst-i Līmū Bū-yi Shīr-i Tāzah [The Smell of Lemon Rind, the Smell of the Fresh Milk]

BAHRĀMĪ, MĪHAN

1968 [1347]. "Bāgh-i Gham" [The Garden of Sorrow] *Jung* 7 (1968 [1347]): 50–65.

1979 [1358]. "Ḥāj Bārik Allāh" [Ḥāj Bārik Allāh] *Nāmah-'i Kānūn-i Nivīsandigān-i Īrān* 2 (1979 [1358]): 85–105.

1979 [1358]. "Saqākhānah-'i Āyinah" *Kitāb-i Jum'ah* 3 (1979 [1358]): 5–21.

1985 [1364]. *Ḥayvān* [The Animal]. 1st ed. Tehran: Intishārāt-i Damāvand. 183 pp. Seven short stories and a discussion of writing (introduction).

"Haft Shakhah-'i Surkh" [The Seven Red Branches], *Kitāb-i Tihrān* 1:1992, pp. 156–170.

Bāgh-i Gham [The Garden of Sorrow]

    'Arūsak Bāzī [Playing with Dolls]

    Tafsīr-i Yak Bālah [The One-Sided Explanation]

    Ḥimāsah-'i Parvāz [The Epic of Flight]

    Ḥayvān [The Animal]

    Āb-i Mutakkā [Pillow Water]

    Saqqākhānah-'i Āyīnah

BAQĀ'Ī KIRMĀNĪ, MALIKAH, 1914–

Baqā'i Kirmānī was born in Kerman. Her father, Mīrzā Shahāb Kirmānī, who died when she was nineteen, was elected as Kerman's Majlis deputy in 1920 as the replacement for his brother, Sayyid Javād Kirmānī, who had been poisoned for reasons unknown to her. After her father's election the family moved to Tehran. Malikah was educated in Iran at Tehran's Dār al-Muʻallimāt High School for girls, where she studied child psychology and education. She continued studying in these fields later through correspondence with Vincennes University in France. She spent most of her professional career working as a self-employed teacher, operating a grade school and a kindergarten of her own for twenty years. Her kindergarten, the Shāhpar School, was the first one to exist in Tajrīsh, a suburb of Tehran. In 1953 she began a six-year legal fight with the Ministry of Education to improve working conditions for teachers, and finally succeeded in obtaining better pay and protection against termination without cause, but at great personal expense. In her fiction, she has tried to express the plight of women, basing her stories on true events. She has also translated the fairy tale collection *Les Contes de Perrault* from French to Persian, but it remains unpublished. Currently residing in St. Louis, Mo., Malikah has three adult children living elsewhere in the U.S., two boys and a girl.[1]

> 1984 [1363]. *Shikastah Bālān* [Those with Broken Wings]. Los Angeles: Ketab Corp. 147 pp. A collection of nine short stories about the Iranian woman.
>
> Ishq u Shahvat [Love and Passion]
> Afsūs [Regret]
> Qalb-i Man az Zabān-i Zan [My Heart from the Woman's Point of View]
> Yād'dāsht'hā-yi Bīnām [Nameless Notes]
> Rāz [The Mystery]
> Qalb-i Man az Zabān-i Mard- i bā Vujdān [My Heart From the Point of View of a Man with a Conscience]
> Chub-i Khudā Ṣidā Nadārad [God's Club Makes No Sound]
> Zan [Woman]
> Jināyat [The Crime]
> Intiqām va Vaẓīfah Shināsī [Revenge and Responsibility]
> Pādāsh [The Reward]

---

[1]Malikah Baqā'ī Kirmānī, personal letters dated Aug 25 and Sep 4, 1986.

BIBLIOGRAPHY

DĀNĀ, MAYMANAT

Born in Shiraz, Maymanat Dānā completed nurse's training in 1935 in Beirut, and later established her reputation and following as a writer on her own, without specific literary training or contact with the literary establishment. Maintaining a lifelong interest in her primary occupation as a nurse, she went to the United States in 1960 and obtained a master's degree in management. She specialized in short stories in her writing, but also translated many works of English literature into Persian. A socially active woman who at one point in her career took a trip around the world, Dānā was President of the Women's Council of Shiraz, President of the Iran-America Society, President of the Shiraz Nurse's Association, and President of the Rivi Hospital Nurse's Association of Shiraz. She was also head nurse at Sa'dī Hospital of Pahlavi Univeristy and Chief of the hospital's health care training unit. A frequent contributor to the magazine *Iṭṭilā'āt-i Bānūvān,* Dānā's works were especially popular among the women of Shīrāz.[2]

1969 [1348]. "'Arūsak-i Shikastah" [The Broken Doll] *Iṭṭilā'āt-i Bān-uvān* 634 (Murdād, 1969 [1348]): 37–38. 62–63, 75. This story was singled out as one of Dānā's most admired in an introductory paragraph.

1969 [1347]. "'Azīzam, Man Bar Gashtah'am" [My Dear, I Have Returned] *Iṭṭilā'āt-i Bānuvān* 615 (Farvardīn, 1969 [1347]): 33, 100, 119–121. The first installment of a series.

1970 [1349]. "Dard-i Pinhān" [The Hidden Pain] *Iṭṭilā'āt-i Bānuvān* 671 (Urdībihisht, 1970 [1349]): NP. Published in installments, check issues for paging.

1970 [1349]. "Kasī Chih Mīdānad?" [What Does Anyone Know?] *Iṭṭilā'āt-i Bānuvān* 670 (Urdībihisht, 1970 [1349]): 32–33, 82.

1970 [1348]. "Man 'Āshiq-i Shuharam Shudam!" [I Fell in Love with My Husband] *Iṭṭilā'āt-i Bānuvān* 605 (Day, 1970 [1348]): 40–41, 58.

1970 [1348]. "Mard-i Yak dar Yak Mīliyūnī Būd" [He Was One Man in a Million] *Iṭṭilā'āt-i Bānuvān* 606 (Day, 1970 [1348]): 34–35, 60, 68.

1966 [1345]. *Āhang-i Judā'ī* [Decision to Separate]. 1st ed. Tehran: Amīr Kabīr. 291 pp. Short stories. First published in various issues of *Iṭṭilā'āt-i Bānuvān.* Second edition 1966, 3d ed. 1969.

---

[2]Fakhrī Qavīmī, *Kārnāmah-'i Zanān-i Mashhūr-i Īrān* (Tehran: Vizārāt-i Āmuzish va Parvarish, 1352/1973 or 1974), pp. 228–229. *Iṭṭilā'āt-i Bānuvān* 634 (15 Murdād 1348 [6 Aug 1969]): 26. *Chihrah- 'i Maṭbū'āt-i Mu'āṣir* [The Face of the Contemporary Press] (Tehran: Pris Agint, 1351 [1972]), p. 82.

Javāhirī dar Lābilā-yi Gūnī-yi Pārah [Jewelry in a Torn Gunny Sack]

'Arūsak-i Shikastah [The Broken Doll]

Āyā Bāz Ham Ū rā Khvāham Dīd [Will I See Him Again?]

Ghurūr Ham Ḥaddī Dārad [Pride Also Has its Limits]

Ātash-i Zīr-i Khvākistar [Fire Beneath the Ashes]

Hamah Gul

Māh-i 'Asal-i Dubārah [Second Honeymoon]

Ārizū-yi Maḥāl [The Impossible Wish]

'Arūs-i Sīyāh Pūsh [The Bride in Black]

'Ishq va Junūn [Love and Madness]

Āhang-i Judāī [A Decision to Separate]

DĀNISHVAR, SĪMĪN, 1921–

1981 [1360]. "Anīs" [Anis] *Ārash* 5.5 (Murdād, 1981 [1360]): 32–47.

1962 [1340]. *Shahrī chun Bihisht* [A Land Like Paradise]. 1st ed. Tehran: 'Alī Akbar 'Ilmī. 250 pp. First printed 1962, Ali Akbar Ilmi, 250p. Reprinted 1975 by Kitāb-i Mawj, 170p. Third edition, Khwārazmī, 1980.

   Shahrī Chūn Bihisht [A Land Like Paradise]

   'Ayd-i Īrānī'hā [The Iranian Festival]

   Sar Guzasht-i Kūchah [The Story of a Street]

   Bībī Shahr'bānū [Sharbanoo the Lady]

   Zāymān [Childbirth]

   Mudil [The Model]

   Yak Zan bā Mard'hā [A Woman With Men]

   Dar Bāzār-i Vakīl [At the Vakil Bazar]

   Mardī kih Bar Nagasht [The Man Who Did Not Come Back]

   Ṣūrat'khānah [The Playhouse]

1959 [1338]. *Bih kī Salām Kunam* [Whom Should I Greet?]. 2nd ed. Tehran: Khavarazmī. 299 pp. 2nd printing, 1959. Third ed. 1983. 4th ed. 1986. Four of the ten stories in this collection were published earlier in the journal *Alifbā* between 1973 and 1975, although there were modifications made before they appeared in this collection.

   Tīlah-i Shikastah [The Broken Marble]

   Taṣāduf [The Accident]

   Bih Kī Salām Kunam [Whom Should I Greet?]

   Chishm-i Khuftah [The Squinting Eye]

   Mār va Mard [The Snake and the Man]

Anīs [The Companion]
Dard Hamah Jā Hast [There Is Pain Everywhere]
Yak Sar va Yak Bālīn [The Perfect Marriage]
Kayd al-Khā'inīn [The Trick of Traitors]
Sūtrā [The Sutra]
1948 [1327]. *Ātash-i Khāmush* [The Dead Fire]. Tehran: [s.n.]. 168 pp.
Ashk'hā [Tears]
Ātash-i Khāmūsh [The Dead Fire]
Yād'dāsht'hā-yi Yak Khānum-i Ālmānī [A German Lady's Notes]
Kilīd-i Sul
Ān Shab-i 'Arūsī [That Wedding Night]
Shab-i 'Aydī [New Year's Eve]
Guzashtah [The Past]
Kalāgh-i Kūr [The Blind Crow]
Yak Pardah az Tiātr-i Zanāshūī Mard'hā 'Avaz Nimīshavand [A
    Scene from the Marriage Drama "Men Don't Change"]
Nāshinās [Unknown]
'Atr-i Yās [The Lilac Perfume]
Jāmah-i Arghavānī [The Purple Garment]
'Ishq-i Ustād-i Dānishgāh [The University Professor's Love]
'Ishq-i Pīrī [The Love of Old Age]
Sāyah [The Shadow]

FARJĀM, FARĪDAH

1972. *The Crystal Flower and the Sun*. Minneapolis: Carolrhoda Books.
24 pp. An original Persian folk story. Story by Faridah Fardjam.
Pictures by Nikzad Nojoomi. Translated by Mansoor Alyeshmerni.
Translation of Gul-i bulur va khvurshid. Dreading the six months
of Arctic darkness, an ice flower begs to travel with the sun to take
light to the world. Reprinted in bilingual format by Mazda in
1983.

1972. *Uncle New Year*. Minneapolis, Minn.: Carolrhoda Books. 24 pp.
An original Persian folk story. Story by Faridah Farjam and Meyer
Azaad. Pictures by Farsheed Meskali. Hoping he will make her
young, an old woman awaits the arrival of Uncle New Year, who
comes to Persia on the first day of spring. A translation of *'Amū
Naw Rūz*. Reprinted in bilingual format by Mazda in 1983 and
renamed *Uncle Noruz*.

GULISTĀNĪ, MIHRĀNDUKHT

1972 [1351]. *'Asalī va Rangīn.* Tehran: Padīdah. 12 pp.
'Asalī va Rangīn

GULISURKHĪ, FARĪDAH

Born in 1934, Gulisurkhī holds a master's degree from Tehran University. She began working as a writer and translator for *Ittilā'āt-i Bānuvān* in 1956.[3]

1969 [1347]. "Ān Zan" [That Woman] *Ittilā'āt-i Bānuvān* 611 (Bahman, 1969 [1347]): 32–33, 64–65. An installment.

1969 [1347]. "Ān Zan" [That Woman] *Ittilā'āt-i Bānuvān* 612 (Isfand, 1969 [1347]): 42. An installment.

1969 [1348]. "Āvā-yi Firishtigān, Qalb-i Divānah" [Voice of an Angel, Heart of a Lunatic] *Ittilā'āt-i Bānuvān* 631 (Tīr, 1969 [1348]): 54–55, 64. Part of a series.

1969 [1348]. "Āvā-yi Firishtigān, Qalb-i Divān" [Voice of an Angel, Heart of a Lunatic] *Ittilā'āt-i Bānuvān* 632 (Tīr, 1969 [1348]): 50–51. Part of a series.

1969 [1348]. "Hargiz 'Āshiq Nakhvāham Shud" [I Will Never Fall in Love] *Ittilā'āt-i Bānuvān* 645 (Mihr, 1969 [1348]): 24, 61, 64, 70–71.

1969 [1348]. "Lāk Pusht" [The Turtle] *Ittilā'āt-i Bānuvān* 636 (Murdād, 1969 [1348]): 24, 56, 58–59.

1969 [1348]. "Nāzparī va Mardān" [Nazpari and the Men] *Ittilā'āt-i Bānuvān* 617 (Farvardīn, 1969 [1348]): 18–19, 78. First of a series.

1969 [1348]. "Nāzparī va Mardān" [Nazpari and the Men] *(Ittilā'āt-i Bānuvān* 618 (Farvardīn, Urdībihisht, 1969 [1348]): 34–35, 60–61/30–31, 67, 71/24–25, 69. Second, third, and fourth of a series.

1969 [1348]. "Nāzparī va Mardān" [Nazpari and the Men] *(Ittilā'āt-i Bānuvān* 621 (Urdībihisht, 1969 [1348]): 24–25, 88. Part of a series.

1969 [1348]. "Nāzparī va Mardān" [Nazpari and the Men] *Ittilā'āt-i Bānuvān* 621 (Urdībihisht, 1969 [1348]): 24–25, 88/54, 72. Last two parts of a series.

1969 [1348]. "Nifrīn-i Jādūgar-i Siyāh" [The Curse of the Black Sorcerer] *Ittilā'āt-i Bānuvān* 623 (Urdībihisht, 1969 [1348]): 30, 67.

1969 [1348]. "Vaqtī kih Mujasammah'sāz az Gur bar Khāst" [When

---

[3]*Chihrah-'i Maṭbū'āt-i Mu'āṣir,* p. 124.

the Sculptor Arose from the Grave] *Iṭṭilā'āt-i Bānuvān* 642 (Mihr, 1969 [1348]): 20–21, 58–59, 69.

1970 [1348]. "Ān Zan" [That Woman] *Iṭṭilā'āt-i Bānuvān* 610 (Bahman, 1970 [1348]): 26–27, 62–63, 66.

1970 [1348]. "Akhgarī az Khākistar'hā" [Embers from Ashes] *Iṭṭilā'āt-i Bānuvān* 651 (1970 [1348]): NP. Published in a series of installments, check issues for paging.

1971 [1350]. "Afsūn dar Bihisht" [Magic in Heaven] *Iṭṭilā'āt-i Bānuvān* 720 (Farvardīn, 1971 [1350]): 36–37, 78.

KASHKŪLĪ, MAH'DUKHT

1981 [1360]. "Dukmah-'i Kandah Shudah" [The Missing Button] *Ārash* 5.3 (Urdībihisht, 1981 [1360]): 91–97. Written in Summer 1978.

1981 [1360]. "Tabrīk va Taslīyat" [Congratulations and Condolences] *Ārash* 6 (Shahrīvar, 1981 [1360]): 32–47.

1977. *Afsānah-i Bārān dar Īrān* [The Legend of Rain in Iran]. 1st ed. Tehran: Tilivīzīyūn-i Āmūzishī, Sāzmān-i Rādiyū Tilīvīziyūn-i Millī-yi Īrān. 29 pp. Illustrated by Ḥusayn Maḥjūbī.

KHĀNLARĪ, ZAHRĀ, 1915 OR 1916–1991

1933 [1312]. *Parvīn va Parvīz, Rahbar-i Dawshīzigān* [Parvin and Parviz, A Guide for Young Ladies]. Tehran: Mehr. Two volumes in one.
Parvīn va Parvīz
Rahbar-i Dawshīzigān

1958 [1337]. *Dāstānhā-yi Dilangiz-i Adabiyāt-i Fārsī*. Tehran: Intishārāt-i Nīl. 245 pp. Prose adaptations of Persian literary classics, done for students. Introduction by Parvīz Nātil Khālarī. Also published in a larger edition of 9, 220 p. 25 cm. Republished by Tūs in 1982–83, 232 pp.
Baktāsh va Rābi'ah [Baktash and Rab'ah]
Shaykh-i Ṣan'ān [Sheikh Sanan]
Dāstān-i Siyāvush [The Story of Siyavosh]
Bahrām Nāmah [The Story of Bahram]
Manīzhah va Bīzhan [Manizheh and Bizhan]
Iskandar va Kayd-i Hindī [Alexander and the Indian Impostor]
Qiṣṣah-'i Bakhtyār [The Story of Bakhtiar]
Yūsif va Zulaykhā [Josef and Zoleikha]

Humāy va Humāyūn [Homay and Homayoon]
Khusraw Shīrīn [Khosrow Shirin]
Bahrām dar Gunbad-i Sīyāh [Bahram in the Black Dome]
Dāstān-i Khayr u Shar [A Story of Good and Evil]

KHĀṬIRAH-'I PARVĀNAH

Parvānah had a career as a singer, in addition to her writing activity.[4]

1970 [1349]. "Biguzār dar 'Ayn-i Khvushbakhtī Bimīram" [Let Me
Die Happy] *Iṭṭilā'āt-i Bānuvān* 675 (Khurdād, 1970 [1349]): 77–80.
1964 [1342]. *Lālā-yi Zindagī* [The Lullaby of Life]. Tehran: Amīr
Kabīr. 267 pp.

Ā'īn-i Pahlavāni [The Heroic Custom]
Bikujā Parad Kabūtar [Where Does the Pigeon Fly?]
Ṣifr'hā-yi Hizār Āfarin
Shākh'hā va Pā'hā [Branches and Legs]
Lālā-yi Zindagī [The Lullaby of Life]
Ranj-i Imrūz va Āfat-i Fardā [Today's Pain and Tomorrow's Dis-
aster]
Parandah-'i Āshiyān Parast [The Nest-Bound Bird]
Luṭf-i Zindagī [The Kindness of Life]
Biguzārīd Giryah Kunam [Let Me Cry]
Chih Ḥaqqī, Chih Ḥisābī
Budan yā Nabudan [To Be or Not to Be]
Buru Vāsah-'i Khudat [Go on Your Own Behalf]
Ruṭaylī Bidurushtī-yi Fīl
Shabdar-i Chahārpar [The Four-Leaf Clover]
Lāmrūtā īn Zanamah
Ṣadā-yi Sarnivisht [The Voice of Fate]
1964 [1343]. *Kirishmah-'i Sāqī* [The Cup-Bearer's Flirtation]. Tehran:
Amīr Kabīr. 284 pp.

Hanūz Sham' Rawshan Būd [The Candle Was Still Burning]
Ākhih Mardī Guftan va Zanī
Dāgh-i Bāṭilah [Journal Regrets]
Jādū-yi Marg [The Magic of Death]
Rū'yā-yi Tū manam
Kirishmah-'i Sāqī [The Cup-Bearer's Flirtation]
'Aks'hā-yi Ārizū [Photographs of Hope]
Rusvā [Disgraced]

---

[4]*Iṭṭilā'āt-i Bānuvān* 675 (Urdībihisht 1349 [1970]): 78.

BIBLIOGRAPHY

Har Kas bā Naṣīb-i Khudash [To Each His Own]
Ā'īn-i Dilnavāzī [The Agreeable Custom]
'Ishq-i Nijātbakhsh [The Saving Love]
Taqallā'hā [The Struggles]
Ḥālā Bibīn Chih Mazah Dārah [Now Look How Good it Is]
Mu'jizah-'i Yak Gunāh [The Miracle of a Sin]
Vaqtīkih Dilī Biraqṣ Āyad [When a Heart Dances]

KASRĀ, LAYLĀ, 1939–1989

Laylā Kasrā did graduate work in administrative sciences at King's College in Cambridge, England, after which she returned to Iran and found employment in the National Iranian Petrochemicals Company. She began writing in 1956, and eventually became a member of the editorial staff of *Iṭṭilā'āt-i Bānuvān*. She also worked for the journals *Umīd-i Īrān* and *Rawshanfikr*. She has published three collections of poems, one of which, *Faṣl Matraḥ Nīst*, won a prize for Book of the Year in 1969 from the Iran National Television Organization. She traveled widely in the United States and Europe, and at the age of thirty-six began a long and successful career, mostly in the United States, as a singer under the name Hidīyah. At the age of thirty-seven she contracted cancer, from which she died in 1989. She is survived by her husband, Iskandar Afshār, and three children.[5]

1969 [1347]. "Dunyā-yi bī Bahār-i Man" [My World without Springtime] *Iṭṭilā'āt-i Bānuvān* 615 (Farvardīn, 1969 [1347]): 37, 90–91.

1969 [1348]. "Hamīshah, Shabānah Rūz Bīst u Chahār Sā'at Ast" [There Are Always 24 Hours in a Day] *Iṭṭilā'āt-i Bānuvān* 619 (Urdībihisht, 1969 [1348]): 20–21, 59.

1969 [1348]. "Pas az Sāl'hā-yi Intiẓār" [After Years of Waiting] *Iṭṭilā'āt-i Bānuvān* 650 (Āzar, 1969 [1348]): 28–29, 62–64.

1970 [1348]. "Agih Bigī Dūstat Dārām" [If You Say I Love You] *Iṭṭilā'āt-i Bānuvān* 610 (Bahman, 1970 [1348]): 26–27, 59.

LAṬĪFĪ, SHAHLĀ

Born in 1944, Shahlā Laṭīfī holds a bachelor's degree in language and literature from Paris University. She began her career as a writer in 1965, working as a writer of short stories and a translator. She has visited Lebanon and Europe, and has one child.[6]

---

[5]*Chihrah-'i Maṭbū'āt-i Mu'āṣir*, pp. 121–122, and *Āshiqānah* 51 (July, 1989):51.

1969–70 [1348]. "Raqs-i Sarnivisht" [The Dance of Fate] Ittilā'āt-i Bānuvān 656 (Day, 1969–70 [1348]): NP. Published in installments, check issues for paging.

1974 [1352]. Raqs-i Sarnivisht [The Dance of Fate]. 1st ed. Tehran: Ibn-i Sīnā. 120 pp.

Qissah-i Nātamām [The Unfinished Story]
Bidard-i Zindagī-yi Talkh Sākhtam Bī Tu [I Tolerated the Bitterness of Life without You]
Tasvīr-i ū[His Image]
Bīgānah Dūstat Dāram [Stranger, I Love You]
Raqs-i Sarnivisht [The Dance of Fate]

MAJLISĪ, FARZĀNAH

1958 [1337]. "Ujāq-i Kūr" [The Barren Woman] Sukhan 9 (Isfand, 1958 [1337]): 1163–1165. Winner of the second prize in Sukhan's story-writing contest.

MĪRZĀDAH'GĪ, SHUKŪH

1979?. Āghāz-i Duvvum [A Second Beginning]. Intishārāt-i Tūs, 184. Tehran: Intishārāt-i Tūs. 148 pp. MiU TxU

Chishmah-'i Sārān [The Starling Spring]
Intahā-yi Nakh'hā-yi Sīyāh [The End of the Black Threads]
Almās'hā-yi Man [My Diamonds]
Nāmah [The Letter]
Khākistarī [Gray]
Tadā'ī, Bulūgh va Gharīzah-'i Sharqī [The Eastern Challenge, Maturity and Instinct]
Rūh-i Khudā [The Spirit of God]
Dar Ānsū-yi Fanā [On the Other Side of Annihilation]
Tā Bu'd-i Chahārum [To the Fourth Dimension]
Andīshah-'i Rahā'ī [The Idea of Release]
Vāqi'īyat-i Malmūs [Tangible Reality]

MUZHDAH

1969 [1348]. "Dar Intizār-i Lahizāt" [Awaiting the Moments] Ittilā'āt-i Bānuvān 621 (Urdībihisht, 1969 [1348]): 20, 59–60.

---

[6]Chihrah-'i Matbū'-āt-i Mu'āsir, p. 125.

1969 [1348]. "Izdivāj-i Ḥisāb Shudah" [The Calculated Marriage] *Iṭṭilā'āt-i Bānuvān* 648 (Ābān, 1969 [1348]): 28, 54.

1970 [1349]. "Bāzgasht" [The Return] *Iṭṭilā'āt-i Bānuvān* 673 (Urdībihisht, 1970 [1349]): 18–19, 67.

1970 [1349]. "Bihtarīn Hidīyah" [The Best Gift] *Iṭṭilā'āt-i Bānuvān* 666 (Farvardin, 1970 [1349]): 20–21.

1970 [1349]. "Dukhtar-i Man va Pisar-i Mardum" [My Daughter and the Vagabound] *Iṭṭilā'āt-i Bānuvān* 678 (Khurdād, 1970 [1349]): 23, 68.

1970 [1349]. "Lakah'i dar Guzashtah'hā" [A Stain in the Past] *Iṭṭilā'āt-i Bānuvān* 698 (Ābān, 1970 [1349]): 18–19, 85.

1970 [1349]. "Sharlī" [Charlie] *Iṭṭilā'āt-i Bānuvān* 700 (Ābān, 1970 [1349]): 14–15, 84.

1970 [1349]. "Taqdīm Bitaw, Mādar . . ." [Dedicated to You, Mother] *Iṭṭilā'āt-i Bānuvān* 704 (Āzar, 1970 [1349]): 8, 102.

1971 [1349]. "Naw Rūz dar Wīskānsīn" [New Year's in Wisconsin] *Iṭṭilā'āt-i Bānuvān* 717 (Isfand, 1971 [1349]): 28–29, 95.

NĪKKHVĀH, GHUNCHAH

1959 [1338]. *Āhang-i Zindagī* [The Melody of Life]. UNK: [s.n.]. 57 pp. Two girls, one named Mahtāb, a simple country girl, the other named Javānah, an urban girl with chronic misfortunes, both fall in love with a young boy named Sa'id. The boy is ill and bedridden, and they renew his will to live. In the end Javānah and Mahtāb come face-to-face and Javānah voluntarily relinquishes her claim to Sa'id in favor of Mahtāb. Then Sa'id and Mahtāb begin life together with high hopes.

NĪKZĀD, GĪTĪ

1988. "Sang-i Fīrūzah'ī va Gūshmāhī-yi Ṣuratī va Sifīd" [The Turquoise-colored Stone and the Pink and White Seashell] *Chishmandāz* 5 (Fall, 1988): 129–130.

1988. "Zindagī-yi Dilkhvāh-i Āqā-yi F" [The Ideal Life of Mr. F] *Chishmandāz* 5 (Fall, 1988): 126–129.

1989. "Qiṣṣah-'i Khargūsh va Gawjah-Farangī" [The Tale of the Rabbit and the Tomatoes] *Ādīnah* 35 (June, 1989): 54–55.

PĀRSĪPŪR, SHAHRNŪSH

1977. *Āvīzah'hā-yi Bulūr* [Crystal Hangings]. 1st ed. Qiṣṣah'hā va dāstānhā-yi jahān, 26. Tehran: Rāz. 83 pp.
Bahār-i Ābī-yi Kātmāndū [The Blue Spring of Katmandu]
Hamzād [The Twin]
Hamkārān [Colleagues]
Āvīzah'hā-yi Bulūr [Crystal Hangings]
Yak Jā-yi Khūb [A Good Place]
Kushtār-e Guṣsfand'hā [The Slaughter of Sheep]
Garmā dar Sāl-i Ṣifr [Heat in the Year Zero]
Sārā
Āqāyān [The Gentlemen]
Dar Chigūnigī-yi Taḥavvul-i Yak Khānivādah [How to Change a Family]
Zindagī-yi Khūb-i Junūbī [The Good Southern Life]
Bārān [Rain]

QAHRAMĀN, ANVAR

1961 [1340]. *Afsānah-'i Dunyā va Tajallī-yi Khudā* [The Legend of the World and the Glory of God]. 1st ed. Tehran: Kitāb'furūshī-yi Furūghī. 134 pp.
Afsānah-i Dunyā [The Legend of the World]
Gul-i Zindagi [The Flower of Life]
Īn Ashk'hā Rū-yi Sīnah-i Kih Birīzad [On Whose Breast Will These Tears Fall]
Dar Ārizū-yi 'Ishq [Hoping for Love]
Tajallī-yi Khudā [The Glory of God]

RAHGŪ, BAHĀR, 1946–

The daughter of Fasā sugar-cube manufacturer 'Abbās Rahgū and descended from a family of Safavid poets and ministers, Rahgū, with the help of Farīdūn Tavallalī, published a collection of stories entitled *Dar Bazm-i Gul'hā* [At the Feast of the Flowers] in 1961 at fifteen years of age after two years of writing.[7]

---

[7]Farīdūn Tavallalī, introduction to *Dar Bazm-i Gul'hā* (Tehran: Ibn Sīnā, 1340 [1961]), pp. 3–4.

BIBLIOGRAPHY

1961 [1340]. *Dar Bazm-i Gul'hā* [At the Feast of the Flowers]. 1st ed.
Tehran: Ibn-i Sīnā. 99 pp.
Dar Bazm-i Gul'hā [At the Banquet of the Flower]
Khāṭirah [The Memory]
Khaṭā [The Mistake]
'Ilm Yā Dīn [Science or Religion]
Dīdī kih [You Saw of Course]
Qalam [The Pen]
Ārizū [Desire]
Chirā [Why]
Tarānah [The Melody]
Vidā' [The Farewell]
Afsūn-i Yak Tarānah [The Spell of a Melody]
Sarāb-i Gham [The Mirage of Sadness]

RĀZI, FARĪDAH

1974 [1353]. "Gurbah'am'rā Kushtam" [I Killed My Cat] *Sukhan* 24.3
(Isfand, 1974 [1353]): 298–301.
1976. "Qallādah" [The Dog Collar] *Sukhan* 25.3–4 (Murdād,
Shahrīvar, 1976): 351–301.
1978. "Lakandah" [The Lame Chicken] *Sukhan* 26.5–6 (Farvardīn,
Urdībihisht, 1978): 27–29. Written in Dey 2536.

RIYĀḤĪ, LAYLĪ

1981 [1359]. "Gul-i Kāktūs" [The Cactus Flower] *Ārash* 5.1 (Isfand,
1981 [1359]): 93–102. Written in Summer of 1977 in Bandar Abbas.
1981 [1360]. "Sāz-i Chap" *Ārash* 5.3 (Khurdād, 1981 [1360]): 55–78.
Written in 1981.

SĀLĀRĪ, NŪSHĪN

1981 [1360]. "Dāshdī Dāgh" [The Stone Furnace] *Shūrā-yi
Nivīsandigān va Hunarmandān-i Īrān* 4 (1981 [1360]): 75–83.
1981 [1360]. "Shādī-yi Avval-i Māh-i Mih" [The Joy of May Day]
Shūrā-yi Nivīsandigān va Hunarmandān-i Īrān 4 (1981 [1360]): 83–90.

SĀZGĀR, ZHĪLĀ

1968 [1347]. "'Arūsak'hā-yi Barfī" [The Snowmen] *Iṭṭilā'āt-i Bānuvān* 604 (Day, 1968 [1347]): 27,91.

1969 [1348]. "Armaghān'hāyi har Āftāb" [The Gifts of Every Sun] *Iṭṭilā'āt-i Bānuvān* 618 (Farvardīn, 1969 [1348]): 22, 66.

1969 [1348]. "Bār-i Dīgar . . . tā Intiẓār'hā-yi Sard" [Once More . . . Until Cold Expectations] *Iṭṭilā'āt-i Bānuvān*) 616 (Farvardīn, 1969 [1348]): 18–19, 77.

1969 [1347]. "Bīrāhah" [The Lost Woman] *Iṭṭilā'āt-i Bānuvān* 611 (Bahman, 1969 [1347]): 14–15, 86.

1969 [1347]. "Daqāyiq-i Sīyāh-i Iẓṭirāb" [Black Moments of Agitation] *Iṭṭilā'āt-i Bānuvān* 612 (Isfand, 1969 [1347]): 20, 76–77.

1969 [1347]. "Dars-i Avval" [Lesson One] *Iṭṭilā'āt-i Bānuvān* 614 (Farvardīn, 1969 [1347]): 19, 83.

1969 [1347]. "Dīvār-i Chahārum" [The Fourth Wall] *Iṭṭilā'āt-i Bānuvān* 615 (Farvardīn, 1969 [1347]): 18–19, 118.

1969 [1348]. "Man va Āyinah'hā" [The Mirrors and I] *Iṭṭilā'āt-i Bānuvān* 622 (Urdībihisht, 1969 [1348]): 27, 66.

1969 [1347]. "Rūz'hā-yi Gīj" [Dizzy Days] *Iṭṭilā'āt-i Bānuvān* 613 (Farvardīn, 1969 [1347]): 14–15, 71.

1969 [1348]. "Taṣvīr'hā-yi Farsūdah" [Faded Images] *Iṭṭilā'āt-i Bānuvān* 635 (Murdād, 1969 [1348]): 22, 60–61.

1970 [1348]. "Ān Sū-yi Dīvār-i Shīshah'ī" [The Other Side of the Glass Wall] *Iṭṭilā'āt-i Bānuvān* 605 (Day, 1970 [1348]): 20–21, 72, 79.

1970 [1348]. "Bahānah-'i Sādah'ī kih Būd" [Simple Pretext Though It Was] *Iṭṭilā'āt-i Bānuvān* 610 (Bahman, 1970 [1348]): 18–19, 74.

1970 [1348]. "Laḥzah'hā-yi Zindah" [Living Moments] *Iṭṭilā'āt-i Bānuvān* 607 (Day, 1970 [1348]): 17, 77, 85.

1970 [1348]. "Shāyad Dīvanigī Būd" [Perhaps It Was Insanity] *Iṭṭilā'āt-i Bānuvān* 606 (Day, 1970 [1348]): 20–21, 73.

1970 [1348]. "Suzan'hā-yi Ṭalā'ī" [Golden Needles] *Iṭṭilā'āt-i Bānuvān* 665 (Bahman, 1970 [1348]): 22–23.

1970 [1348]. "Tā Bāvarī-yi Dīgar" [Until the Next Belief] *Iṭṭilā'āt-i Bānuvān* 610 (Bahman, 1970 [1348]): 18–19, 74.

1970 [1349]. *Pas az Marg-i Māhī'hā* [After the Fish Die]. Tehran: Amīr Kabīr. 212 pp.

Ḥaqīqatī Vujūd Nadārad [There Is No Truth]
Pas az Marg-i Māhī'hā [After the Fish Die]
Khafaqān [Palpitation of the Heart]
Yak Shahr va Yak Rahguzar [A City and a Traveler]

BIBLIOGRAPHY

Rūzhā-yi Gīj [Dizzy Days]
Hāshūr-i Nūr bar Dīvār'hā-yi Sīyāh [Rays of Light on Black Walls]
Laḥzah'hā-yi Zindah [Living Moments]
Payvand [The Link]
Dīvār-i Chahārum [The Fourth Wall]
Bār-i Dīgar tā Intiẓār'hā-yi Sard [Once again Until Cold Expectations]
Musāfir [The Traveler]
Ānsū-yi Dīvār-i Shīshah'ī [The Other Side of the Glass Wall]
Daqāyiq-i Sīyāh-i Iẓtirāb [Black Moments of Agitation]
Dars-i Avval [The First Lesson]
Bīrāhah [A Devious Path]
Shāyad Dīvānigī Būd [Maybe It Was Madness]
Man va Āyinah'ha [The Mirrors and I]
Armaghān'ha-yi har Āftāb [The Gifts of Every Sunshine]
Tā Bāvarī Dīgar [Until Another Belief]
Mātādur Nifrīn bar Tu [Damn You, Matador]

SHAHRZĀD

1979 [1358]. "Ā, Bābā, Qīqām" *Kitāb-i Jum'ah* 2 (Isfand, 1979 [1358]): 33–36.

TARAQQĪ, GULĪ, 1939–

1967 [1346]. "Khvushbakhtī" [Prosperity] *Andīshah va Hunar* 5.10 (Murdād, 1967 [1346]): 1579–1586.

1967 [1345]. "Panjarah" [The Window] *Andīshah va Hunar* 5 (1967 [1345]): 1020–1026.

1967 [1346]. "Safar" [The Journey] *Andīshah va Hunar* 5.10 (Murdād, 1967 [1346]): 1572–1578.

1967 [1346]. "Yak Rūz" [Someday] *Jahān-i Naw* 2.8–10 (1967 [1346]): 83–90.

1967 [1346]. "Ziyāfat" [The Party] *Andīshah va Hunar* 5.10 (Murdād, 1967 [1346]): 1565–1571.

1979 [1358]. "Buzurg Bānū-yi Rūḥ-i Man" [The Great Lady of My Soul] *Kitāb-i Jum'ah* 5 (Shahrīvar, 1979 [1358]): 38–50.

1969 [1348]. *Man Ham Chih Guvārā Hastam* [I Am Also Che Guevara]. Tehran: Murvārīd. 160 pp.

Khvushbakhtī [Good Fortune]
Muṣād
Safar [The Journey]
Tavallud [The Birth]
Yak Rūz [Someday]
Dirakht [The Tree]
Ziyāfat [The Party]
Man ham Chih Guvārā Hastam [I Am Also Che Guevara]

TAVALLALĪ, MAHĪN

The wife of poet Farīdūn Tavallalī.

1953 [1332]. "Bābā-yi Madrasah" [The Old Man of the School] *'Ilm va Zindagī* 2.4 (Tīr, 1953 [1332]): 308–317.

1955 [1334]. "Gumshudah" [Lost] *Sukhan* 6 (Ābān, 1955 [1334]): 789–793.

1955 [1334]. "Nāmah-'i Yildā" [Yilda's Letter] *Sukhan* 6 (Khurdād, 1955 [1334]): 335–338.

1955–56 [1334]. "Tanhā'ī" [Loneliness] *Sukhan* 6 (Day, 1955–56 [1334]): 1014–1020.

1957 [1336]. "Ābilah Kūb" [The Shot Giver] *Sukhan* 8.5 (Shahrīvar, 1957 [1336]): 442–445.

1959 [1338]. *Sanjāq-i Murvārīd* [The Pearl Brooch]. Shiraz: Mūsāvī. 169 pp. Ten short stories, the first and perhaps only volume published by this author. These stories had appeared previously in *Sukhan*.

Bābā-yi Madrasah
Ishmayt-i Bāstān Shinās
Nī Nī Kūr
Gumshudah
Nāmah-'i Yildā
Ābilah-Kūb
Sanjāq-i Murvārīd
Nīlī
Marzā

VĀLĀ, LU'BAT

Lu'bat Vālā completed her high school education, studied journalism for one term at Tehran University, then went to San Francisco for further studies in journalism. She began working as a journalist in 1948, and served as managing editor for the journal *Tihrān-i Muṣavvar*. She was elected to membership of the Board of Directors in the first round of elections by the Iran Press Association. Her writing consists primarily of short stories and poetry, usually written under the pseudonym 'Fitnah.' She has traveled to the United States, Canada, the Soviet Union, Europe, and Asia. Vālā has one daughter and one son.[8]

> 1969 [1348]. "Chishm'hā" [Eyes] *Ittilā'āt-i Bānuvān* 650 (Āzar, 1969 [1348]): 22, 60, 68.

ZARNĀZ

> 1968 [1347]. "Qiṣṣah-'i Ghuṣah'hā-yi Zindagī" [A Story of the Sadness of Life] *Ittilā'āt-i Bānuvān* 604 (Day, 1968 [1347]): 31, 88.
> 1969 [1347]. "Bīmārī dar Jahannam" [Illness in Hell] *Ittilā'āt-i Bānuvān* 611 (Bahman, 1969 [1347]): 26–27, 59, 71.
> 1969 [1347]. "Rāndah Shudah" [Driven] *Ittilā'āt-i Bānuvān* 613 (Farvardīn, 1969 [1347]): 32–33, 61–62.
> 1969 [1347]. "Raqṣ-i Andūh" [The Sad Dance] *Ittilā'āt-i Bānuvān* 615 (Farvardīn, 1969 [1347]): 40–41, 124–125.
> 1969 [1347]. "Sīyāh Chāl-i Sukūt" [The Black Pit of Silence] *Ittilā'āt-i Bānuvān* 612 (Isfand, 1969 [1347]): 22, 73–74.

---

[8]*Chihrah-'i Maṭbū'āt-i Mu'āṣir*, p. 143. *Ittilā'āt-i Bānuvān* 650 (5 Āzar 1348 [26 Nov 1969]): 21.